# KABUKI
A Mirror of Japan

JAPAN LIBRARY

Plate 1. *Shibaraku*
The hero Kamakura Gongorō (Ichikawa Danjūrō XII) confronts the *uke* villain, Kiyohara no Takehira (Ichikawa Sadanji IV). A household ledger is displayed beside Takehira. (Performed at the Kabuki-za in May 2003. Photo courtesy of Shochiku Co., Ltd.)

Plate 2. *Kuruwa Bunshō*
Ruined by debauchery, Izaemon (Sakata Tōjūrō IV) is reduced to wearing a paper kimono but manages to visit his lover Yūgiri (Nakamura Kaishun II) after a long absence. (Performed at the Kabuki-za in November 2008. Photo courtesy of Shochiku Co., Ltd.)

Plate 3. *Kanadehon Chūshingura*
Hayano Kanpei (Onoe Kikugorō VII) regrets that a tryst with his lover Okaru prevented him from coming to his lord's help when needed. He conveys his feelings to Senzaki Yagorō (Sawamura Tōjūrō II) and Hara Gōemon (Kawarasaki Gonjūrō III) while committing suicide. (Performed at the National Theatre in December 1973. Photo courtesy of the National Theatre.)

Plate 4. *Sanmon Gosan no Kiri*
Standing atop an ornate temple gate that rises on the central trap lift, Ishikawa Goemon (Onoe Shōroku II) admires the spring scenery with his famous line, "Such a stunning view!" before encountering his arch enemy Mashiba Hisayoshi (Onoe Baikō VII) for the first time. (Performed at the Kabuki-za in February 1989. Photo courtesy of Shochiku Co., Ltd.)

Plate 5. *Tsumoru Koi Yuki no Seki no To*
Ōtomo Kuronushi (Ichikawa Danjūrō XII) in black aristocratic attire wields a giant battleax against his comely enemy Sumizome (Bandō Tamasaburō V), who executes an impressive *ebizori* (shrimp arch) backbend at the climax of the dance. (Performed at the National Theatre in January 1991. Photo courtesy of the National Theatre.)

Plate 6. *Tōkaidō Yotsuya Kaidan*
Her face disfigured by poison, Oiwa (Nakamura Utaemon VI) still wants to look her best and combs her hair, but it falls out in great clumps. (Performed at the Kabuki-za in September 1973. Photo courtesy of Shochiku Co., Ltd.)

Plate 7. *Sannin Kichisa Kuruwa no Hatsugai*
Oshō Kichisa (Ichikawa Danjūrō XII, center) intercedes as Ojō Kichisa (Onoe Kikugorō VII, left) and Obō Kichisa (Nakamura Kichiemon II, right) squabble over 100 ryō. Realizing that they all are named Kichisa, though, they become blood brothers, with Oshō as their leader. (Performed at the Kabuki-za in February 2000. Photo courtesy of Shochiku Co., Ltd.)

# KABUKI
## A Mirror of Japan

Ten Plays That Offer a Glimpse
Into Evolving Sensibilities

### Matsui Kesako

Translated by
David Crandall

Japan Publishing Industry Foundation for Culture

Translation Note
The Hepburn system of romanization is used for Japanese terms, including the names of persons and places. Except in familiar place names, long vowels are indicated by macrons. The local custom of placing the family name first has been followed for the names of Japanese persons. Historical figures such as kabuki actors are often referred to by their personal names to distinguish them from the many other members of their house (*ie*) sharing the same family name. Example: Danjūrō for Ichikawa Danjūrō.


*Kabuki, a Mirror of Japan: Ten Plays that Offer a Glimpse into Evolving Sensibilities* by Matsui Kesako. Translated by David Crandall.

Published by
Japan Publishing Industry Foundation for Culture (JPIC)
3-12-3 Kanda-Jinbocho, Chiyoda-ku, Tokyo 101-0051, Japan

First edition: March 2016

© 2010 by Matsui Kesako
English translation © 2016 by Japan Publishing Industry Foundation for Culture
Illustrations by Kobayashi Wakuna

All rights reserved.

Originally published in the Japanese language as *Kabuki no Naka no Nihon* by NHK Publishing, Inc., in 2010.

Jacket and cover design by Niizuma Hisanori
Front and cover photo: The restored Konpira Grand Theater (Kyū Konpira Ōshibai, also known as the Kanamaru-za) in the town of Kotohira, Kagawa Prefecture, prior to undergoing a major renovation in 2004. (© JAPACK/orion/amanaimages, Yoshi/PIXTA)

As this book is published primarily to be donated to overseas universities, research institutions, public libraries and other organizations, commercial publication rights are available. For all enquiries regarding those rights, please contact the publisher of the English edition at the following address: japanlibrary@jpic.or.jp

Printed in Japan
ISBN 978-4-916055-58-3
http://www.jpic.or.jp/japanlibrary/

Contents

Preface to the English Edition

vii

Introduction

1

*Chapter One*
**Shibaraku**
A HERO IN THE NICK OF TIME

7

*Chapter Two*
**Kuruwa Bunshō**
DESCENDENTS OF HIKARU GENJI, THE SHINING PRINCE

23

*Chapter Three*
**Sugawara Denju Tenarai Kagami**
PLAYS OF SUBSTITUTE SACRIFICE

37

Chapter Four

**Yoshitsune Senbonzakura**

HUMANS SEEN THROUGH
ANIMAL FANTASIES

51

Chapter Five

**Kanadehon Chūshingura**

MORE THAN JUST A TALE OF
FEUDAL LOYALTY

65

Chapter Six

**Natsu Matsuri Naniwa Kagami**

THE BIRTH OF CHIVALRY

91

Chapter Seven

**Sanmon Gosan no Kiri**

A MONTAGE OF STAGE EFFECTS

103

*Chapter Eight*

**Tsumoru Koi Yuki no Seki no To**

A SOPHISTICATED FAIRY-TALE DANCE

117

*Chapter Nine*

**Tōkaidō Yotsuya Kaidan**

QUEEN OF JAPANESE HORROR

153

*Chapter Ten*

**Sannin Kichisa Kuruwa no Hatsugai**

BONNIE AND CLYDE, JAPANESE STYLE

169

Notes

183

*Plates follow half title page.*

# Preface to the English Edition

This book, originally published in Japanese in March 2010, is based on the text I wrote for an NHK educational series that was broadcast in 2009. Because the availability of images was a major consideration in selecting the plays I discussed, I chose to focus on pieces that are often performed today and used them to describe kabuki's various attributes.

Another factor in the selection process was the plays' ability to provide insight into the historical evolution of kabuki's content and form. By examining the kind of human drama and plot development that appealed to audiences throughout the Edo period and by highlighting the storytelling methods that are still used today, I tried to clarify some of the intellectual, emotional, and aesthetic sensibilities of the Japanese people that have evolved through time.

From its inception through its flowering in the Edo period, kabuki never enjoyed the backing of the ruling samurai class. On the contrary, it was only through popular support that kabuki managed to survive repeated attempts at suppression. In this sense, kabuki is an invaluable tool in understanding the sentiments of the common people. It would be very gratifying

PREFACE TO THE ENGLISH EDITION

if this English edition can help convey the essence of those sentiments to an international audience.

To reach as many people as possible, I purposely wrote the original Japanese in an informal style and reserved the more scholarly information for the notes. The fine translation team for this English edition includes translator David Crandall and editor Kawamoto Nozomu, both of whom are professional noh practitioners with a deep knowledge of Japanese performance culture. I feel fortunate that they have lent their expertise to the task of introducing kabuki and fostering a deeper understanding of Japanese culture to a wider readership outside Japan.

# Introduction

When faced with the difficulty of formulating a concise definition of the Japanese stage art of kabuki, the literary polymath Tsubouchi Shōyō (1859–1935) likened it to a chimera, the three-headed monster of Greek mythology. This hints at just how challenging it is to make a single, generalized statement. I would like to propose a different approach, however.

    The kabuki we see today is in no way a unified, consistent entity created in a single moment in time according to some master blueprint. Rather, it's the distillation of a vast repertory that has been performed over the course of hundreds of years. Therefore, if we seek an appropriate simile, we might say that kabuki resembles a cross section of geological strata. At the bottom we find a layer of trilobites; higher up, ammonites; and higher still, the fossils of dinosaur bones. If we examine the kabuki repertory in the chronological order in which the surviving plays were originally created, it becomes very easy to understand the genre's rich diversity.

    The word "kabuki" is derived from the term *kabukimono*, which referred to people who sported flamboyant, vanguard fashions and drew attention to themselves with their unconventional behavior. This suggests that many of the pieces making up the repertory today were on the cutting edge of entertainment when they were first developed. Just as television programming has evolved dramatically from the time TV sets first appeared, pieces in the kabuki repertory display very different characteristics depending on the era in which they were made. This is only natural. Just as television offers many different channels, kabuki was performed in a variety of theaters. From the staggering number of pieces presented over the years, only a relatively few have navigated the tides of time to become the kabuki that we enjoy today.

Before becoming a novelist, I wrote kabuki scripts. When I mention this to people, they often ask, "Kabuki scripts? Hasn't kabuki been around for centuries?" Well, yes, but someone had to write the plays in the past for them to exist now, and we must remember that they haven't remained static. They've undergone a gradual process of revision to accommodate changing times, and this is what has enabled them to survive.

I sense a tendency among the Japanese to view their own culture, not just kabuki, as if it did not belong to them. Many people who watch kabuki seem to think it has no direct connection with them at all and apparently feel it's worth appreciating simply because it's been around for a long time. I believe this is misguided. We should recognize that kabuki was in fact created by our own ancestors, so it's a part of us.

The kabuki we see today has been washed by the waves of bygone eras, and the pieces now remaining have proven to be the most popular over the course of centuries. In this sense, kabuki is a great mirror that reflects the popular sentiments of the Japanese people through time.

When we watch kabuki, we develop insight into the stories, situations, and expressive methods that were preferred by our forebears. This may in turn lead us to a greater understanding of our own sensibilities.

INTRODUCTION

Kabuki adeptly incorporates and preserves for us various performing arts that were both preexisting and contemporaneous, as well as prevailing cultural elements and customs. For example, there are many common objects that were used by our ancestors on a daily basis that can now only be seen on the kabuki stage. Or, tracing the relationship in reverse, we can find many expressions in common use today that originated with kabuki.[1]

The Japanese history taught in our schools focuses almost exclusively on heroic figures and the achievements of the great and mighty. This alone isn't enough for a complete historical understanding, however. For a novelist such as myself, kabuki provides an important glimpse into the lifestyles and attitudes of ordinary people who lived in past eras.

Understanding kabuki is thus nothing less than understanding ourselves as Japanese. In a long-gone era when movies, television, computers, and other forms of entertainment did not exist, what was it that fascinated Japanese audiences and excited their passions as they packed themselves into local theaters? Contemplating this while watching performances is yet another way to enjoy this stage art.

As I noted earlier, kabuki is easier to understand if we think of it as a cross section of geological strata and examine the layers in chronological order from oldest to newest. With that in mind, I'll focus on 10 famous plays in the current repertory and examine them from the "bottom" up. By considering how the plays are constructed and how they were received by audiences of the day, I'll identify certain Japanese sensibilities and mentalities that have remained fairly constant, while highlighting others that have undergone significant change. In the process, I hope to help readers rediscover the appeal of kabuki, a stage art that was engendered by those very sensibilities.

# Kabuki Timeline and Book Structure

| Date | Event | Description |
|---|---|---|
| Keichō 8 (1603) | Ieyasu establishes the Tokugawa shogunate in Edo | Okuni from Izumo dances *kabuki odori* in the riverbed at Shijō Road in Kyoto. Other performers imitate her and *yūjo kabuki* (prostitute kabuki), an imitation of Okuni's revue, becomes popular. *Yūjo kabuki* is banned and *wakashu kabuki* (youth kabuki) becomes popular. |
| Kan'ei 14 (1637) | Shimabara Rebellion | *Wakashu kabuki* is banned, ushering in the era of *yarō kabuki* (men's kabuki) performed by young men with shaved forelocks that signify adulthood.<br>• Ichikawa Danjūrō originates the *aragoto* (bravura) style in Edo. |
| | **Chapter 1** | **A Hero in the Nick of Time—*Shibaraku*** |
| Genroku Era | | Chikamatsu Monzaemon leads the golden age of kabuki in Osaka and Kyoto.<br>• Sakata Tōjūrō pioneers the *wagoto* (gentle) style in Osaka and Kyoto. |
| | **Chapter 2** | **Descendants of Hikaru Genji, the Shining Prince—*Kuruwa Bunshō*** |
| Genroku 15 (1702) | Akō Incident | |
| Kyōhō 1 (1716) | Kyōhō Reforms | Double-suicide plays are banned.<br>Many *Gidayū kyōgen* (kabuki adaptations of popular *jōruri* puppet plays) are performed.<br>• Historical plays become popular. |
| | **Chapter 3** | **Plays of Substitute Sacrifice—*Sugawara Denju Tenarai Kagami*** |
| | **Chapter 4** | **Humans Seen through Animal Fantasies—*Yoshitsune Senbonzakura*** |

| | | |
|---|---|---|
| An'ei 1 (1772) | **Chapter 5** | More than Just a Tale of Feudal Loyalty—*Kanadehon Chūshingura* |
| | | • "Chivalrous commoner" plays become popular. |
| | **Chapter 6** | The Birth of Chivalry—*Natsu Matsuri Naniwa Kagami* |
| Tanuma Okitsugu becomes a senior counselor | | Namiki Shōza completes development of the revolving stage. Other set improvements continue to evolve. |
| | | • Birth of "sedition" plays. |
| | **Chapter 7** | A Montage of Stage Effects—*Sanmon Gosan no Kiri* |
| | | • Dance-drama reaches its peak. |
| Tenmei 7 (1787) | **Chapter 8** | A Stylish Fairy-Tale Dance—*Tsumoru Koi Yuki no Seki no To* |
| Kansei Reforms | | |
| Bunka/ Bunsei Eras | | • Tsuruya Nanboku develops *kizewa* (raw domestic) style. |
| | **Chapter 9** | Queen of Japanese Horror—*Tōkaidō Yotsuya Kaidan* |
| Tenpō 12 (1841) | | |
| Tenpō Reforms | | • Kawatake Mokuami is active as a playwright. "Bandit" plays become popular. |
| Kaei 6 (1853) | | |
| Commodore Perry arrives in Japanese waters | **Chapter 10** | "Bonnie and Clyde," Japanese Style—*Sannin Kichisa Kuruwa no Hatsugai* |
| Keiō 3 (1867) | | |
| *Taisei hōkan* (Return of Political Rule to the Emperor) | | Theater reform movements arise and kabuki comes to be regarded as a "classical" stage art. |

CHAPTER ONE

# *Shibaraku*

## A Hero in the Nick of Time

### A Show of Strength

The kabuki pieces that survive today have stood the test of time and won over successive generations of theatergoers. They've also evolved over the years, undergoing repeated revision and improvement. This process has kept them modern and fresh, which is one reason they're still with us today. The piece *Shibaraku* (Stop Right There!) belongs to the oldest stratum of kabuki's geological cross section and exemplifies the kinds of changes that have occurred.

As today's kabuki fans well know, "shibaraku" is the phrase spoken by the hero when he makes his grand entrance. His hair is splayed out like giant spider legs in the *kurumabin*[1] style and his face is decorated in the dynamic stripes of *sujiguma*[2] makeup, which symbolizes his great strength. He enters the stage in a two-piece *suō*[3] costume with gigantic sleeves, bearing a huge sword more than two meters long. When people think of kabuki, this is often the iconic image that comes to mind.

The story as performed today is very simple. A dastardly villain plotting to usurp the imperial throne captures virtuous men and women who stand in his way and orders his minions to behead them. But just in the nick of time, we hear a voice boom out "Stop!" from the back of the theater, and the hero strides down the *hanamichi* bridgeway to save the day. With clever repartee and physical might, he punishes the evildoer, rescues the prisoners, and gallantly continues on his way. Although that's all there is to the plot, this vivacious play is full of distinctive characters, including the *haradashi* ("bare-bellied") minions with their bright red faces and protruding red bellies, and the comic sidekick villain Namazu Bōzu (catfish priest), with his absurdly long sideburns hanging down like pigtails.

Interestingly, *Shibaraku* was not originally the title of a play or the name of a role, but referred to the type of character that entered using the "Stop right there!" catchphrase. First appearing at the end of the seventeenth century, the original type belongs to the oldest stratum of kabuki but has undergone gradual change with the years. Let's examine where it first appeared, how it was received by audiences of the time, and what aspects of it have survived to the present day.

## Fresh New Star

The first to play the *Shibaraku* hero was an actor named Ichikawa Danjūrō I. Shortly before that debut, from around the middle of the seventeenth century, a form of puppet theater called *Kinpira jōruri*[4] was very popular in Edo (now Tokyo). "Kinpira" refers to Sakata no Kinpira, the protagonist in many of these puppet plays, which featured violent action that included puppets' heads being torn off and characters beating each other. Danjūrō I is said to have painted his whole body red to bring the role of Sakata no Kinpira to the kabuki stage. In today's terms it would be like an actor taking on the role of an anime action hero in a live action film. The

## Typical Kumadori Makeup Patterns

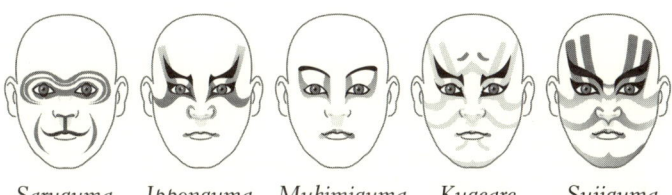

Saruguma   Ipponguma   Mukimiguma   Kugeare   Sujiguma

bigger-than-life acting technique Danjūrō I employed for this role came to be called the *aragoto* (bravura) style of acting.

Danjūrō, of course, used the bright red body paint to infuse the heroic role with childlike vitality. One is reminded of a comment made by the internationally acclaimed contemporary artist Murakami Takashi, who asserts that one of Japan's most distinctive charms for the world is its "culture of cuteness."[5] *Shibaraku* marked the birth of a cute, new hero brimming with youthful energy. It also provided a launching pad for Danjūrō himself.

## Otherworldly Authority versus the People's Hero

Let's turn now to the first time that Danjūrō I performed *Shibaraku*, which was a scene in the play *Sankai Nagoya*. The story is preserved in an illustrated synopsis (*e-iri kyōgen bon*)[6] dating from the time.

A man is hanging his business ledger at a Shinto shrine as a votive offering when a villain appears to tear it down. Just as the villain is about to pull down the offering, the hero calls out "Shibaraku!" to prevent the offense.

The villain justifies his actions, saying that a ledger is a common item found in any merchant's home and is therefore unfit to serve as a shrine offering. But the hero comes to the man's defense. In extremely ornate and difficult language, he argues that, just as the bow and arrow are always found in the home of a samurai, ledgers are always found in the homes of commoners, making them highly prized treasures worthy of being used as an offering. The villain is ultimately overwhelmed by the hero's hairsplitting repartee.

The role of the villain is called *uke* (literally, "receiver") because it's the job of that character to take the verbal jabs hurled by the hero as he enters along the *hanamichi* bridgeway. The villain is dressed in a style conventionally associated with an aristocrat of the imperial court. The first actor to play the *uke* role was Yamanaka Heikurō,[7] who is said to have possessed a terrifying visage. According to one *yakusha hyōbanki*[8] guidebook, which comments on the acting skills and popularity of kabuki actors, "his ferociousness is almost inhuman."[9] His costume as a court aristocrat would have been unfamiliar to most townspeople in Edo, lending him a demonic air as if he'd come from a different world. A modern equivalent of such a character may be Darth Vader in *Star Wars*. Defending ordinary people against unearthly authority and power, the hero outwits the villain using nonsensical arguments. This is the essence of *Shibaraku*.

*Sankai Nagoya* is the oldest extant synopsis we have of a play that features a *Shibaraku* scene. Other early plays with this scene also feature a ledger. Observant modern playgoers have probably noticed that a ledger is always displayed near the *uke* role even today as a vestige of this early practice (see plate 1), even though it no longer has any relevance to the plot.

Audiences in the Edo period (1600–1868) believed that kabuki plays should be placed within the context of an older tale, so the first step in creating a play was to decide what tale to use as the background "world."[10] Naturally, the characters to be featured would vary depending on what world was chosen.

Today, the hero depicted in *Shibaraku* is customarily identified as Kamakura Gongorō Kagemasa, but in the Edo period his name would change depending on the "world" that was being portrayed. Suppose, for example, the backstory was provided by the *Gikeiki*, a chronicle of the exploits of the great warrior Minamoto no Yoshitsune. In this case the character making the *Shibaraku* entrance would be identified as Yoshitsune's trusted retainer, Musashibō Benkei. From this we can see that *Shibaraku* was originally a vignette that could be inserted into different plays and take on various specific features depending on the context.

Ichikawa Danjūrō I

Danjūrō I played the *Shibaraku* hero Kamakura Gongorō Kagemasa with a bright red face and body like a modern-day action figure. (From the print series *Ichikawa Danjūrō Daidai* [Generations of Ichikawa Danjūrō] by Ichiyōsai Toyokuni.)

The character Kamakura Gongorō Kagemasa emerged early in kabuki history, and Danjūrō I himself is known to have played the role. It was not until the time of Danjūrō IX at the end of the nineteenth century, however, that *Shibaraku* solidified into a one-act play with a fairly standardized script. Danjūrō IX performed *Shibaraku* three times during his career, and the script he used in his last performance of it forms the basis for the piece we have today.

## *Shibaraku* as a Symbol of Resurrection

It was Danjūrō II who took his father's original *Shibaraku* character and gave it the costume we know and love today.

## Shibaraku

Danjūrō I was murdered in the theater by another actor while Danjūrō II was still in his teens. Initially, Danjūrō II was shunned by the theater after the incident, but the tragedy ultimately spurred him to great heights as an actor. Before he died peacefully at the age of 71, he reigned supreme in the theater world and was hailed for surpassing his father. It was Danjūrō II who etched the Danjūrō name in the pantheon of famous kabuki actors in Edo.

The basic look of the *Shibaraku* hero created by Danjūrō II incorporated a *sumimaegami* (shaved forelock) wig that was normally used for youths who had not quite reached adulthood. The main costume element was a brick-red, two-piece *suō* suit made of linen. The *suō* used in today's performances with its gigantic sleeves requires 60–100 meters of cloth — enough material to make ordinary kimonos for five to eight people. When the hero enters, his sleeves are suspended and displayed like kites on rattan sticks. Although Danjūrō II's costume was apparently not quite that extreme, we do know that the use of the *suō* itself, as well as the large

Ichikawa Danjūrō I
The *Shibaraku* hero Kamakura Gongorō Kagemasa as portrayed by Danjūrō II in his youth (print by Torii Kiyomine). Photo courtesy of Hiraki Ukiyoe Foundation.

Danjūrō's post-illness depiction of the *Shibaraku* hero. Note the shaved forelock wig and *sujiguma* makeup (print by Utagawa Toyokuni III).

sword, shaved forelock wig, and striped *sujiguma* makeup, all started with him.

Danjūrō II did not adopt this look from the start, however. An illustration included in one actors' guidebook[11] and other sources show that, when he was in his twenties, he sported a clean-shaven pate and had mustaches angled sharply upward, a style indicating a grown man.

The name "Danjūrō" is associated with physically large, narrow-faced men, but Danjūrō II was a small man with a boyish face, according to one guidebook.[12] It seems that his youthfulness was what made him popular, at least in his early years. When he reached his forties, he encountered career difficulties. Either because audiences grew tired of him or he just fell into a personal slump, he stopped enjoying the hits he had achieved earlier, and his reputation among critics gradually declined. At age 48 he suffered a further blow when he grew seriously ill and was forced to stop acting for about five months to recuperate. After his recovery he resumed his performances but did so using the name Ichikawa Ebizō.

"Ebizō" was the childhood name of Danjūrō I. Danjūrō II's childhood name had been Kuzō, so his use of "Ebizō" meant he was going back in time and adopting his father's childhood name. Significantly, it was just before his fiftieth birthday that he changed the look of his *Shibaraku* character by adopting the shaved forelock wig. His audiences are likely to have interpreted this change as proof of his own resurrection and of his desire to express youthful vigor.

In his first stage appearance after his recovery, the newly renamed Ebizō reportedly addressed the audience directly, telling them that he had conquered his illness by eating many carrots. A published critique of that performance[13] reports that "the entrance cry of 'shibaraku, shibaraku' resounded throughout Edo with tremendous success," suggesting the wild enthusiasm with which the denizens of Edo embraced the actor's rebirth. Personally, I've always suspected that it was precisely this enthusiasm that established the shaved forelock wig as the customary look of the *Shibaraku* hero. Some scholars recognize a folkloric significance in Ebizō's decision to give the hero a younger appearance. As a novelist, though, I couldn't help but think about Ebizō's personal life as I read through the research materials. The joy of being resurrected after struggling five months with illness must have been thrilling for himself, his family and friends, and his legions of fans. Even now I well up with emotion when I think of it.

## Character Development and Variations

After overcoming illness and being reborn with his new name Ebizō, Danjūrō II went on to dominate the theater scene in Edo for many years, living to a ripe old age of 71. He nurtured and trained many younger actors, including Danjūrō IV, an apprentice turned son-in-law who inherited and continued the *Shibaraku* tradition.

It's interesting to note that Danjūrō IV was well-suited for villains' roles. One anecdote relates how, while playing the *uke* with another actor doing the *Shibaraku* hero, he made an inside joke. As the catchphrase was being boomed out by the

A Hero in the Nick of Time

*Kurumabin* is cited in *Shibai Kinmō Zui* as the wig used in *Shibaraku*.

other actor on the bridgeway he asked, "Why is someone out there prattling 'shibaraku' when I'm right here?" That's the extent to which *Shibaraku*'s lead role had come to be associated with the Danjūrō name.

The splayed *kurumabin* hairstyle now used for the *Shibaraku* hero was probably first adopted by Danjūrō V (1741–1806), as it appears in an illustrated encyclopedia called *Shibai Kinmō Zui* published in 1803 that details various aspects of kabuki and theater life.[14]

The woodblock prints depicting Danjūrō VII (1791–1859) in the *Shibaraku* role show costumes and wigs that are virtually identical to those used today. It was this Danjūrō who, with the intention of establishing the works of his forebears as a classical repertory, identified the *Kabuki Jūhachiban* — the "18 Favorite Plays" of the Danjūrō line of actors, which includes *Shibaraku*.

While the costume was exaggerated in various ways as it evolved into its present form, the content of the play itself also developed many variations. Danjūrō IV's performance of the *uke* role cited above can be counted as one example.

15

The 18 Favorite Plays

1. *Fuwa* (Fuwa)
2. *Narukami* (Narukami)
3. *Shibaraku* (Stop Right There!)
4. *Fudō* (Fudo the Wisdom King)
5. *Uwanari* (Jealousy)
6. *Zōhiki* (Pulling the Elephant)
7. *Kanjinchō* (The Subscription List)
8. *Sukeroku* (Sukeroku)
9. *Oshimodoshi* (The Demon Repeller)
10. *Uirō Uri* (The Medicine Peddler)
11. *Ya-no-Ne* (The Arrow Sharpener)
12. *Kan'u* (Kan'u)
13. *Kagekiyo* (Kagekiyo)
14. *Nanatsumen* (Seven Masks)
15. *Kenuki* (Tweezers)
16. *Gedatsu* (Salvation)
17. *Jayanagi* (Snake Willow)
18. *Kamahige* (Sickle Beard)

During the Tenpō era (1830–1844) Ichikawa Danjūrō VII selected these 18 plays as the representative works performed by the Danjūrō line of actors. Including major hits highlighting the artistry of this lineage, they showcase the *aragoto* (bravura) style of acting, which originated with the Ichikawa clan. The fact that he was brash enough to claim that his family's art was the best that kabuki had to offer not only shows Danjūrō VII's robust self-regard but also suggests that the time had come for kabuki to be recognized as a "classical" art form.

Another, more extreme example is the play *Shitennō Ubuyu no Tamagawa* (The Four Guardian Kings at the Ubuyu and Tama Rivers),[15] in which Danjūrō VII performed the *Shibaraku* scene as a play within a play, portraying himself. There was also a variation called *Onna Shibaraku* (Woman *Shibaraku*)[16] tailored to an era when popular *onnagata* (male actors who play women's roles) emerged. Apparently, there was even a version that did away with the "shibaraku" phrase altogether, but this evidently proved unpopular and did not survive. In all other cases, however, the hero (or heroine) always arrived in the nick of time and made a grand entrance after calling out "Shibaraku!" from behind the curtain on the bridgeway.

## Vehicle for an All-Star Cast

Once the content of *Shibaraku* was more or less set, its place in kabuki programming was also established. The *Ehon Shibai Nenjū Kagami* (Illustrated Compendium of Annual Theater Practices)[17] published in 1803 notes that *Shibaraku* was always performed as the "third act" (*mitateme*) of the first main play in the first program of the theater season. Before the "third act," it was customary to perform a prelude (*jobiraki*) and a "second act" (*futatsume*), usually a short comic skit. The *mitateme*, then, was the opening act of the program's main presentation. Thus we see that by the end of the seventeenth century, *Shibaraku* was already firmly established in the kabuki repertory. With a few exceptions, theater professionals and audiences alike had come to expect its performance in the first program of the theater season.

In the Edo period, actors signed annual contracts, and the first program of each season was a star-studded event called the *kaomise* (literally, "face showing"). Because the *kaomise* was designed to introduce that year's star performers, preposterous and illogical storylines were tolerated as long as the actors were shown in the best possible light.

In Danjūrō I's time, *Shibaraku* was a new vignette that might be performed any time of the year. Beginning with Danjūrō II, however, it came to be customarily performed in *kaomise* programs. Though it became rather stereotyped, it endured because it provided an excellent vehicle to display the talents of each new season's actors. In fact, it was an advantage to have the audience eagerly anticipate the well-known entrance of the *Shibaraku* hero. Today, the hero might interpolate jokes like "Well, here I am again" when he makes his entrance, which of course is premised on the fact that it's a yearly event that audiences have grown to expect.

Danjūrō II once performed *Shibaraku* by having a character in the preceding comic skit open a letter attached to an arrow that was shot onto the stage. The letter bore the single Chinese character for "shibaraku," and provided the cue for the hero to make his entrance. Precisely because the piece became stereotyped, many variations, including exaggerated costuming, were explored as a means of surprising and delighting audiences.

## The Context of an Urban Festival

During the Edo period, the *kaomise* program that marked the beginning of the new theater season was always presented in the eleventh month of the lunar calendar, which corresponds with the Chinese New Year dating to the Zhou dynasty. It was the time of the winter solstice and the longest nights of the year.

Some researchers say that Christmas was superimposed on the winter solstice holidays of ancient Rome, a fact that illustrates just how important the solstice is to people everywhere. The darkest, longest night of the year also serves as the starting point for a renewed journey into light and is a time that people mark with festivals. Kabuki's *kaomise* program can be considered the winter festival of the city of Edo, and *Shibaraku* can be viewed as that festival's essential star character.

Try to imagine the theater on those dark winter nights. With no electric lighting, it must have been much darker than the theaters we have today. Then imagine the *Shibaraku* hero striding out to vanquish the demonic villain in a scene that was repeated year after year. There was something there that thrilled the hearts of ordinary people. It's not just that the

Japanese are fond of one-pattern storylines. Whether it's the TV period drama *Mito Kōmon* or the science fiction series *Ultraman*, we want to see a hero fight for justice by appearing in the nick of time to save the day. Common people could not possibly strike the blow themselves and only had a vague conception of power and authority. They longed for a hero who, however improbably, could decisively punish formidable evildoers. That's the secret of *Shibaraku*'s popularity.

More than anything, *Shibaraku* is founded on the premise of youth. There's meaning in the fact that, at the age of 48, Danjūrō II earned enthusiastic accolades when he used a shaved forelock wig to portray the hero as an adolescent. In fact, the hero is treated as a child in the script, at one point being told, "Out of my way, youngster." His hairsplitting repartee with the villain has an extremely childish flavor, and the fact that the entire piece is suffused with a childlike atmosphere is part of its appeal. In the context of an urban festival during the darkest time of the year, *Shibaraku* provided a moment of joy and excitement that accompanied the entrance of a hero bursting with youthful vitality. Watching this play today, I fancy I can hear the echoing applause of the people of old Edo.

# Generations of Danjūrō

### Danjūrō I (1660–1704)
Founder of the Ichikawa Danjūrō lineage. His birth surname was Horikoshi and his "shop name" (*yagō*) was Naritaya. Descended from samurai stock in Kōshū, he knew how to use a sword and battleax, which proved useful when he developed the *aragoto* style. He authored plays under the pen name Mimasuya Hyōgo, including *Sankai Nagoya*, which contained the original *Shibaraku* vignette. A proud and difficult man, he offended a fellow actor named Ikushima Hanroku, who stabbed him to death in a theater.

### Danjūrō II (1688–1758)
Oldest son of Danjūrō I. Adopting the Danjūrō name at age 17 after his father was murdered, he went on to become one of the leading actors of the Kyōhō era (1716–1736). He premiered such works as: *Ya-no-Ne* (The Arrow Sharpener), with Soga Gorō as the protagonist; *Sukeroku*, which incorporated the *wagoto* (gentle) style that was popular in Kyoto and Osaka; and *Uirō Uri* (The Medicine Peddler), which highlighted oratory and word play. He also wrote a diary under his haiku name Hakuen that vividly conveys the life of an Edo-period actor.

### Danjūrō IV (1702–1778)
Adopted son of Matsumoto Kōshirō I, and husband of Danjūrō II's adopted daughter. It was also rumored that he might be the illegitimate son of Danjūrō II himself. Before assuming the Danjūrō name he specialized in villains' roles, but he later broadened his artistic scope to include realistic portrayals. After retiring at age 66, he devoted his energies to nurturing young actors. He established a study group on acting that met in his home in Fukugawa Kiba that earned him the sobriquet, "Godfather of Kiba."

### Danjūrō V (1741–1806)
Son of Danjūrō IV. Like his father, he came to the Danjūrō name after being called Matsumoto Kōshirō. He had a versatility that ranged from *aragoto* roles to *onnagata* female roles and was lionized by the leading cultural figures of Edo during the Tenmei and Kansei eras (1781–1801), when Edo's urban culture reached full maturity. A true man of letters and a haiku poet, he was a follower of Bashō and wrote many satirical *tanka* short poems under the tutelage of Ōta Shokusanjin.

### Danjūrō VII (1791–1859)
Grandson of Danjūrō V and adopted son of Danjūrō VI. He received the Danjūrō name when just 10 years old, after the premature death of Danjūrō VI. A master of *aragoto*, *wagoto*, and realistic acting styles, he dominated the Edo theater scene in the first half of the nineteenth century. However, his extravagant lifestyle ran afoul of the sumptuary laws enacted as part of the Tenpō Reforms of 1842, inflicting on him the hardship of being banished from Edo for more than seven years.

### Danjūrō VIII (1823–1854)
The oldest son of Danjūrō VII, he assumed the Danjūrō name at age 10. Oval-faced and very handsome, he revitalized the theater district in Edo, which by then had relocated to Asakusa Saruwakachō. The part of Kirare Yosaburō in the play *Yowa Nasake Ukinano Yokogushi* (or *Kirare Yosa, Scarred Yosa*) became his signature role. In 1854 he visited his father in Osaka and, just before he was to perform there, committed suicide under mysterious circumstances.

### Danjūrō IX (1838–1903)
Fifth son of Danjūrō VII, he assumed the Danjūrō name in 1874. Famous as a master of all kabuki styles including men's and *onnagata* roles, villains, period pieces, contemporary pieces, and dance, he dominated the theater world in the late eighteenth and early nineteenth centuries. An avid reformer, he championed historically accurate plays that were based on true events, identified a new set of "18 Favorite Plays," and built the foundation for modern kabuki.

# Successive Danjūrō Generations Carry on the *Aragoto* Acting Style

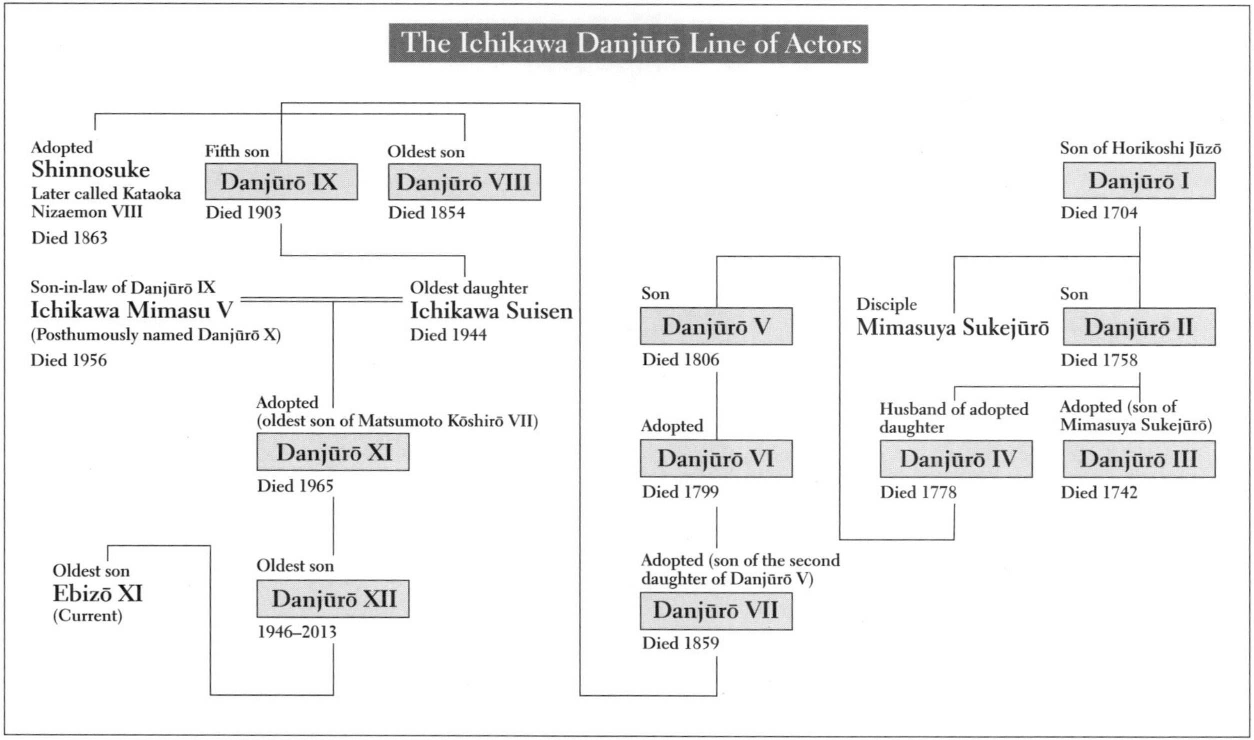

## The Ichikawa Danjūrō Line of Actors

**Danjūrō I** — Son of Horikoshi Jūzō — Died 1704

↓ Son

**Danjūrō II** — Died 1758

- Disciple → **Mimasuya Sukejūrō**
- Adopted (son of Mimasuya Sukejūrō) → **Danjūrō III** — Died 1742
- Husband of adopted daughter → **Danjūrō IV** — Died 1778

↓ Son

**Danjūrō V** — Died 1806

↓ Adopted

**Danjūrō VI** — Died 1799

Adopted (son of the second daughter of Danjūrō V) → **Danjūrō VII** — Died 1859

- Adopted → **Shinnosuke**, Later called Kataoka Nizaemon VIII — Died 1863
- Fifth son → **Danjūrō IX** — Died 1903
- Oldest son → **Danjūrō VIII** — Died 1854

**Danjūrō IX** — Oldest daughter → **Ichikawa Suisen** — Died 1944

Son-in-law of Danjūrō IX → **Ichikawa Mimasu V** (Posthumously named Danjūrō X) — Died 1956

Adopted (oldest son of Matsumoto Kōshirō VII) → **Danjūrō XI** — Died 1965

Oldest son → **Danjūrō XII** — 1946–2013

Oldest son → **Ebizō XI** (Current)

CHAPTER TWO

# Kuruwa Bunshō

## Descendents of Hikaru Genji, the Shining Prince

### A Memorial Service for a Courtesan

Danjūrō's *Shibaraku* provided a glimpse of the oldest stratum of kabuki in Edo. Now let's look at *Kuruwa Bunshō* (Love Letters from the Licensed Quarter), a play still popular today that dates back to the earliest days of kabuki as performed in Kyoto and Osaka.

First, a little historical context. In the seventeenth century, a courtesan by the name of Yūgiri[1] became so famous for her beauty that when she moved by boat from Kyoto's Shimabara brothel district to Osaka, crowds of spectators gathered on the riverside to get a glimpse of her. Courtesans in those days were more than prostitutes; they were celebrities.

In his *Kōshoku Ichidai Otoko* (The Life of an Amorous Man), the seventeenth-century poet and popular fiction writer Ihara Saikaku[2] described Yūgiri as a courtesan "peerless since the age of the gods." But in a tragedy that shocked the nation, this young beauty died at the age of 25. There's a tradition in kabuki dating back to its founding by Okuni (see chapter 8) in which the deceased are memorialized onstage. Yūgiri was

23

resurrected in this way in a very successful play titled *Yūgiri Kyōgen* (The Yūgiri Play).

The lead role in this play was performed by Sakata Tōjūrō I.[3] He did not portray Yūgiri herself, however—he played the part of Yūgiri's lover, the playboy Fujiya Izaemon. The piece was so successful that Tōjūrō starred in 18 different production runs of it during his lifetime, allowing him to share the stage with a glittering (though deceased) celebrity and making him a top star in his own right. Tōjūrō had already gained considerable fame thanks to plays written originally for the puppet theater by Chikamatsu Monzaemon.[4] Teaming up with that playwright, he went on to generate many more hits in the Genroku era (1688–1704), which is considered the golden age of kabuki.

*Kuruwa Bunshō* is an adaptation of a scene from *Yūgiri Kyōgen* and gives us a glimpse of how the full-length play was performed by Tōjūrō I. It depicts the disinherited and penniless Izaemon visiting his former lover Yūgiri in a ragged, paper kimono (see plate 2). Yūgiri had become ill after Izaemon left her, but she has returned to work at the restaurant-brothel Yoshidaya, whose owner kindly allows Izaemon to enter. Yūgiri is engaged with another patron, however, and Izaemon must wait to see her. Growing increasingly impatient and jealous, he sulks and picks a fight when she finally appears. Their interaction until they settle their lovers' quarrel is performed as a dance drama.

The paper kimono, incidentally, was something poor people wore to fend off the cold and was indicative of just how far Izaemon had fallen. He was the scion of a wealthy family but had spent all of his money on women in the pleasure quarters. He returns to his woman, but only to sulk and complain—one can hardly call him admirable, and yet he's the hero of the play. I call this type of character the "profligate hero," and

I'd like to take a moment to consider why *kamigata* (western Japan) theatergoers found this kind of protagonist so endearing.

## Penniless, Debauched Young Men

Although a specific model for the Izaemon character hasn't been identified, quite a few people like him did in fact exist. This can be deduced from the fact that many episodes in *Saikaku Okimiyage* (Saikaku's Parting Gift)[5] describe men who ruined themselves by spending their fortunes on courtesans.

Saikaku's bestselling *Kōshoku Ichidai Otoko*[6] was an immensely popular fictional biography of a playboy named Yonosuke. After dallying with all kinds of women over many years, he sails to a happy ending on a mythical island inhabited only by women. In stark contrast, *Saikaku Okimiyage*, written in the author's later years, focuses on men who were ruined because of their relationships with women.

This change probably reflects a general shift in the economy. Japan in the last decades of the seventeenth century experienced a bubble that quickly burst in the early eighteenth century. In *Saikaku Okimiyage* the author writes: "People have recently become frugal with their entertainment, unlike the free-spending past."

In *Nippon Eitaigura* (The Eternal Storehouse of Japan),[7] Saikaku observed that the wealthy class used to consist of enterprising men who founded their own successful businesses, but the only skill their sons and grandsons appeared to have was dissipating their inheritances through licentious extravagance. This was the world that prevailed when the author wrote *Saikaku Okimiyage* late in life. There were many real-life examples of men who had fallen into ruin. Plays that featured such "profligate heroes" probably seemed quite realistic and struck a chord with audiences.

One anecdote provides a fascinating insight into Tōjūrō's acting style. A rural man came to town and, at the urging of a friend, went to see Tōjūrō perform. Asked for his impressions, the man said, "I must have gone on a bad day. Tōjūrō spent the whole time having a meeting onstage and never got around to performing a play."[8] What he saw, though, was the very essence of Tōjūrō's art.

Tōjūrō was not interested in bigger-than-life action heroes. The types of plays he specialized in were called *ikyōgen*,[9] which roughly means "sitting kabuki." It was centered on dialogue and presented scenes from daily life. So it wouldn't be surprising if someone unfamiliar with this style failed to understand his art. He did enjoy an enthusiastic following among the upper class in Genroku-era Kyoto, however, and was often featured in *hyōbanki* guidebooks and other contemporary publications.

In 1712, three years after Tōjūrō's death, Chikamatsu wrote the play *Yūgiri Awa no Naruto* (Yūgiri and the Awa Whirlpool) for the puppet theater. By this time he had left kabuki behind and was writing almost exclusively for the puppets. But this play features the character Fujiya Izaemon as the protagonist—the very role that had made his friend Tōjūrō famous.

Here's a summary of the plot. The disinherited and destitute Izaemon visits Yūgiri at the brothel where she works. As in earlier plays featuring these characters, he quarrels with her for making him wait while she serves another patron. It turns out, though, that the patron is not a man but Oyuki, the disguised wife of a samurai named Hiraoka Sakon from Awa province. Oyuki has agreed to adopt the love child of Yūgiri and Izaemon and raise him as Sakon's son. Understanding Yūgiri's difficult position, Oyuki also agrees to ransom her freedom from the brothel and hire her as a nursemaid. Izaemon secretly follows Yūgiri and is able to meet his son, but this angers Sakon, who cuts all ties with the boy. Yūgiri returns to the brothel and falls critically ill. Just as she's bidding a final farewell to Izaemon and their son on her deathbed, Izaemon's mother appears, reverses his disownment, and announces that Yūgiri shall be his wife. The joyous news prompts Yūgiri's recovery, and the play ends happily.

The first scene of the puppet play *Yūgiri Awa no Naruto* was fashioned into the independent kabuki play *Kuruwa Bunshō*. Thus, the original hit kabuki play *Yūgiri Kyōgen* was rewritten as *Yūgiri Awa no Naruto* for the puppets, and then brought back to the kabuki stage in the form of *Kuruwa Bunshō*.

## From Realistic Dialogue to Dance

Although the story of *Kuruwa Bunshō* hasn't changed, the version we now have is no longer based on Tōjūrō's acting style. Tōjūrō portrayed a realistic quarrel between lovers that was fueled by jealousy, but the piece as performed today is a dance drama. Let's look at how this change came about.

In the 1740s, a popular song called *Yukari no Tsuki* (Moonlight of Love) was incorporated into the play:

> I met a sweet man in Osaka
> But, oh, the ways of the world are harsher than a locked gate
> My love is trapped by a man who cares nothing for me
> Like a still, murky pond in wild Nozawa Marsh
> How my heart longs for the clear moonlight of his love.

Even today, this song is performed as background music for the scene in which Izaemon waits for Yūgiri to appear, played by *geza*[10] musicians as a *nagauta*[11] piece. Songs like this were equivalent to pop songs today. Cast in *bungo-bushi*[12] and other singing styles of the time, they became contributing elements in the birth of kabuki dance drama.

Kabuki dance, which I'll discuss in more detail in chapter 8, first flourished in Edo under the influence of the famous dancer Ichimura Uzaemon IX.[13] Subsequently, dance was added to *Kuruwa Bunshō* by Nakamura Tomijūrō I,[14] Segawa Kikunojō III,[15] and Nakamura Utaemon III.[16] One interesting detail is that both Kikunojō and Tomijūrō were *onnagata* (male actors playing female roles), but each had experience playing both the Izaemon and Yūgiri roles and sometimes performed the play together. The staging we have today may well have evolved through their interaction. To the choreography developed by the two *onnagata* actors, Utaemon III[16] added a comical touch, thereby creating many variations that survive to this day.[17]

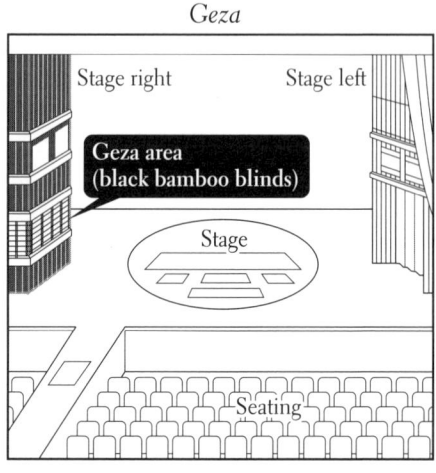

In outlining the plot of *Kuruwa Bunshō* above, I mentioned the use of a paper kimono. In modern performances, one would never guess the costume was meant to signify poverty without some prior explanation. In Tōjūrō's day the dialogue was delivered so realistically that untutored playgoers mistook it for a run-through. This commitment to realism extended to the costume, which was actually made of paper.

Once dance was incorporated into the piece in the mid-eighteenth century, however, the costume changed.

According to one contemporary *hyōbanki* guidebook, Ichimura Uzaemon IX wore "a *kosode* (small-sleeved) kimono patterned like a quilt of stitched-together papers embroidered with love poems."[18] Already by this time, the costume was not made of actual paper but featured a pattern that suggested paper. A hundred or so years after Tōjūrō first performed the Izaemon role at the end of the seventeenth century, the costume had become quite ornate, and the play itself had become a splendidly showy dance drama quite unlike the original dialogue-based work performed in the Genroku era.

## The Elegance of Shabbiness

"Profligate heroes" continued to appear in many plays after the debut of the Izaemon character. Typically, they are philandering scions of wealthy families who fall on hard times, meet with former concubines, and fall into lovers' quarrels. It's important to note that kabuki audiences had a deep fondness for plays about such characters. To help explain this phenomenon, I'd like to return to Sakata Tōjūrō I, who was called the "Father of *Yatsushi-goto*." What exactly is *yatsushi-goto*?

The verb *yatsusu* was an everyday expression in western Japan until very recently. It means to look good or dress sharply, and people equated it with being stylish. But its original meaning was to be haggard or worn out, and it was used to describe a seedy or shabby appearance. This transformation in meaning can be traced to the *yatsushi-goto* style of kabuki acting, with roots deeply embedded in the aesthetic sensibilities of the Japanese.

The idea of a high-born person relegated to a lowly position can be found in cultures throughout the world. In Greek mythology, for example, there are many stories of gods disguising themselves as humans or even animals. Stories similar to that of Mark Twain's *The Prince and the Pauper* can also be found universally. Cultural anthropologists might point to a popular fascination with "strangers" from outside the community or, from a different perspective, might interpret the tale as a rite of passage for a ruler who falls from grace and must undergo trials before being restored to his rightful place.

The folklorist Orikuchi Shinobu[19] called this motif *kishu ryūri*, or the wayfaring noble. Found in many Japanese tales, it typically portrays an exalted person who is forced by circumstance to wander aimlessly. The *yatsushi-goto* theme in kabuki is another example of this archetype.

## Tōjūrō as Hikaru Genji

The premise of *yatsushi-goto*, with the protagonist portrayed in a guise far less exalted than his actual station in life, was a staple of Genroku-era kabuki. The play *Keisei Hotoke no Hara* (The Courtesan on Buddha Plain),[20] which Sakata Tōjūrō I premiered in the lead role, is representative of the genre. This was a spectacular hit written by Chikamatsu specifically for Tōjūrō, but all that remained of it was an illustrated synopsis. I worked with the late author and playwright Kinoshita Junji[21] to develop a script based on the synopsis, and a revival was staged by the Chikamatsu-za troupe in 1987. The lead role was played by Sakata Tōjūrō IV, who at the time was known as Nakamura Senjaku.

The protagonist in *Keisei Hotoke no Hara* is Umenaga Bunzō, the heir of a powerful daimyo clan. Infatuated with a courtesan and betrayed by villains who exploit his weakness, he finds himself disinherited. As he miserably wanders about wearing only a paper kimono, he reencounters the woman who was the cause of his downfall. She has meanwhile been redeemed from the brothel and has become the mistress of a

# Sakata Tōjūrō and Chikamatsu Monzaemon: Founders of the *Wagoto* Style

Chikamatsu Monzaemon was the premier playwright for the *jōruri* puppet theater during the Genroku era. He was also active for a time as a writer of kabuki plays, nearly all of which were written for Sakata Tōjūrō I. *Keisei Hotoke no Hara* (The Courtesan on Buddha Plain) was one of their greatest successes, making paper kimonos and old straw hats the symbols of the *wagoto* (gentle) acting style.

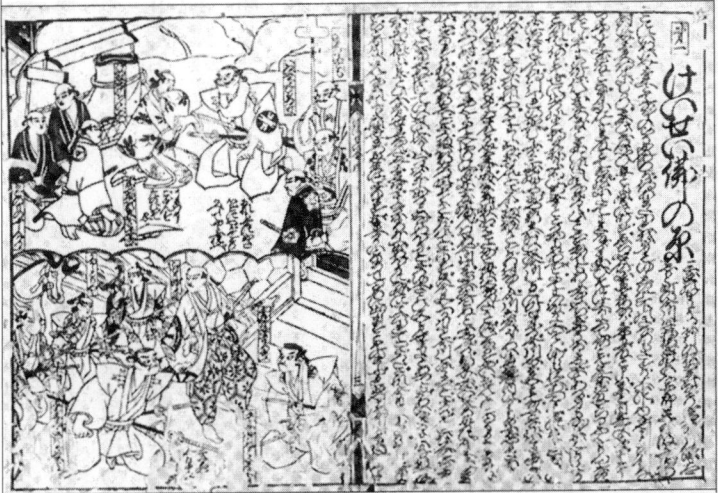

The illustrated synopsis of Chikamatsu Monzaemon's *Keisei Hotoke no Hara*, performed at the Miyako Mandayu-za in Kyoto in the first month of 1699. Found in Ōkorienshū (Collection of the Ancient Pear Orchard).

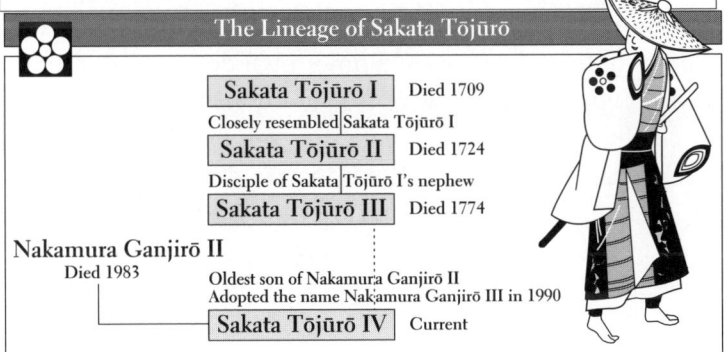

### The Lineage of Sakata Tōjūrō

| Sakata Tōjūrō I | Died 1709 |
|---|---|
| Closely resembled Sakata Tōjūrō I | |
| Sakata Tōjūrō II | Died 1724 |
| Disciple of Sakata Tōjūrō I's nephew | |
| Sakata Tōjūrō III | Died 1774 |

Nakamura Ganjirō II
Died 1983
  Oldest son of Nakamura Ganjirō II
  Adopted the name Nakamura Ganjirō III in 1990

| Sakata Tōjūrō IV | Current |
|---|---|

feudal lord. Though shocked by Bunzō's bedraggled appearance, she tells him that no matter how pitiful he may look, it's in a woman's nature not to abandon a man she loves. This is one important message of the play.

The guidebook *Yakusha Mai Ōgi* (The Actor's Dance Fan) published in 1704 contains the following comment: "Tōjūrō, like Genji before him, shows the people the Way of Dampness."

"Genji" probably refers to Hikaru Genji, the fictional hero of *The Tale of Genji* written by Murasaki Shikibu in the early eleventh century. The "Way of Dampness" refers to carnal relations between men and women. To describe such relations at the level of a "way," as one might describe judo as the "Way of Gentleness," seems like a distinctively Japanese way of thinking. The gist of the quoted comment is that Tōjūrō and Genji both taught the people the quintessence of romantic love. In this sense Tōjūrō can be considered an early modern version of the Shining Prince.

## Dashing, Even in Humble Disguise

Many illustrated and annotated editions of *The Tale of Genji* were published during the Edo period, including the *Kogetsushō* (Moon on the Lake Commentary).[22] The Shining Prince was therefore well known among the general population. Copies of the tale were sometimes included in brides' trousseaus, and courtesans were frequently named after Genji's lovers. Just as we in Japan today are rediscovering the charms of Edo culture, people of the Edo period were fascinated by the Heian period (794–1185). Like their own time, the Heian period was an era of extended peace, and the love affairs of the ancient court had a nostalgic appeal.

One of the most famous episodes in *The Tale of Genji* is the chapter about Genji's lover Yūgao, in which Genji deliberately dresses in a shabby travel cloak and changes his appearance when visiting her. This was because Yūgao, while not exactly poor, lived in a rather ramshackle house. Genji was sensitive enough to know that were he to visit her in his customary splendor, he and Yūgao would be unable to meet on equal terms. In accordance with the Japanese view of romantic love, he needed to adopt a humble disguise—*yatsusu*—to enter into an amorous relationship with her.

Perhaps two even more famous episodes in *The Tale of Genji* among Japanese readers are the *Suma* and *Akashi* chapters. Before being banished from the capital, Genji voluntarily withdraws to the shores of Suma, where he's described as having become a person of no rank. Wearing an everyday robe without a family crest in a most nostalgic and humble disguise, he nonetheless cuts a dashing figure.

Edo-period devotees of *The Tale of Genji* readily understood that men disguised below their true station in life could be "dashing." This is the sensibility, sustained over centuries in the Japanese psyche, that contributed to the birth to *yatsushi-goto*, and it was Tōjūrō I who brought that sensibility to aesthetic life on the kabuki stage.

## A Legendary Actor Performs the Ideal of Romantic Love

Another important aspect of the *yatsushi-goto* hero is that, no matter how dire the circumstances, his spirit is never broken. In *Keisei Hotoke no Hara*, Bunzō proudly declares that his thin, paper kimono is more precious than the most resplendent of 12-layer kimonos. "It was my true desire to become like this because of you, my courtesan," he says. "I was born naked, so having nothing more than paper to wear is still a blessing." Similarly, Izaemon in *Yūgiri Awa no Naruto* proudly announces: "In all Japan, only I, Fujiya Izaemon, can claim to withstand the burden of 700 *kanme* of debt and buy paper apparel without batting an eye." Whether it's Genji or Izaemon, these high-born ladies' men have one trait in common: they never give in to adversity.

As a footnote, let me share an interesting anecdote that I heard from sociobiologist Hasegawa Mariko concerning primate behavior.[23] It seems that solitary alpha males that have been forced out of their leadership role in their own troupes often find that they attract females when they come into contact with other troupes. Apparently attraction to unknown males coming from outside the home group is a female sexual strategy not limited to humans.

Fundamentally, the Edo period imposed many regulations on romantic love because it was viewed as a threat to the era's social class structure. In Edo-period drama, love among commoners often ended unhappily—sometimes tragically in double suicide—while romance among the samurai class was castigated for being immoral. But true love by its nature is blind to class and status. This is precisely why, in a period that suppressed romantic love, Tōjūrō's *yatsushi-goto* dazzled crowds as if the Shining Prince himself had appeared before their eyes.

Tōjūrō I apparently enjoyed an extremely luxurious lifestyle. Many anecdotes describing his wild excesses have come down to us, although we don't know how true they are. For example, when he performed in Osaka, he reportedly had all of his drinking water delivered to him from Kyoto[24] and spent a fortune on crane meat only to use it for soup stock.[25] One especially grand story relates how, when someone he was visiting asked him if there was anything he desired, Tōjūrō casually replied, "that pine tree you have is nice." When the tree was duly delivered to his home, Tōjūrō demolished his garden wall so that the tree could be planted there.[26] It seems that he had a larger-than-life persona both onstage and off.

Tōjūrō was not the only actor who performed *yatsushi-goto* roles in his time, but he was the only one of his peers whose legacy continued to grow after death. As I mentioned earlier, his was a subtle art not well understood by everyone in his lifetime, so we might say that his acting style was an acquired taste. Perhaps because of the strong yet peculiar impression he made on audiences, many books about what he said and did were published after he passed away, turning him into a legendary symbol of the *belle époque* that was the Genroku era.

CHAPTER THREE

# Sugawara Denju Tenarai Kagami

## PLAYS OF SUBSTITUTE SACRIFICE

### A Boom in Historical Plays

*Sugawara Denju Tenarai Kagami* (Sugawara and the Secrets of Calligraphy)[1] concerns the ninth-century aristocrat-scholar named Sugawara no Michizane (called Kan Shōjō in the play) who was banished from the capital by political rivals and forced to accept a minor post in Dazaifu. We'll be focusing specifically on a scene from this play called *Terakoya* (The Temple School), which is now often performed as an independent piece, but first I'll provide a quick overview of the play as a whole.

Triplet boys are born to a commoner family in a farming village and are named Umeō-maru (Plum), Matsuō-maru (Pine), and *Sakura-maru* (Cherry). As triplets are highly unusual, they are noticed and become the retainers of three different lords, with duties that today might be performed by personal valets. Umeō serves Sugawara no Michizane (Kan Shōjō); Matsuō serves Fujiwara no Tokihira (called Shihei in the play), who becomes Kan Shōjō's political enemy and is cast as the play's villain; and Sakura serves Prince Tokiyo.

37

The brothers become entangled in the conflict between Kan Shōjō and Shihei, leading to tragic consequences.

In the *Terakoya* scene, Kan Shūsai, the young son of the banished Kan Shōjō, has taken refuge with temple schoolmaster Takebe Genzō, one of Kan Shōjō's disciples. The villain Shihei discovers Kan Shūsai's whereabouts and orders him beheaded. Genzō is determined to save the son of his master, but this means he must kill another boy instead. Meanwhile, Shihei's retainer Matsuō is ordered to accompany the retinue sent to kill the boy and verify the identity of the victim because he and his brothers were born in the domain of Kan Shōjō (who was the first to celebrate their birth) and knew what Kan Shūsai looked like. But Matsuō is wracked with guilt because of the shameful behavior of his lord, and cannot bring himself to kill the son of his benefactor Kan Shōjō. So, he sends his own son Kotarō to the temple school, knowing that Genzō will kill him instead of Kan Shūsai.

Since the play features events that happened in an earlier epoch from the perspective of Edo audiences, it falls within the category of *jidai-geki*, or historical plays. The term *jidai-geki*—now often used to describe samurai dramas—is relatively new. Originally, historical plays in kabuki were called *jidai-goto* (historical matters) and later *jidai-mono* (historical pieces). I'd like to briefly discuss the term *jidai-goto*.

*Sugawara Denju Tenarai Kagami* was written in the 1740s, about half a century after the Genroku era when Sakata Tōjūrō I was active (see chapter 2). The term *jidai-goto* began to appear in *hyōbanki* guidebooks shortly before the 1740s. The Genroku bubble had burst, causing the merchant economy to shrink and prompting the feudal rulers to impose increasingly stringent measures. Much like contemporary Japanese during the recent recession, people felt dispirited and trapped in the face of a stagnant economy. They longed for the good old days, and historical plays were no doubt just the thing to satisfy their craving.

The art of chanting military epics became very popular during this time. In addition to the fourteenth-century *Taiheiki* (Chronicle of Grand Pacification) about the civil war in Japan between the Northern and Southern Courts—which had been performed since medieval times—other favorite chronicles included the *Taikōki* (Biography of Toyotomi Hideyoshi), *Kōyō Gunkan* (Military Exploits of the Takeda Clan),[2] and *Sangokushi* (Records of the Three Kingdoms).

With audiences looking to the past, kabuki artists found it difficult to develop appealing stories set in contemporary times. Riding the boom in military epics, they created and performed many plays that were set in bygone days. Their strategy was similar to that which fuels the many adaptations of popular historical novels for movies and television programs today.

The counterpoint to *jidai-goto* was *sewa-goto* (domestic matters), a term that came into use at about the same time. Plays in this category deal with the events and mores of the times in which they are written. Before historical *jidai-goto* became popular, the kabuki repertory focused on dramas depicting rival factions of fictional feudal clans. *Sewa-goto* pieces dealing with such sensational topics as double suicides and murders were added to the program almost as an afterthought and simply reenacted like skits in a variety show.

## Hints from the Puppet Theater

The *jōruri* puppet theater[3] was extremely popular in Osaka in the 1740s, when *Sugawara Denju Tenarai Kagami* was written. Its ascendancy over kabuki was noted by one contemporary commentator who observed, "The puppets are gradually gaining in popularity to the point where kabuki hardly matters."[4] The boom in historical dramas initially spurred the production of many original kabuki plays, but as new material dried up, kabuki producers turned to the puppet theater, which was a treasure house of plays depicting historical events. Gradually, kabuki artists realized that they could expand their repertory simply by adopting puppet plays "as is."

The puppet play *Sugawara Denju Tenarai Kagami* was first performed in August 1746, and quickly debuted as a kabuki play the following month. This became a common pattern, with many puppet play premieres being followed immediately by kabuki versions. The plays in question became major

---

### Kabuki Play Categories

#### *Jidai-mono*
(Historical Pieces)

Plays featuring samurai families and set in such pre-Edo times as the Kamakura and Muromachi periods.

#### *Sewa-mono*
(Domestic Pieces)

Plays based on the daily lives of Edo-period townsfolk. Those that portray the lives of commoners with gritty realism are called *kizewa-mono* ("raw" domestic pieces).

#### *Shosa-goto*
(Dance Matters)

Pieces in this category are danced to a variety of accompaniments, including *gidayū-bushi*, *tokiwaza-bushi*, *kiyomoto-bushi*, and *nagauta*.

additions to the kabuki repertory and are still performed today. All three of the plays regarded as the greatest kabuki masterpieces of all time were written during this period and first staged as puppet plays: *Sugawara Denju Tenarai Kagami*, *Yoshitsune Senbon Zakura* (Yoshitsune and the Thousand Cherry Trees) (see chapter 4), and *Kanadehon Chūshingura* (The Treasury of Loyal Retainers) (see chapter 5).

*Sugawara Denju Tenarai Kagami* is set in about the tenth century, but its most famous scene features a "temple school," which didn't exist until about the eighteenth century. Some might be puzzled by this, but we should bear in mind that anachronisms are quite common in art, regardless of time or place, including the paintings of the Rembrandt school[5] and the plays of Shakespeare. In the West as in Japan, the concept of anachronism didn't become a major issue until the nineteenth century. Audiences before that time were not as concerned with historical accuracy as they are today.

It's interesting to note that the Meiji government issued a remonstrance concerning anachronisms in kabuki in 1872. The dramatist Kawatake Mokuami (about whom I write in chapter 10) and his colleagues were called to the First Ward Office of Tokyo Province and instructed, among other things, to use historically accurate names for the characters they portrayed. A newspaper article from the time reports that this type of promulgation was founded on the idea that theater was a kind of "primary school" for teaching the public about history.[6]

## Drama as a Window on Exotic Japan

*Terakoya* exerted a strong influence on Western audiences, who viewed it as quintessentially Japanese drama. For example, when it was performed in Cologne, Germany, in 1907, German critics[7] noted that the local cast and crew expressed an almost "fanatical" Japanese sense of loyalty transcending even the devotion depicted in *The Song of the Nibelungs*.[8] In 1908, the play was performed in Berlin under the direction of one of the leading modern directors of the time, Max Reinhardt.[9] Critics of that production compared the story with the Old Testament account of Abraham's willingness to sacrifice his son Isaac to Jehovah.[10]

But why was *Terakoya* performed overseas at all? One background factor might be the Russo-Japanese War of 1904–05. That war had just ended, and the world was fascinated by this exotic Far East nation that had defeated Russia. Just a decade earlier, the First Sino-Japanese War of 1894–95 had similarly sparked international interest in *Bushidō: The Soul of Japan* by Nitobe Inazō (whose face once graced our 5,000 yen note).[11] Perhaps it's not surprising that non-Japanese turned to *Terakoya* for clues about Japan after the Russo-Japanese War. This phenomenon might be compared to the attention Japan received in the 1980s when it had become an economic juggernaut.

In 1916, an adaptation of *Terakoya* by M.C. Marcus titled *The Pine Tree* was staged in the United States. This was subsequently "re-imported" to Japan, where it was performed under two competing productions: one by a troupe of kabuki actors led by Bandō Jusaburō[12] and the other by a *shingeki*[13] (new theater) ensemble.[14] In the Bandō production, the retinue sent by the villain to confirm the death of Kan Shōjō's son performs a piece called *Ōedo Nihonbashi* that mixes Japanese and Western styles, and the final requiem, popularly called *Iroha Okuri*, incorporates *Ave Maria*. From all reports, it was a truly unusual production.[15]

These performances are almost completely forgotten today, but we should remember that Westerners at the time frequently had *Terakoya* in mind when they thought about Japan. The play became an object of Western Orientalism.

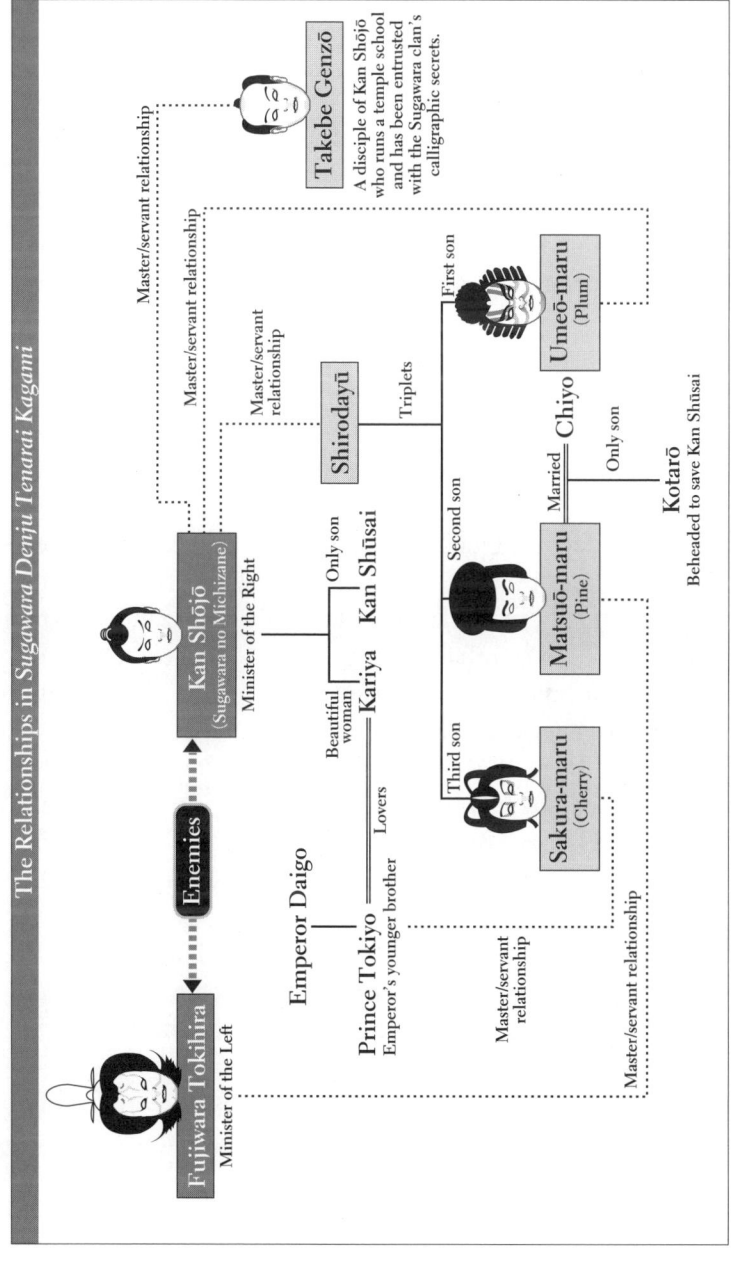

*Sugawara Denju Tenarai Kagami*

## The Old Trick of Substitute Sacrifice

What, then, made *Terakoya* so popular in Japan? One answer to this question can be found in the concept of substitute sacrifice.

As you'll recall, the villain Shihei dispatched Matsuō to verify the beheading of Kan Shūsai. Shihei didn't trust Matsuō completely, however, so he assigned a second retainer to accompany him and assist in verification. This reflected actual practice in Edo times; a system of mutual monitoring was in place so that two people were generally assigned to every task.

The second verifier, Shundō Genba, warns Genzō, "Don't attempt to present a substitute head just because the face changes after death and you think we won't know the difference. That won't fool us. Don't try a tired old trick that you'll regret."

These lines indicate that the dramatic device of substitution was already an old-fashioned cliché by the time *Terakoya* premiered. The fact that substitution was an entrenched convention also suggests that Matsuō really had no choice but to sacrifice his own son in place of Kan Shōjō's.

Matsuō knew that the substitution wouldn't work unless the sacrificed boy had the look of a refined aristocrat. He also knew that Genzō would be unable to find such a boy on his own, which is why he sent his own son. There can be little doubt that having the verifier's own son serve as a stand-in was a shocking plot twist for initial audiences. The modern-day equivalent would be to have one's son killed by his elementary school teacher so that another child could be saved. That such a horrifying plotline was used is perhaps indicative of just how common the theatrical pattern of substitute beheadings had become by the middle of the eighteenth century.

## Two Traditions of Substitution

The oldest surviving example of this theatrical device in Japan is the noh play *Nakamitsu* (also called *Manjū*).[16] There was also a piece by the same title in the repertory of a genre of dance drama called *kōwakamai*,[17] which developed at about the same time as noh. Both versions tell the same story. The tenth-century general Minamoto no Mitsunaka (commonly called Manjū), infuriated by his son Bijo-maru's refusal to apply himself to his studies, violently proclaims that such a ne'er-do-well should be executed. Manjū's retainer Nakamitsu hears this reckless command and finds himself in a quandary, since he can't bring himself to kill the son of his lord. But Nakamitsu's own son Kōju-maru freely volunteers to take the place of Bijo-maru and is tragically beheaded by his father.

Such stories of substitute deaths thus already existed in *kōwakamai* and noh, which developed during the medieval period. This was an era of ongoing internecine warfare, so the scenario may have appeared quite realistic — medieval warriors were naturally expected to die on the battlefield for the sake of their lords.

Plays involving substitute sacrifice were incorporated early in the kabuki repertory and often performed in Edo, which had a large samurai population. In 1702, for example, the Yamamura-za in Edo staged *Onigajō Onna Yamairi* (Woman of Demon Castle Enters the Mountains). It features the same Bijo-maru character who appears in *Manjū*, but in this case the murdered substitute is a woman who loved him — a romantic twist that no doubt appealed to Edo-period audiences. In *Kantō Koroku* (Koroku of Kantō), performed at the Nakamura-za in 1698, a loyal retainer who kills his own child

*Sugawara Denju Tenarai Kagami*

Matsuō (Matsumoto Kōshirō IX) inspects the severed head. Benzō (Nakamura Kichiemon II) and his wife Tonami (Nakamura Kaishun II) look on with great anxiety. (Performed at the Kabuki-za in September 2006. Photo courtesy of Shochiku Co., Ltd.)

to save the life of his young lord is castigated and ridiculed by friends and family because they were misled into thinking that he in fact killed the son of his lord. That play ends in unremitting tragedy as the protagonist's father, who had heaped scorn on his son but is now mortified to learn the truth, laments his own foolish ignorance and commits suicide. A similar pattern is found in *Wakoku Gosuiden* (Green Palace of Japan), performed at the Morita-za in 1700. The wife of a chief retainer kills her own son in place of their young lord, but her husband, who doesn't know that she made the switch, berates her for betraying their lord.

Despite its similarity to all of these plays, however, *Terakoya* has features that belong to a slightly different lineage. For one thing, it premiered in western Japan, which had a different tradition of substitute deaths than Edo. There are several *kojōruri* (old *jōruri*)[18] plays dating from the early days of the puppet theater that present this theme, including *Amida no Munewari* (Splitting Open the Chest of Amida Buddha) and *Kiyomizu Kannon Rishō Monogatari* (The Beneficence of the Bodhisattva Kannon of Kiyomizu Temple). One can almost guess the plots of these plays from their titles.

In *Kiyomizu Kannon Rishō Monogatari*, the son of a wealthy family becomes deathly ill and can be saved only if he eats a raw human liver. In a storyline that brings to mind the modern-day issue of human organ trafficking, the liver of an impoverished boy is procured. However, the boy is ultimately saved because Kannon, the bodhisattva of mercy, sacrifices herself so that the boy may live. Stories about people in dire straits who are saved through divine intervention were quite common in plays staged in Kyoto and Osaka.

In *Terakoya*, when Matsuō falsely attests that the head belongs to Kan Shūsai, Genzō's wife Tonami says, "Perhaps the Golden Buddha took his place." That line carries with it a hint of the tradition of western Japan. We might say that *Terakoya* is a product of both narrative traditions of substitute death: that of the warrior popular in Edo in the east and that of Buddha popular in Kyoto and Osaka in the west.

## The Tragedy of Organizational Obligations

One line from *Terakoya* that is crucial to an understanding of the play is, "Woe unto them who serve the rulers of the land." It's uttered by the schoolteacher Genzō, who must kill one of his students to protect the son of his lord. The boy to be sacrificed is unknown to him at first and has just entered the school as a pupil. It's an absurd and cruel deed, but Genzō steels himself to do it, at which point he says the line in a moment of bitterness. He regrets putting himself in the position of serving a powerful man.

This line was used verbatim in other plays before *Terakoya*. It appears, for example, in Chikamatsu's plays *Higashiyama-dono Ne no Hi no Asobi* (Collecting Herbs at the Silver Pavilion on the Day of the Rat)[19] and *Chūshin Migawari Monogatari* (The Tale of Loyal Self-Sacrifice),[20] as well as in the *kojōruri* play I mentioned earlier, *Kiyomizu Kannon Rishō Monogatari*. In all cases, the line is spoken just at the point where the substitute child must be killed. So it had already become something of an idiomatic phrase by the time *Terakoya* was written.

In a sense, the expression encapsulates the tragic theme of *Sugawara Denju Tenarai Kagami* as a whole. It was precisely because they became the retainers of great lords that the triplets Sakura, Matsuō, and Umeō became embroiled in political strife. Sakura was forced to commit ritual suicide, and Matsuō had to kill his own son. Woeful, indeed, was the fate of the characters called upon to serve powerful men with unswerving loyalty.

Let me emphasize here that audiences watching these plays in the Edo period never thought it was natural for children to be killed as substitutes for the offspring of powerful men. For them—as for us today—the plays were set in the past, so they viewed the stories with a certain amount of detachment, thinking how terrible it must have been to live in olden times. However, there's a reason why *Terakoya* has remained popular through the centuries. No matter what the era, people have continued to harbor a suspicion that working for or belonging to an organization compels them to make unreasonable choices.

The phrase "Woe unto them who serve the rulers of the land" was once a common expression, as familiar to the

Japanese as *Hamlet*'s "To be or not to be" is among English speakers. The sentiment expressed by the phrase no doubt widely permeated Japanese society until quite recently.

## Hearts that Cry for Murdered Children

There are many kabuki plays besides *Terakoya* that depict children's lives being sacrificed. This fact highlights a question worth considering: why were so many children killed, even if only in plays on stage? I once gave a talk that touched on this question, and a woman in the audience made the following observation.

In former days, economic hardship and food shortages contributed to frequent miscarriages and abortions, and even if the children were born they were often subject to infanticide. Illness also commonly took children's lives to an extent that is difficult to imagine today. It was safe to assume, then, that many people watching these plays would have actually experienced the loss of a child, giving rise to a sense of guilt and need for atonement. Perhaps watching a play about a child being killed and shedding tears over the death helped them to find some peace of mind.

This is an insight that could only have come from a mother. Indeed, several edicts were issued during the Edo period that prohibited child abandonment and abortion, which is evidence that such practices were quite common.

In 1925, the folklorist Yanagita Kunio[21] observed in his essay "Imo no Chikara" (The Power of Women)[22] that the practice of lovingly caring for children had only recently become firmly established in rural Japan. I remember being shocked when I read this. Yanagita states that the dissemination of cow's milk had reduced infant mortality, as compared with earlier times when suckling babies often died if their mothers failed to produce breast milk. He noted that willingness to buy cow's milk for their children was a great change in the mentality of rural parents.

In fact, there was a kabuki play called *Chimorai* (Seeking Milk)[23] based on the idea that if a mother was unable to breastfeed, milk had to be sought from other nursing mothers. If that couldn't be done, the death of the child was considered inevitable. No one seemed to question the underlying premise that only children who could survive the natural rearing process would in fact be raised. How different the sensibilities of that time compared with our own era as we work to reverse the decline in Japan's birthrate.

We must remember that the original audiences for *Terakoya* lived in a time when children frequently died, a fact that explains why plays depicting the death of children had such a strong impact. Audience members who had lost children of their own may have had a visceral feeling that, just as Buddha could become a sacrificial substitute, their children too died so that they themselves could live. The extreme popularity of these plays of substitute sacrifice might well be explained by the perception on the part of audience members that their own existence had been given to them through the saving grace of their children.

And let's not forget the line "Woe unto them who serve the rulers of the land," which honestly expressed people's anguish. In their daily lives, many Edo commoners probably resigned themselves to the fact that, in order to protect the people at the top, those at the bottom often had to pay an unreasonable price. Watching characters onstage contend with extreme examples of this reality elicited great sympathy. I believe this is the secret to *Terakoya*'s continued popularity over the centuries.

CHAPTER FOUR

# Yoshitsune Senbonzakura

## HUMANS SEEN THROUGH ANIMAL FANTASIES

### The Puppet Theater's Contributions to Kabuki

Like *Terakoya*, *Yoshitsune Senbonzakura* (Yoshitsune and the Thousand Cherry Trees)[1] is a play of enduring popularity that was originally written for the puppet theater. In fact, about 70 percent of the plays now considered classics of the kabuki repertory were first staged in *ningyō jōruri* form. Kabuki producers began tapping the puppet repertory for material after the 1715 premiere of Chikamatsu Monzaemon's *Kokusen'ya Kassen* (The Battles of Coxinga),[2] a blockbuster hit that enjoyed an unprecedentedly long run. The kabuki version of that work became a sensation simultaneously in Kyoto, Osaka, and Edo.

As I mentioned in the last chapter, one critic in the 1740s observed that "the puppets are gaining in popularity to the point where kabuki hardly matters." In just the two years of 1747 and 1748, three puppet masterpieces were premiered in succession and quickly adapted for the kabuki stage: *Sugawara Denju Tenarai Kagami* (Sugawara and the Secrets of Calligraphy), *Yoshitsune Senbonzakura*, and *Kanadehon Chūshingura* (The Treasury of Loyal Retainers).

*Yoshitsune Senbonzakura*

*Ningyō Jōruri*
*Yoshitsune Senbonzakura* Scene Structure

| Act I | |
|---|---|
| Kuchi | Palace Grounds |
| Naka | Hermit's Retreat in Kitasaga |
| Kiri | Horikawa Palace |

| Act II | |
|---|---|
| Kuchi | Fushimi Inari Shrine |
| Naka | Tokaiya Shop |
| Kiri | Daimotsu-ura Bay |

| Act III | |
|---|---|
| Kuchi | The Oak Tree |
| Naka | Death of Kokingo |
| Kiri | The Sushi Shop |

| ACT IV | |
|---|---|
| Kuchi | Travel Dance |
| Naka | Zaō Hall in Yoshino |
| Kiri | Kawazure Hogen's Manor (Fox/Tadanobu) |

⋯⋯⋯⋯⋯⋯ (**Shi no Kiri**)

| Act V | |
|---|---|
| | Yoshino Mountains |

There's something about the puppet theater of the Edo period that reminds me of today's anime. The films of Miyazaki Hayao, for example, can be enjoyed by adults, and the grand sweep of their stories and themes arguably outshines that of live-action films. Similarly, there was a time during the Edo period when the dramatic appeal of the puppet theater greatly surpassed that of live-action kabuki.

Kabuki borrowed more than just storylines from the puppets. It also incorporated the *jōruri* style of chanted narration and musical accompaniment, additions that significantly changed the way that kabuki was performed. Acting techniques such as *ningyōburi* (puppet style), in which actors move like marionettes or robots in pantomime, obviously developed under puppet influence. These and other puppet-inspired kabuki innovations went on to influence the puppet theater itself, creating a cycle of mutual stimulus that resulted in the performance arts we see today.

*Yoshitsune Senbonzakura* can be termed one of the most puppet-like of all the plays that were borrowed by kabuki. It's an extremely long work, and the last section, which is often performed as an independent piece, is frequently referred to as *Shi no Kiri* (End of Act IV) for reasons I'll explain below. The protagonist is a shape-shifting fox who impersonates the warrior Satō Tadanobu.

The term *shi no kiri* is derived from the way puppet plays are traditionally structured. They usually have five acts, but the fifth act is often more of an epilogue, so that plays are basically configured in four acts. The climax usually comes in the third act, which depicts deeply tragic human drama; the fourth act often presents a showy finale.

Each act is generally divided into three segments respectively called *kuchi* (opening), *naka* (middle), and *kiri* (ending). Even within an act, a distinction is made between the lightly paced opening and the segments that follow. Sometimes an act will consist of just the opening and ending, but in all cases the ending is the most substantial segment of the act. *Shi no kiri*, then, refers to the ending segment of the fourth act of any four-act puppet play. *Terakoya* for example, which we examined in the previous chapter, is the *shi no kiri* segment of *Sugawara Denju Tenarai Kagami*. Today, however, when *Shi no Kiri* is used as a proper noun, it's understood to refer to the scene in *Yoshitsune Senbonzakura* that features the Fox/Tadanobu character.

## A Tale of a Hand Drum

The title character of *Yoshitsune Senbonzakura* is the great twelfth-century warrior Minamoto no Yoshitsune, although Yoshitsune himself doesn't figure very prominently in the play. Rather, the spotlight falls on the incidents involving various characters around him.

Before focusing on *Shi no Kiri*, I'll provide a quick overview of the whole play. The story is set in the aftermath of the war between two rival clans in the late-Heian period: the Taira and the Minamoto. In that war, the Taira clan and its three great generals—Tomomori, Koremori, and Noritsune—are vanquished by the Minamoto general, Yoshitsune. In this play, however, all three are still alive and in hiding. Yoshitsune has received secret orders from the cloistered emperor Go-Shirakawa to rebel against the shogun Yoritomo, who is Yoshitsune's older half-brother. Wishing to avoid a family war, Yoshitsune sets sail from Daimotsu-ura Bay to Kyushu, but Tomomori is disguised as the boat captain and attacks Yoshitsune with forces still loyal to him. Yoshitsune defeats Tomomori and takes into his care the infant emperor Antoku, whom Tomomori had been sheltering. The defeated Tomomori ties an anchor around his waist and throws himself into the sea. This brings us to the end of Act II.

Meanwhile, Koremori is hiding with a former retainer who now runs a sushi shop, but Yoritomo's forces have gotten wind of this and are closing in. The sushi chef's dissolute son Gonta sees the situation as a chance to redeem himself in his parents' eyes. He sacrifices his own wife and child to save Koremori and his family, but his parents misunderstand his actions and tragically kill him. Act III ends with Koremori lamenting the uncertainty and transience of human life and becoming a Buddhist monk.

The fox Minamoto no Kurōgitsune (Nakamura Kanzaburō XVIII) receives the drum from Yoshitsune, who sympathizes with his plight. The rejoicing fox frolics among the blossoming cherry trees. (Performed at the Minami-za in December 2006. Photo courtesy of Shochiku Co., Ltd.)

Act IV takes us to the mountains of Yoshino, where Yoshitsune is attacked by Noritsune—now disguised as the evil warrior monk Yokawa no Kakuhan—and his minions. Yoshitsune easily defeats the villain with the help of a fox who takes the form of his trusted retainer Satō Tadanobu.

One key theme running throughout the play is the Japanese notion of *hōgan biiki*, which can loosely be translated as "rooting for the underdog." *Hōgan* refers to the court rank that Yoshitsune held, and it is by this title that he is widely known; *biiki* means "sympathy" or "preference." Despite his military successes against the Taira clan, Yoshitsune incurred the wrath of his powerful older brother Yoritomo and was hunted down. *Hōgan biiki* thus came to mean sympathizing with the losing (and often more charismatic) side. The phrase, for instance, was until recently used to describe the unwaveringly loyal fans of the Hanshin Tigers baseball team, which always seemed to lose the pennant to the Yomiuri Giants. Although *Yoshitsune Senbonzakura* doesn't depict Yoshitsune's defeat, the entire play is infused with the spirit of *hōgan biiki*. Ironically, the sympathy elicited is not for Yoshitsune himself but for the Taira generals Yoshitsune defeated, as is evident in the storylines of Acts II and III. But now let's turn our attention to *Shi no Kiri*, the ending of Act IV.

As a reward for Yoshitsune's heroic exploits in defeating the Taira clan, the cloistered emperor Go-Shirakawa presents him with a two-sided hand drum called Hatsune no Tsuzumi. Reputedly made at the order of Emperor Kanmu (737–806) for use in rainmaking prayers, the drum is thought to have magical powers. Its heads are made from the hides of a pair of brother foxes with the front head—the side struck when played—belonging to the older brother. Go-Shirakawa's gift thus carries an implicit order for Yoshitsune to "strike" his older brother Yoritomo.

It turns out, though, that the drumheads were actually not made from the skins of brother foxes but from a fox husband and wife. As long as the drum remained inside the Imperial Palace, the son of that couple could not approach it. But as soon as the drum passed into Yoshitsune's hands, the fox son began to follow the drum around to be near his beloved parents.

To avoid having to fight his brother's soldiers, Yoshitsune decides to flee Kyoto. He bids farewell to his lover Shizuka and gives her the drum for safekeeping. As soon as he does so, Yoshitsune's trusted retainer Satō Tadanobu,[3] who had been recovering from battle wounds in his hometown, appears. Yoshitsune orders him to act as Shizuka's bodyguard, but this Tadanobu is actually the fox son in disguise. He accompanies Shizuka (and the drum) to the mountains of Yoshino to await Yoshitsune's return.

When Shizuka and Yoshitsune are reunited in Yoshino, the real Tadanobu arrives, now recovered and ready to resume service to his lord. Naturally, this casts doubt on the true identity of Fox/Tadanobu. Unmasked at last, he recounts how his parents had been killed to make the drum, and then suddenly disappears. Yoshitsune feels sorry for the fox, who loves and misses his parents, and tells Shizuka to strike the drum to call the fox back. She does so, but the drum no longer makes a sound. The highlight of the play is the fox son's sorrowful account of his parents' deaths, but perhaps even more dramatic is the moment Shizuka strikes the drum and no sound comes.

In a noh play called *Tenko* (The Heavenly Drum)[4] that is set in China, a drum falls from heaven and is given into the care of a youth. The emperor hears about the celestial drum and orders it to be brought to him. When the youth refuses to surrender it, he's killed, and the drum is taken to the palace. But no matter who strikes it, it remains silent. The emperor seeks out the youth's father and commands him to strike the drum, whereupon it sounds again. Moved to pity by this miracle, the emperor realizes how cruel he's been, showers the father with gifts, and sends him home.

Chikamatsu used the title of this noh play for a puppet play of his own. The story is very different, of course, as befits a puppet play: A princess owns a drum that is a family heirloom. The drumheads are made from the skin of the wife of an old fox, who aids and protects the princess and vanquishes villains. It may very well be that the authors of *Yoshitsune Senbonzakura* created the character of Fox/Tadanobu by combining the noh and puppet versions of *Tenko*.

## Other Fox Tales

When the drum fails to sound in *Shi no Kiri*, Shizuka says poignantly, "Though not human, how deeply they feels for their child." Yoshitsune murmurs in response, "I, too, am moved by the love and compassion of these living creatures."

Later, Yoshitsune laments that his efforts to serve his much older half-brother by fighting the Taira clan as his general only made Yoritomo turn against him. After their father Yoshitomo was killed in the Heiji Rebellion,[5] Yoshitsune had looked upon Yoritomo as a father and tried to win his love. But the harder he tried, the stronger their enmity seemed to grow.

Yoshitsune sympathizes with the orphaned fox because he himself feels deserted and alone. Even animal families can display deep affection for one another; why, then, should so much hatred arise between human siblings? The foxes have something to teach humans about compassion, and this is one of the play's most important morals.

Yet in the kabuki version of the play, the fox is of course played by a human. The actor wears a special fox suit and wig, and he plays the role not only with distinctive fox-like gestures but with a special type of *jōruri* chanting technique called *kitsune kotoba* (fox words). One wonders if audiences of the time found it unnatural to see a live actor play an animal role originally intended for puppets.

Foxes appear in other performance genres, including the kyōgen play *Tsurigitsune* (Fox Trapping). A common saying about the training of *kyōgen* actors is that "(Training) begins with a monkey and ends with a fox." (The monkey in question appears in the play *Utsubo-zaru* (The Monkey-Skin Quiver).[6] *Tsurigitsune* is considered a very difficult piece that only the most seasoned and skilled of actors can perform. To properly depict a fox, the actor must maintain an extremely uncomfortable posture and walk in a special way known as *kemono ashi* (beast feet).

The story centers on a fox that is saddened because all of his friends are being killed by a human hunter. The fox (which in Japanese folklore has magical powers) disguises himself as the hunter's uncle and admonishes him to follow the Buddhist precept against taking life. On his way home, however, the fox comes across a trap baited with fried mouse meat. The delicious smell of it makes him revert to his bestial nature, and he gets caught in the trap.

Going back even further in history, foxes appear in *Konjaku Monogatari* (Tales of Times Now Past),[7] a collection of stories believed to have been compiled in the twelfth century. The fox in *Tsurigitsune* says, "Treat someone as an enemy, and an enemy you shall have; treat someone with compassion, and compassion shall be granted you." This sentiment can be traced directly back to the older anthology.

*Kyōgen* plays are at heart comedic skits, and as such they present many different kinds of animals, including cows, horses, foxes, and monkeys, as well as more unusual creatures like crabs, octopi, and even mosquitoes. Because the plays are

*Yoshitsune Senbonzakura*

comedies, audiences have no trouble accepting actors who play animal roles in cartoonish costumes.

Since *Yoshitsune Senbonzakura* was originally a puppet play, audiences probably had no difficulty accepting the appearance of an animal there, either. The kabuki version of the play combines elements from both of these performance genres to create Fox/Tadanobu, a character that occupies a special place in the kabuki repertory.

## Animals on Stage: Is Japan Different from the West?

Many other animals have been portrayed on the kabuki stage. *Shibai Kinmō Zui*, the parody of an illustrated encyclopedia written by Shikitei Sanba[8] that I mentioned in chapter 1, lists the many animal roles that have appeared: a lion, tiger, cow, horse, monkey, rat, and boar, among others. This indicates just how common it was to see animal roles in kabuki.

This made me wonder about the role of animals in Western theater, so I asked Matsuoka Kazuko,[9] a noted translator of Shakespeare, if she knew of any instances where actors dressed up as animals in Shakespeare's plays.

One example she gave is the final line in *Richard III*: "A horse! a horse! my kingdom for a horse!" In the production of this play directed by Ninagawa Yukio, actors were hidden inside a large stage horse that looked much more realistic than the horse costumes used in kabuki. Ninagawa also directed *Hamlet*, which was performed in England. When the character of the Norwegian crown prince Fortinbras made his entrance riding a horse puppet, the audience burst into laughter.

Matsuoka says that if a horse is to be used in a play by Shakespeare, British theatergoers are likely to expect a live animal onstage. She notes that there are just two instances in Shakespeare when an actor dresses up like an animal: the

# Kabuki Animals Shown in *Shibai Kinmō Zui*

## *Shibai Kinmō Zui*
## (Encyclopedia of Theater)

Shikitei Sanba published this humorous work in 1803 aimed at children and others unfamiliar with theater. Using charming illustrations, it categorizes and explains various aspects of the theater world.

character of Bottom, who is comically transformed into an ass in A Midsummer's Night Dream, and the bear that appears in A Winter's Tale. In the latter case, the bear symbolizes the fact that all of the tragic occurrences depicted to that point in the play constitute a fairy tale, so that when the bear appears the audience, as expected, bursts into laughter.

In kabuki, low-ranking actors are called "horse legs," indicating just how common it is for horse costumes to be used. Sometimes, these horses play major roles, as in *Ichinotani Futaba Gunki* (A Chronicle of the Battle of Ichinotani)[10] and *Dantoku-sen* (Mount Dantoku). Parenthetically, the playwright Namiki Gohei once used a live horse in one of his plays, but discontinued the practice after the animal relieved itself onstage.

## A Sensibility that Ascribes Love to Animals

As we'll see in more detail in chapter 8, human actors can play plants as well as animals in kabuki. One can discern in this the vestiges of animism, which is the belief that all living beings are imbued with spirit. Although animism was found all over the premodern world, I think it's rare to find examples of it in plays meant to be viewed by modern audiences.

In the medieval narrative genre *sekkyō-bushi* (sermon-ballad chanting),[11] there's a piece called *Shinoda-zuma* (The Fox Wife of Shinoda) that also depicts a fox in disguise. That piece was the basis for the puppet play *Ashiya Dōman Ōuchi Kagami* (Sorcerer Ashiya Dōman at the Palace),[12] which later became a popular kabuki play. The kabuki version as performed today is called *Kuzunoha*.

The play is based on the legend of the sorcerer Abe no Seimei,[13] who was purportedly the son of a human father and fox-spirit mother. The fox mother's grief at having to say farewell to her son is full of tender pathos. The fascination this drama exerts on audiences resides in the way that a fox is able to arouse feelings of human compassion more powerfully than a human character could do.

We observed this phenomenon earlier in *Yoshitsune Senbonzakura*, where the fox character displays much more filial piety than do the feuding half-brothers.

These dramas, which allow people to reflect on themselves through the images of animals, are premised on the idea that animals and plants possess a more "human" emotional element than do human beings themselves. I feel this is the product of a distinctively Japanese sensibility characterized by a modest willingness to learn from animals and nature—a gentle sensibility that is in turn the product of Japanese attitudes toward the richness of the natural world. Indeed, the Japanese continue to produce works that accord with this sensibility, including TV programs that feature animals. Perhaps viewers who watch TV shows about animals forced to part ways with their offspring share a sensibility with theatergoers who "root for the underdog" in a kabuki play.

CHAPTER FIVE

# Kanadehon Chūshingura

## MORE THAN JUST A TALE OF FEUDAL LOYALTY

### Modern Images of Chūshingura

Kanadehon Chūshingura (The Treasury of Loyal Retainers) is so deeply woven into the cultural fabric of Japan that until quite recently there was hardly anyone who didn't know the story. Based on a historical vendetta known as the Akō Incident that occurred in 1702, the play has spawned spin-off works in many other genres, including a storytelling series called Gishi Meimei Den (Biographies of Loyal Retainers)[1] that was popular in the second half of the eighteenth century. These and other variants often developed subsidiary storylines that had very little to do with the original play.

After the Russo-Japanese War of 1904–05, the popular *naniwa-bushi* narrative singer Tōchūken Kumoemon[2] scored a hit with the song Gishiden (Legend of the Loyal Retainers). This entertainer had the backing of a right-wing group called the Black Ocean Society, which tinged his Chūshingura story with ultra-nationalistic ideals of loyalty and patriotism. In the lead up to World War II, this nationalistic flavor had evolved to the point where the story was featured prominently in government-mandated textbooks for elementary schools. It was extolled as the "revenge of loyal retainers that lifted our hearts," providing an "antidote" to a complacency that had supposedly set in during the Genroku era because of prolonged peace. For Japanese of a certain age today, this is the decisive image evoked by *Chūshingura*.

As a postwar corrective, the play was banned by the Occupation authorities immediately after World War II, and it wasn't until 1947 that it was revived on the kabuki stage. The ban was lifted on cinema in 1952, after which movie companies competed to produce *Chūshingura* films on a yearly basis, resulting in many variants.[3]

Of all the movies and television programs created on the *Chūshingura* theme after World War II, perhaps the most widely watched was the NHK Taiga Drama series *Akō Rōshi* (Forty-Seven Ronin) broadcast in 1964, the year of the Tokyo Olympics.[4] Television was quickly permeating Japanese households at the time, and this series became extremely popular, perhaps in part because programming was still quite limited. I believe that the high rate of economic growth being experienced at the time was a contributing factor to the show's success. Audiences no doubt felt that although the Japanese may be weak as individuals, by working together—just like the heroes of the TV series—the nation could recover from the devastating wartime defeat and overcome adversity. This romanticized image of *Chūshingura* has been an inspiration for the Japanese people ever since.

In the 1980s, when Japan became internationally recognized as an economic powerhouse,[5] author Maruya Saiichi[6] published his much-talked-about *Chūshingura to wa Nanika* (What Is *Chūshingura*?), probably out of a perceived need to discuss the tale in a way that was divorced from right-wing sentiments of loyalty and patriotism. Incorporating ethnological theories of ancestor worship and discourse from cultural anthropology focused on carnival practices, Maruya brilliantly elucidated the secret to *Chūshingura*'s enduring popularity.

On a practical level, *Chūshingura* inspired such a vast number of films and television programs because it's so rich in potential plots, with 47 loyal retainers to choose from in addition to peripheral characters. All kinds of stories can be told in virtually endless variations, featuring characters who are so well known that little exposition is needed. It's little wonder that the play has proven so attractive to producers.

## *Kanadehon Chūshingura* as Domestic Drama

In 1701, Asano Naganori, lord of the Akō domain, drew his sword in the Corridor of the Pines in Edo Castle and wounded Kira Yoshinaka, a senior shogunal official.[7] As a result of this infraction the Asano clan was abolished and Naganori himself was forced to commit ritual suicide. The next year, former retainers of the dead lord, led by Ōishi Kuranosuke, broke into Kira's mansion and murdered him in revenge. This incident became known as *Chūshingura* solely because of the popular success of the play *Kanadehon Chūshingura*.[8]

Initially produced as a puppet play in 1748, *Kanadehon Chūshingura* later achieved great success as a kabuki play. Although there were many earlier plays that dealt with the same material, the popularity of this version was unprecedented. To clarify the reasons behind this, I'll begin by providing a broad overview of the plot. I believe this tale is easier to understand if we view it as a tapestry of three or four interwoven domestic dramas.

The first drama, obviously, is the tragedy of the Asano clan. To avoid shogunal censorship, the incident was set in the past, with the protagonist Asano Naganori cast as En'ya Hangan,[9] a historical figure who lived in the fourteenth century.

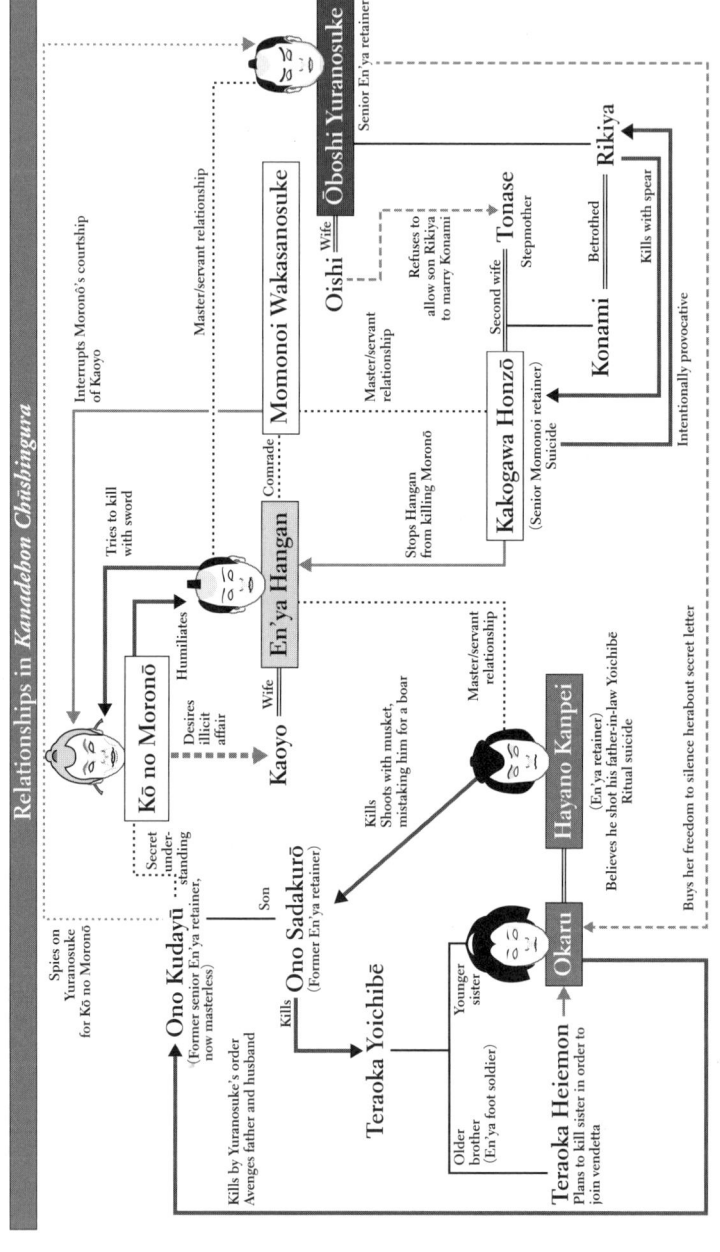

His story is told in Volume 21 of the *Taiheiki* (Chronicle of Grand Pacification) in an episode titled *En'ya Hangan Zanshi no Koto* (The Slander and Death of En'ya Hangan). In that episode, the shogunal official Kō no Moronō[10] lusts after Hangan's beautiful wife and asks Yoshida Kenkō, the famous author of *Tsurezuregusa* (Essays in Idleness) to write her a love letter on his behalf. When his advances are rebuffed, the furious Moronō humiliates Hangan by slandering him in front of the shogun. This outrageous incident provides the starting point for *Chūshingura*.

In the opening scene, the smitten Moronō tries to give Hangan's wife Kaoyo a love letter but is foiled by Hangan's comrade Wakasanosuke of the Momonoi clan. Resentful, Moronō mercilessly insults Wakasanosuke, who, infuriated, vows to kill Moronō the next day at the shogunal palace. He shares his intentions with his old retainer Kakogawa Honzō, who expresses false support for the plan by cutting a limb off a pine tree and urging his hot-tempered young lord to likewise cut his enemy down without hesitation. In fact, however, Honzō goes to the palace and bribes Moronō to make peace with Wakasanosuke.

Honzō's ruse works. When Moronō next meets Wakasanosuke, he apologizes so profusely that Wakasanosuke cannot bring himself to draw his sword, thus avoiding further trouble. Honzō, who secretly watches the exchange, breathes a sigh of relief. But immediately afterwards Hangan appears and unwittingly gets embroiled in the conflict when he delivers a letter from his wife. The letter, written in response to Moronō's unwelcome advances, contains a classical poem that reads, "My night kimono already feels heavy. How then could I add another layer not my own?" Kaoyo's roundabout rejection further enrages Moronō, who had ignobly prostrated himself before Wakasanosuke just moments before. The brunt of Moronō's fury falls on Hangan, who has no idea what is happening or why. Moronō mercilessly browbeats and humiliates him to the point where he is driven to drawing his sword. At that moment, Honzō emerges from hiding and restrains Hangan.

Hangan is forced to commit ritual suicide without the satisfaction of striking down his enemy. Just before he dies, he entrusts his blood-stained short sword to his senior retainer Ōboshi Yuranosuke, (the character based on the real-life Ōishi Kuranosuke) who has just arrived from their home domain. Lamenting the death of her husband, Kaoyo becomes a nun and surrenders Hangan's castle. The young retainers in her service are spoiling for a fight, but Yuranosuke restrains them for the time being while secretly vowing to avenge their lord's death.

This, then, is the tragedy that befalls the En'ya family. As described in the *Taiheiki* source text, the underlying cause is the sexual harassment that Moronō inflicts on Hangan's beautiful wife. We must not forget, however, that the loyalty of the old retainer Kakogawa Honzō to the Momonoi clan was the direct, albeit inadvertent, source of the En'ya clan's demise and created the thirst for revenge. If Honzō had allowed Hangan to kill Moronō, no vendetta would have been needed. Also, it was the bribe that Honzō paid Moronō to protect his lord Wakasanosuke that brought Moronō's wrath down upon Hangan in the first place.

## The Tragedy of the Teraoka Family

The first family affected by the En'ya clan's demise is that of Teraoka Heiemon, whose younger sister Okaru is in love with Hayano Kanpei, an En'ya retainer. Though assigned to Lord Hangan, Kanpei was with Okaru when the incident with

Kanpei (left) mistakes Sadakurō (right) for a boar and shoots him with a musket (from *Kanadehon Chūshingura* woodblock print series by Utagawa Kunisada I). Photo courtesy of Tsubouchi Memorial Theatre Museum.

Moronō occurred. His failure to come to his lord's aid in his time of need was considered a capital offense. Ashamed of his dereliction of duty, Kanpei decides to commit ritual suicide but is talked out of it by Okaru. She convinces him to flee with her to her parents' house and live as a hunter. Always anxious to redeem himself, Kanpei wants to join Hangan's other retainers when he learns of their plot to mount a vendetta against Moronō.

The avengers need money to fund their plan, so Okaru's father Teraoka Yoichibē sells Okaru into prostitution and donates the money to the cause. The Teraokas were originally farmers; although the oldest son Heiemon is ostensibly a retainer serving the En'ya clan, he is only a lowly foot soldier, and Okaru had been Kaoyo's chamber maid. For her to be courted by a proper samurai like Kanpei, who could be

Okaru (Onoe Baikō VII) reads the secret letter addressed to Ōboshi Yuranosuke (Nakamura Kanzaburō XVII) using a hand mirror. Meanwhile, Ono Kudayū (Suketakaya Kodenji) also furtively reads the letter while hidden under the veranda. (Performed at the National Theatre in December 1973. Photo courtesy of the National Theatre.)

welcomed as a son-in-law, was a matter of great pride for the Teraoka family. They were anxious to see Kanpei regain his former samurai status, which is why they agreed to sell Okaru and fund the vendetta.

Yoichibē receives 50 ryō for Okaru as a down payment and is on his way home when he's beset by a brigand named Ono Sadakurō, himself a former retainer of the En'ya clan who had stooped to robbery to support himself after Hangan's death. Sadakurō kills Yoichibē and steals his money but is then immediately killed himself by Kanpei, who is out hunting and shoots him with a musket, mistaking him for a boar. The incident happens at night, and though Kanpei realizes he has accidentally shot a man, he knows nothing of the preceding circumstances. He tries to tend to Sadakurō's two bullet wounds, but Sadakurō has already died. Kanpei then discovers the money in the dead man's purse and impulsively takes it home with him.

Once home, Kanpei learns that his father-in-law Yoichibē is expected to return soon with the down payment he received for selling Okaru. When Yoichibē's body is brought home instead, Kanpei realizes that the purse he took from Sadakurō's body in fact belonged to Yoichibē. Even so, Kanpei tries to donate the money to support the vendetta cause, but his mother-in-law becomes convinced that Kanpei was the one who killed Yoichibē and stole the money for himself. The Teraoka family thus believes that Kanpei betrayed the generosity they had shown him and revile him for being inhuman. The loyal retainers hear of it and refuse to take Kanpei's money. In despair, Kanpei commits ritual suicide while offering a final apology. It then comes to light that Yoichibē died of a stab wound, not bullet wounds, making it clear that Kanpei had in fact avenged Yoichibē by killing his enemy Sadakurō. To reward that achievement, the loyal retainers add Kanpei's name to their roster of avengers, and Kanpei dies with his mind at ease.

The Teraoka family is in ruins. The family head Yoichibē and the son-in-law Kanpei are both dead, and the daughter Okaru has been sold into prostitution. Only Okaru's brother Heiemon and their mother are left to live out a lonely existence.

Meanwhile, Okaru has begun working at the Ichiriki geisha house in Gion, where Ōboshi Yuranosuke, who was once Hangan's senior retainer, spends every night in wild debauchery while secretly plotting revenge. Teraoka Heiemon visits him to ascertain Yuranosuke's true intentions but can't seem to penetrate the depths of his heart. Okaru happens to see a secret letter alluding to the vendetta that was delivered to Yuranosuke. When this is discovered by Yuranosuke, he suddenly offers to buy her freedom and send her home.

Okaru encounters her brother Heiemon at Ichiriki and tells him what had just happened. Heiemon surmises that Yuranosuke is indeed planning to avenge Hangan's death and furthermore intends to kill Okaru because she saw the secret letter. Heiemon resolves that if Okaru is fated to die to keep the plan secret, he will kill her himself so that he may be accepted as a participant in the vendetta. Being a lowly foot soldier, he feels he must "display a most valiant heart to be admitted into their ranks." Though he bitterly rues it, he tries to kill his own sister in order to earn Yuranosuke's trust. At first Okaru resists, but when she learns that her husband Kanpei has committed suicide, she loses her will to live and meekly accepts her fate. Knowing all of this and understanding that Heiemon is trustworthy, Yuranosuke steps in at the last minute and saves Okaru. He gives her the opportunity to kill Sadakurō's father Ono Kudayū, who as Moronō's spy had also read the secret letter. Yuranosuke also grants Heiemon permission to join the vendetta conspiracy. This is the story of the Teraoka family's fate following the tragedy of the En'ya clan.

## The Kakogawa and Ōboshi Families

Next comes what happened to the family of Kakogawa Honzō, the man responsible for the En'ya tragedy in the first place. Honzō was the one who paid a bribe to protect his lord, which resulted in En'ya Hangan unwittingly becoming the target of Moronō's ire. Also, it was Honzō who held Hangan back when he tried to kill Moronō, forcing Hangan to commit suicide unavenged.

Prior to the incident, plans were in place for a marriage between Honzō's daughter Konami and Yuranosuke's son Rikiya, which would have united the Kakogawa and Ōboshi families. Although Hangan's demise has made the Ōboshi

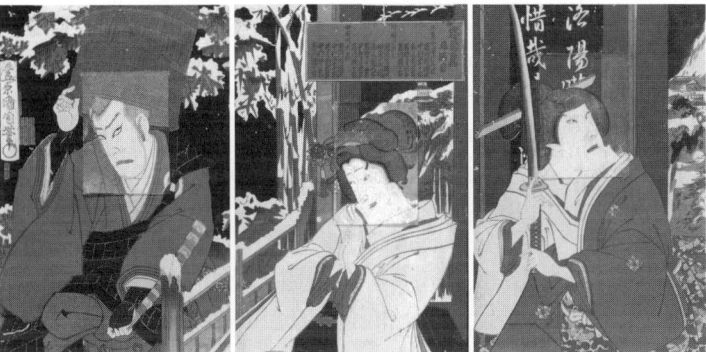

When the betrothal of Konami (center) and Rikiya is called off, Konami's stepmother Tonase (right) decides to kill Konami and commit suicide. Outside the gate, Honzō (left), who's disguised as a begging priest, watches as the scene unfolds. In these pictures, various actors are portrayed in each of these three roles, indicating that *Chūshingura* was performed with an interchangeable cast. (Woodblock print from *Chūshingura*, Act IX, by Toyohara Kunichika.)

men masterless and itinerant, Konami still hopes to marry Rikiya, so she travels with her stepmother Tonase to Yamashina in Kyoto, where the Ōboshi family lives.

Unfortunately, the two are given a cold reception by Oishi, Yuranosuke's wife, who calls off the wedding plans. She naturally refuses to allow her son to marry the daughter of a man who betrayed their lord, En'ya Hangan. Konami persists, saying that she wants to be with Rikiya, but her stepmother Tonase is at a loss and resolves to commit double suicide with Konami. Just then Honzō himself appears and, in an argument with Oishi, verbally abuses the Ōboshi family to the point where Rikiya stabs him with a lance. Honzō has provoked the attack intentionally, hoping that his own death will help Konami get her way. With Honzō on his deathbed, Yuranosuke finally reveals the revenge plot, and Honzō provides him with the ground plans of Moronō's mansion.

With his dying words, Honzō deeply laments what he calls the "shallow and ill-advised"[11] actions of En'ya Hangan, whose hot temper caused the fall of such a fine samurai as Yuranosuke. It may be that Honzō was castigating himself as well.

The next act focuses on the family of a merchant named Amakawaya Gihei, who procures the armaments needed for the vendetta. Gihei is so dedicated to maintaining secrecy that he has separated from his wife and children, but despite this Yuranosuke and his comrades disguise themselves as government officials to test his loyalty. This clever but somewhat unsympathetic storyline has not proven very popular, so that this act was gradually cut from performances. The final act is the well-known vendetta scene, but in Edo times it seems that it, too, was often cut; its original staging has not been properly transmitted, so that today we have instead a series of showy fight scenes that are far removed from the original script.

This overview of the kabuki play is probably enough to demonstrate just how far the modern image of *Chūshingura* has strayed from the original story. With this in mind, let's explore why the original play was such a tremendous success among Edo-period audiences.

## An Ultra-Popular Play

The book *Kokon Iroha Hyōrin* (Critical Primer of Past and Present) published in 1785 lists and critiques all of the actors who performed in *Chūshingura* in Kyoto, Edo, and Osaka starting in 1748—the year it premiered as a kabuki play. From this work we know that the play was mounted 41 times in just 38 years between 1748 and 1785.

The common practice at that time was to present a new play with each new production, so this repeated mounting of *Chūshingura* was an anomaly and probably explains why the book was published. It includes the following comment: "People flock to see how actors perform the play in each new run." This might seem unexceptional to modern audiences, who are interested in how particular actors interpret roles performed by many others before them, but in the world of Edo-period kabuki it was highly unusual.

Tatekawa Enba (1743–1811), the founder of the Tatekawa hereditary line of *rakugo* raconteurs and a key mentor responsible for the revival of the art of *rakugo* storytelling, published *Hana no Edo Kabuki Nendaiki* (Annals of Kabuki in Glorious Edo) in 1811. In it, he describes *Chūshingura* as "the *dokujintō* of theater." *Dokujintō* is a type of Chinese medicine containing ginseng that was considered a powerful tonic for the treatment of bloody sputum or bowel discharge. So Enba was saying that *Chūshingura* served as a booster shot that could cure a moribund theater suffering from the illness of empty seats. It's not clear whether this turn of phrase originated with Enba himself or was already current in his time, but it was a familiar characterization of the play among theater professionals until quite recently.

## Earlier Dramatizations

The Akō Incident was dramatized and performed in many other plays before *Kanadehon Chūshingura*. One account tells of a play presented at the Nakamura-za in Edo immediately after the incident occurred. That rendition was cast in the form of a vendetta carried out by the Soga brothers in 1193. However, the source cites letters written by Takarai Kikaku[12] and Chikamatsu Monzaemon, two completely different people, which casts doubt on its authenticity. Scholars tend to agree that the account is probably a forgery inserted at a later date. For one thing, it's highly unlikely that any dramatization could be staged in Edo that even obliquely referred to such an incident so soon after it occurred. There are extant illustrated synopses and other sources, however, that seem to indicate that Chikamatsu did write dramatizations of the story for performance in western Japan at a very early date.[13]

Two of Chikamatsu's two-part puppet plays deal squarely with the incident: *Kenkō Hōshi Monomi Guruma* (The Sightseeing Carriage of Priest Kenkō)[14] and *Goban Taiheiki* (Chronicle of Grand Pacification Played on a Chessboard). As one can surmise from the titles, Chikamatsu set the incident in the world of the *Taiheiki*, a work from the fourteenth century. A retainer of En'ya Hangan named Hachiman Rokurō appears in the *Taiheiki*, and it is this character who leads the vendetta in *Kenkō Hōshi Monomi Guruma*.

In *Goban Taiheiki*, however, the leader's name is Ōboshi Yuranosuke. The low-ranking samurai Teraoka Heiemon infiltrates the mansion of Kō no Moronō as a spy sent by Yuranosuke to gather intelligence, but is then ordered by Moronō to spy on Yuranosuke. Heiemon feeds Moronō false information to put him off guard, but Ōboshi Rikiya believes that Heiemon has betrayed Yuranosuke and strikes him down. As he dies, Heiemon reveals that he was in fact a double agent, and his last action is to use a chess board to reveal the layout of Moronō's mansion. This scene has been incorporated into *Kanadehon Chūshingura* at the end of Act IX.

It seems that what fascinated Edo audiences most about the vendetta was how information about the layout of the mansion was obtained before the attack was launched. *Goban Taiheiki* was the first play to answer this question, after which an episode about the mansion's floor plan was always included in works inspired by the *Chūshingura* theme. *Goban Taiheiki* also included a realistic battle scene depicting the vendetta itself.

At about the same time that *Goban Taiheiki* premiered at the Takemoto-za (where Chikamatsu was the resident playwright), a puppet play by Ki no Kaion[15] titled *Onikage Musashi Abumi* (Stirrups of Musashi's Demon Horse)[16] opened at the rival Toyotake-za. In this version of the story, Asano Naganori is transformed into Oguri Hangan,[17] a fictional character who appears in *sekkyō-bushi* (sermon-ballad chanting) and other traditional performance forms. In this work, however, he is explicitly described as "hot-tempered," and the lead-up to the initial sword incident is depicted very realistically.

The vendetta leader in *Onikage Musashi Abumi* is named Ōgishi Kunai, and he is portrayed in one scene as "besotted with alcohol and debauchery" in the pleasure quarters of Kyoto. He buys the freedom of the courtesan Agemaki with the intent to kill her because of her knowledge of the vendetta plot. These elements were later incorporated into Act VII of *Chūshingura*.

There was a kabuki play titled *Onikage Musashi Abumi* that predated the puppet play, so it's assumed that the latter was an adaptation of the former, but the original kabuki script has been lost so we don't know its content in detail. *Chūshingura*'s survival to the present day might be largely due to the fact that it started out as a puppet play, since puppet scripts were properly published. Kabuki scripts were copied haphazardly by hand, with actors usually only writing down their own parts, making it less likely that a complete script would survive. Also, each kabuki theater created scripts that were tailored to individual actors, so that a given script could only be performed by the theater to which the actor belonged. In this sense many original kabuki plays lacked dramatic universality, which might also explain why *Chūshingura* and so many other plays in the classical kabuki repertory originated with the puppets.

It's interesting to note that Namiki Senryū,[18] one of the co-authors of *Chūshingura*, wrote an earlier play titled *Chūshin Kogane no Tanzaku* (The Golden Cards of Loyal

Retainers)[19] that dealt with the same subject matter. In that play he combined the content of Acts VII and IX of *Chūshingura* and introduced a character named Hayano Kanpei for the first time, who gets killed when he tries to ascertain the true motives of the vendetta leader.

## The Appeal of Life-Size Drama

After examining some of its many predecessors, one might feel that *Chūshingura* is almost completely lacking in originality. Why, then, has it survived all these years? One reason might be the times in which it was created. As I noted in chapter 3, the mid-eighteenth century was a time when the puppet theater reigned supreme. Patrons flocked to see it in numbers far higher than when Chikamatsu was still active, and puppet plays were immediately adapted for the kabuki stage.

Still, there were many other outstanding plays being produced at the time, so why did *Chūshingura* stand out above all others? One refreshingly pithy answer is provided by Jippensha Ikku (1765–1831), the famous author of *Hizakurige* (Shank's Mare), who was a highly successful author of puppet plays in Osaka before becoming a writer of humorous light fiction in Edo.

About a half a century after *Chūshingura* premiered, Ikku wrote an informal book of criticism titled *Chūshingura Okame Hyōban* (A Bystander's Look at *Chūshingura*).[20] In the introduction to that work, he sets out some of the characteristics of the play that he believes ensure its abiding popularity. He observes that it has a simple sentence structure throughout; stays focused on the important points in each act and avoids verbosity; and is written carefully to keep the audience engaged at all times. Although many people today might not quite concur with Ikku's claims, it is true that *Chūshingura's* literary style is markedly different from that found in the plays of Chikamatsu and others. Because it has less ornamental language, the story is easy to understand and develops at a rapid pace, leaving no time for the audience to get bored. When we compare *Chūshingura* with other puppet plays, even modern readers will agree to some extent with Ikku's assessment.

I can suggest other aspects that distinguish *Chūshingura* from other puppet plays. One of these is a relatively direct storyline that develops very naturally, even when compared with such related works as *Goban Taiheiki* and *Chūshin Kogane no Tanzaku*. Also, villains in most other puppet plays with historical settings are portrayed as being larger than life. For example, Fujiwara no Shihei, the villain in *Sugawara Denju Tenarai Kagami*, is an evil despot bent on usurping the imperial throne. Such superhuman villains bring great grief to the protagonists in ways that seem far removed from everyday life. In *Chūshingura*, the villain Kō no Moronō is a comparatively realistic character who happens to be a lecherous and foolish bully but is otherwise very human.

*Chūshingura* is also completely free of the bizarre plot twists and false identities that are often found in other puppet plays. In *Yoshitsune Senbonzakura*, for example, the boatman turns out to "actually" be Taira no Tomomori in disguise, and the live-in helper at the sushi shop is "actually" Taira no Koremori. In contrast, *Chūshingura* is based on a historical incident and is closer in tone to a domestic drama. This realistic depiction on a life-size scale is probably the very aspect that transfixed many audience members of the time.

Even today, some might grow angry and resort to violence if they were subjected to the sexual harassment by a malicious boss in the workplace. We can also easily imagine a young worker who has the misfortune of being away from his desk dallying with a lover when he should have been on hand during a company crisis. Nor is it difficult to envision an otherwise stubborn father swallowing his pride and asking a family's forgiveness for the sake of a sweet young daughter who has her heart set on marrying the man of her own choosing. *Chūshingura* presents a story that is so realistic that it can even be transposed into such contemporary situations without too much difficulty.

## It's All about *Ribenji*

Another feature of *Chūshingura* is that the entire tragedy grows out of a trivial scuffle and bad timing. The only reason Hangan suffered Moronō's relentless humiliation was because Moronō himself was in a bad mood, having groveled before Wakasanosuke just moments before. Similarly, Honzō just happened to be there to prevent Hangan from cutting Moronō down on the spot, thereby creating the need for revenge. As for Kanpei's tragedy, things seem to go awry in ways that seem strangely realistic in their randomness.

One might wonder why the dying Kanpei felt content to have his name added to the roster of ronin bent on revenge, even though he himself would not survive to participate in the vendetta. The answer is that he felt it absolved him of his guilt. For him, the greatest sin was not that he accidentally killed someone with his musket but that he failed to come to his lord's aid when needed, as a faithful samurai should do. Kanpei's ardent desire to reinstate himself as a proper retainer motivates all of his actions.

For his part, Honzō felt deep regret that his inappropriate actions—his bribing of Moronō and his stepping in to prevent Hangan from slaying Moronō—caused his daughter grief. This is why he attempted to wipe the slate clean with his own death. In a way he resembles Kanpei, because he, too, attempts to atone for mistakes of the past.

In recent years, the word *ribenji* (revenge) has gained currency in Japanese as a borrowed word from English. It was first used in the sports world in the 1990s to describe "revenge matches," in which one of the contestants tries to redeem a past defeat. Usage of the term has gradually broadened, and with it there has been a softening of the meaning. Today it doesn't mean "retaliation" so much as "making recompense" and is often used without reference to any particular enemy but rather as a description of a desire to correct one's own failures. As so often happens with words borrowed from other languages, the Japanese have put "revenge" to a use that is somewhat removed from its original meaning. The evolution evidenced by the word *ribenji* strikes me as a distinctively Japanese process.

*Ribenji* in the Japanese sense is perhaps *Chūshingura*'s true theme. Of course, retainers loyal to their dead lord Hangan do mount a vendetta against Moronō, but their underlying purpose is not simply to kill their enemy. Each character is trying to restore the world to its proper order, by which means they hope to recover a self that was lost. I think this is why *Chūshingura* reverberates so deeply with so many Japanese.

## Highlights

Before ending this chapter, I'd like to briefly describe some act-by-act highlights that were glossed over in my plot summary.

At the very beginning, a puppet appears before the curtain and introduces the characters of the play. The curtain then opens to reveal the actors looking down with eyes closed. As the *takemoto* narrator[21] calls each character's name, the

the *takemoto* narrator[21] calls each character's name, the corresponding actor uses puppet-like gestures to slowly lift his face and begin to act. This opening sequence symbolizes the fact that *Chūshingura* originated as a puppet play. Today, it's the only play in the kabuki repertoire that begins in this manner.

Act III depicts the confrontation between Hangan and Moronō. Hangan is subjected to merciless ridicule and abuse, and his forbearance is one of the main highlights that modern audiences come to see. A similar scene is found in the puppet play *Kagamiyama Kokyō no Nishikie* (The Color Prints of Kagamiyama),[22] which is sometimes called the women's version of *Chūshingura*. Iwafuji, the chief lady-in-waiting, maliciously insults Onoe, the second lady-in-waiting, who bears it patiently as long as she can before committing suicide. This, too, is a highlight scene, underlining a fondness the Japanese seem to have for a pattern of forbearance that I explore more fully in the next chapter.

Act IV depicts Hangan's ritual suicide in a documentary style that pays great attention to procedural detail. As such it is a highly unusual scene within the kabuki repertory. During performances in Edo-period theaters, it was normal for vendors to walk up and down the aisles selling their wares and for viewers to come and go at will. When this act was performed, however, and this act alone, these distractions were not permitted. For this reason it came to be known as the "no walking scene." The audience has been watching Hangan prepare to die in an extended scene filled with quiet tension. Just as he touches the dagger to his belly, in rushes Yuranosuke, making a great clatter as he enters down the bridgeway. Enjoying a cathartic release, viewers might well be tempted to call out the famous line spoken by Hangan: *Machi kaneta wa yai* (I've been waiting for you!) It's hard to imagine a more dramatic and effective entrance for a hero. The Edo-period

Nakamura Nakazō I in the role of Ono Sadakurō. (Woodblock print by Katsukawa Shunshō.)

author and critic Ikku agrees with this assessment in his *Chūshingura Okame Hyōban*, where he notes that, although audiences are curiously unaware of it, Yuranosuke's entrance is extremely well crafted and one of the high points of the play.

Act V features the character Ono Sadakurō, who originally appeared dressed like a mountain brigand. However, the actor Nakamura Nakazō I[23] changed the costume completely into what we see onstage today — a masterless samurai who could have easily been found walking the streets of Edo. This anecdote is so well known that there's even a *rakugo* story about it. Nakazō created various other costume designs and acting techniques that heightened realism and increased his popularity. From that time onward, Sadakurō ceased to be a mere side character.

In today's productions, Sadakurō leaps with sword drawn out of a stack of rice straw behind Yoichibē. This entrance was not invented by Nakazō, however. It probably dates to the time when the roles of Yoichibē and Sadakurō where played by a single actor who made quick, onstage costume changes. As I noted, *Chushingura* was regarded as a "tonic" for financially ailing theaters, which meant that the cast often lacked an adequate number of good actors. From the early days of kabuki, we see records of productions in which actors made quick costume changes onstage in order to perform more than one role, and this approach was touted as a display of their skill.

Act VI features Kanpei's ritual suicide. According to *Kokon Iroha Hyōrin*, which lists all the actors who performed in *Chūshingura* from 1748 to 1785, there were productions in which both Act V and Act VI were cut because audiences had already seen Hangan's suicide scene, and in any case the storyline at this point was too gloomy and depressing. It wasn't until the success of Onoe Kikugorō III in the role that Kanpei became one of the most important characters in the entire play. Since then, Kanpei has always been portrayed as a peerless pretty boy, an image that was ingeniously refined by Kikugorō III's grandson Kikugorō V[24] and great grandson Kikugorō VI to create the distinctive role so popular among Tokyo audiences today. The main purpose of that staging is to enhance the colorful beauty of Kanpei's appearance in order to brighten up a generally dark scene.

After cutting open his belly, Kanpei launches into a long speech that reveals his inner feelings. This speech is not found in the original puppet play and was inserted later into the kabuki version. Kanpei regrets his erotic interest in Okaru at a time when, unbeknownst to him, his lord's life was at stake. As he delivers the line, "I embarrassed myself with lust," he slaps his own cheek with his bloodstained hand, leaving a red mark. This gesture, attributed to Kikugorō III leaves an impression of terrifying, grotesque beauty that reflects the overripe decadence of the late Edo period (see plate 3).

In Act VII, Okaru is told that both her father Yoichibē and her husband Kanpei are dead. She regards their loss with a frankness that makes her seem like a modern girl, saying: "I'm sorry about father's untimely death, but he was old, after all. Kanpei, though, was barely 30. How sad that he should die, when I wanted to see him so badly." Not all of this speech is delivered by the actor; parts of it are set to a melody and chanted by the *takemoto* narrator while the actor dances. This type of choreographed passage is called a *kudoki*, which I will discuss in more detail in chapter 8.

Yuranosuke's entrance was reputedly first conceived by Sawamura Sōjūrō I[25] for the kabuki play *Ōyakazu Shijūshichi Hon* (Launching of 47 Great Arrows) and then "re-imported" into the puppet version of *Chūshingura*.[26] As one might expect, it has the most kabuki-like feel of all the scenes in the play. Apparently Ōishi Kuranosuke, the real-life model for the Yuranosuke character, actually did frequent geisha houses, so that part of the story has the ring of truth. But having the character spend his days in dissipation in the pleasure quarters in order to throw his enemies off the scent is a quintessentially kabuki-like conceit. A man concealing his true intentions, pretending to be a complete fool who cares nothing for his reputation, and enduring public scorn until the time is ripe to take action is a character type that seems to resonate deeply with the Japanese.

The challenge of this role is to convey Yuranosuke's true desire for vengeance throughout the play. In Act IV, when Hangan's castle has been surrendered and the young samurai are clamoring for revenge, Yuranosuke calms them down. Left alone afterward, he shows his inner resolve by taking out the dagger of his dead lord and gazing at it in silence. When he finally does reveal his intentions after exposing Ono Kudayū to be a traitor in the Ichiriki scene, he allows his long-suppressed anger to explode. This is a moment of great cathartic relief, both for him and the audience.

Act VIII is a dance scene in which Tonase and her daughter Konami travel down the Tokaidō Road. Since limiting the scene to just these two women seemed comparatively drab, the authors added other travelers, including samurai attendants and pilgrims on their way to Ise.[27] These additions lend the scene extra vitality and color.

In Edo productions, another travel scene was created to depict Okaru and Kanpei traveling as newlyweds to Okaru's family home. Called *Ochūdo* (The Fugitives), it is now more often performed than the original travel scene that featured Tonase and Konami. *Ochūdo* is based on Act III of the original puppet play, in which Kanpei is convinced by Okaru not to commit suicide but instead flee home with her. The scene is set in the hills of Totsuka along the Tokaidō, showing Mt. Fuji in the background with cherry blossoms in full bloom. It is truly a stunning dance piece that portrays a beautiful young couple talking of love. Particularly when performed after the dark and somber Act IV, *Ochūdo* provides a moment of light.

The lead character in Act IX is Kakogawa Honzō, who generated a bit of controversy in Edo Japan. Some observers, such as a commentator quoted in *Chūshingura Okame Hyōban*, felt that Honzō was "drunk with love for his daughter and a fool for losing his life because of it." Others felt differently, however. Chikamatsu Hanji,[28] for example, argued articulately that Honzō's "death for the sake of his daughter may not have been the correct path for a samurai but was the true path in light of the situation."

Chikamatsu Hanji was a famous author of puppet plays and one of Jippensha Ikku's mentors. He also wrote several successful kabuki plays, including *Honchō Nijūshi Kō* (Twenty-four

Models of Japanese Filial Piety)[29] and *Imoseyama Onna Teikin* (An Example of Noble Womanhood).[30] His comment concerning Honzō illustrates how much antipathy playwrights of the time felt toward the prevailing ideals of feudal loyalty, and how much they cherished humanistic values.

Modern people tend to associate *Chūshingura* with right-wing nationalism, but the original play as written for the kabuki stage was not particularly nationalistic. Most of the characters, including Honzō and Kanpei, are simply swept along by natural human emotions. This is a drama about people whose families were destroyed and who suffered deeply because of a single unfortunate incident. In bringing this chapter to a close, I'd like to emphasize just how large a gap there is between modern renditions of the *Chūshingura* story and the kabuki version, *Kanadehon Chūshingura*.

CHAPTER SIX

# *Natsu Matsuri Naniwa Kagami*

## THE BIRTH OF CHIVALRY

### Giving Puppets Bodies

As we've seen, kabuki borrowed many plays from the *jōruri* puppet theater, but the reverse was also true, with "human" elements being introduced into the puppet genre from kabuki. Perhaps the best known example is *Natsu Matsuri Naniwa Kagami* (Summer Festival: Mirror of Osaka), which premiered at the Takemoto-za in Osaka in 1745—around the same time that *Kanadehon Chūshingura* and other masterpieces that I've already covered were first presented.

A commentary on the puppet theater called *Gida Momo Hiki* published in 1777 notes that *Natsu Matsuri* was the first play in which a puppet was dressed in a *katabira* light kimono. A *katabira* is an unlined kimono worn in the summer; in fact, the familiar word yukata (summer kimono) is an abbreviated form of *yukatabira*, which means "unlined kimono for the bath."

This is important because until then, *jōruri* puppets were merely heads attached to costumes. The use of a light kimono made it necessary for the puppets to have bodies, especially since there's a scene that requires the puppets to undress.

*Natsu Matsuri* was therefore the first play in which *jōruri* puppets with bodies were used. Obviously, this was the result of "importing" the play from the kabuki repertory.

*Natsu Matsuri* as it is performed today originated as a live-action piece that was adapted for the puppets and then reintroduced to the kabuki stage. The protagonist Danshichi Kurobē has two friends: Issun Tokubē[1] and Tsurifune no Sabu. These three characters first appeared in a kabuki play from the Genroku era (1688–1704) called *Yadonashi Danshichi* (Homeless Danshichi). In that production, the rascal Danshichi was played by Kataoka Nizaemon I,[2] who depicted villains with tremendous skill. The character was probably based on a real person because the play is cast in the form of a *sewa-mono*, or a contemporary play dealing with the everyday lives of townsmen, a category I briefly discussed in chapter 3.

In the Genroku era, kabuki performed in Kyoto and Osaka often included a type of skit called *kiri-kyōgen* as a bonus feature at the end of the main program. This was how the *sewa-mono* genre originated. These short pieces were created as a form of infotainment, presenting dramatizations of the latest murder or double suicide.[3] Because "Homeless Danshichi" first appears in a *kiri-kyōgen*, scholars have concluded that there must have been a real-life model for the character.

In Osaka, there were many homeless people without registered addresses. This might be another reason why "Homeless Danshichi" remained a familiar name for many years.

## Chivalrous Stars

During the reign of the eighth Tokugawa shogun Yoshimune, who ruled from 1716 to 1745, a new type of kabuki play called *kyōkaku-mono* ("chivalrous commoner" plays) became extremely popular in Kyoto and Osaka. Today, Yoshimune is often portrayed in TV historical dramas as an ideal shogun, but in fact his rule was one in which restrictive laws and regulations put heavy pressure on the lives of townsfolk.

Policies designed to strengthen feudal control brought the merchant economy to a grinding halt, and ordinary people were suffering. As I discussed in chapter 3, the hard economic times inspired a popular interest in historical dramas. But they also sparked the popularity of plays about chivalrous commoners. This marked the beginning of a genre that later spread to many other art forms, including storytelling, shamisen-accompanied *naniwa-bushi* recitation, and films.

One of the early actors who benefitted from this new genre was Anekawa Shinshirō,[4] whose portrayal of the character Kurofune Chūemon propelled him to stardom.

The Kurofune character was modeled on an Osaka man named Nezu Shirōemon, otherwise known as the Old Man of Dōjima. Dōjima was the rice exchange district in Osaka, and the head of the rice brokers who worked in that district was customarily called the Old Man of Dōjima. Shirōemon was respected as a kind of godfather among the rice brokers and became famous because of the following incident.

The Kajimaya family was one of the wealthiest of the many well-to-do merchants that lived in Osaka. One day, a man accosted a Kajimaya apprentice and stole the rice certificates he was carrying, which could be redeemed at a warehouse for rice. The Kajimaya family asked Nezu Shirōemon to negotiate the return of the certificates, and this commission elevated his reputation as a negotiator.

The actor Anekawa Shinshirō created the role of Kurofune Chūemon based on Nezu Shirōemon and subsequently performed many plays that featured the character.

According to one commentary published at the time,[5] Shinshirō was not very good at portraying samurai but extremely adept at playing chivalrous commoner roles. I suspect that he was similar to the modern-day movie star Takakura Ken, who played Ōishi Kuranosuke in the film *Shijūshichinin no Shikaku* (47 Ronin)[6] directed by Ichikawa Kon, which was based on the *Chūshingura* story. Watching that film, I was struck by how ill-suited Takakura was to samurai roles. When he finally stabbed Kira Yoshinaka in the vendetta scene, I could almost hear him recite his trademark line against yakuza villains from his better known *ninkyō* (chivalry movies) produced by Toei: *Shinde moraimasu* (You're going to die). It seems to me that Shinshirō might have been the same type of actor.

Shinshirō's Kurofune plays all follow the same pattern. Although he negotiates successfully, and everything seems to go well at first, Kurofune is later subjected to the villain's vengeful humiliation and assaulted both verbally and physically. Usually, he stoically endures this abuse for the sake of the person he's protecting until he can stand it no longer, at which point he explodes in anger and kills the villain. Although the details of the plot vary from play to play, this basic storyline was repeated over and over as the basis for many works.

One commentary notes that Shinshirō's performances tended to be appreciated more among the "groundlings" (who sat in the "pit" in front of the stage) than by the higher class patrons who sat up in the gallery seats.[7] It was this kind of actor who appealed to theatergoers when townsfolk were struggling in the face of a shrinking economy.

Shinshirō enjoyed a swell of popularity but gradually lost his audience. In his later years he was criticized for lack of innovation as he played the same role over and over again. While such criticism may be justified, it doesn't change the fact that in his prime, his Kurofune provided the foundation for the *ninkyō* movies of later times.

## Layers of Reality

The puppet play *Natsu Matsuri* was created with all the many layered images and patterns provided by kabuki, including the "Kurofune" pattern described above. For this reason it can be considered an importation from kabuki to *jōruri*, instead of the other way around.

Historical plays are the foundation of the puppet theater. Although domestic dramas did exist, they were in no way the mainstay of the repertory. It's true that Chikamatsu Monzaemon produced "double suicide" hits like *Sonezaki Shinjū* (The Love Suicides at Sonezaki),[8] which might be considered a domestic drama. But such plays were banned by authorities in 1723 because of their supposed bad influence on public morals. It was through the medium of chivalry plays that domestic drama was resurrected in *jōruri*.

As one would expect from a domestic drama, *Natsu Matsuri* is based on a true story. About six months before the play's premiere, a fishmonger was murdered in a backstreet in Nagamachi, Osaka. This helps to explain why the protagonist in the play is a fishmonger.

The story is quite easy to summarize. The fishmonger Danshichi Kurobē feels indebted to a certain samurai and has taken on the responsibility of caring for the samurai's son Isonojō and his lover, the courtesan Kotoura. Aided by his stouthearted friends Issun Tokubē and Tsurifune no Sabu, Danshichi succeeds in shielding the pair from a samurai named Sagaemon, who seeks an illicit love affair with Kotoura. Unfortunately, Danshichi's greedy father-in-law Giheiji has been bought off by Sagaemon and fools Kotoura into coming with him. Learning of Giheiji's intentions to deliver Kotoura to Sagaemon, Danshichi overtakes him on the road and offers to pay him to let Kotoura go, despite the fact that he has no money. When Danshichi's false promise is exposed, he ends up killing Giheiji in a fit of anger.

Although Danshichi is something of a roughneck, he's not a villain at heart. He's depicted as a man who values masculine virtues, believes in manly honor, and tries to act with a chivalrous spirit.

The climax of the play comes after Danshichi's promise to pay is exposed as a lie and he's subjected to relentless humiliation by Giheiji. Showing tremendous restraint, Danshichi bears one insult after another until he finally snaps and kills Giheiji in a fit of rage. The murder of a father-in-law was considered patricide and carried a much stiffer penalty than did ordinary murder. The situation that traps Danshichi into committing such a heinous crime is depicted in elaborate detail.

While Danshichi is struggling to bear Giheiji's abuse and keep his cool, a lively festival scene is unfolding with drum and flute music in the background. This highly effective evocation of Osaka's muggy summer heat—so hot that it can easily make people lose their temper—gives the scene a very realistic feel. Danshichi strips down to his waist when he commits the murder, accentuating his elaborate tattoo. It's a stunning visual effect that truly evokes the beauty of a color woodblock print.

## Mud-Splattered Murder

In one powerful scene, Danshichi and Giheiji fall into a mud pool as they fight. It was common practice as early as the middle of the eighteenth century to place mud in a box called a *dorobune* (mud boat)[9] and spread sand over the stage. Unlike the concrete theaters of today, theaters back then were wooden buildings with dirt floors. It was easy to create sand

Danshichi (Nakamura Kichiemon II) about to murder Giheiji (Nakamura Karoku V). Covered in mud, Giheiji gradually expires while performing a series of 13 *mie* poses.

> ## Kabuki Design
>
> Backstreet Nagamachi scene in *Natsu Matsuri Naniwa Kagami*
>
> *Honmizu* (real water)
> After killing his father-in-law, Danshichi draws water from a well and washes off the mud and blood spattered all over him. The use of real water evoked the ambiance of summer while giving audiences a sense of cool refreshment in theaters that had no air conditioning.

and mud pits by cutting through the stage floor and digging holes. This was similar to the approach adopted by the tent theaters of the *angura* (underground) movement that became so popular in Japan in the 1960s. In a near open-air theatrical setting, creating ponds or making mud posed no problem.

Kabuki also used *honmizu* (real water) onstage from quite early on. Already in the Genroku era, *mizu karakuri* (water tricks)[10] were often incorporated into plays performed in the summer. Like the magical illusions presented in modern-day shows, these enhancements helped create a sense of spectacle.

As these examples show, early kabuki artists put a tremendous amount of effort into their stage sets and equipment. In an era without modern machinery, there were few theater traditions in the world that went to so much trouble to create special effects. I'll discuss this aspect of kabuki in more detail in the next chapter.

## "The Culture of Shame" and "The Aesthetic of Forbearance"

As I noted in the previous chapter, kabuki plays often depict situations in which the protagonist explodes in a fit of anger after enduring all kinds of abuse. This became a common pattern for chivalry plays in particular, such as the scene in *Natsu Matsuri* when Giheiji hits Danshichi's forehead with his leather-soled sandal.

The humiliating act of hitting someone in the face with footwear was already a feature of kabuki in the Genroku era. As I discussed in chapter 1, *Sankai Nagoya* was the first play in which Danjūrō I portrayed the *Shibaraku* character, who makes his appearance in Act II. In Act III of that play, that character is humiliatingly beaten with a sandal, after which he commits suicide.

*Ise Ondo Koi no Netaba* (The Vengeful Sword at Ise)[11] is one play that comes to mind when thinking about protagonists whose resentment incites them to murder after being shamed in public. As with other plays of this type, it was based on a true story, a mass murder at the Furuichi brothel in Ise.

The many situations in which public humiliation leads to murder reminds me of the "culture of shame" identified by anthropologist Ruth Benedict.[12] At the same time, the popularity of scenes depicting the hero enduring the unbearable until he finally cracks can be explained by the strong sympathy such scenes elicited from audiences who were themselves being suppressed in various ways.

Yakuza films starring Takakura Ken were tremendously popular in the 1960s and early 1970s, even among students protesting the US-Japan Security Treaty. Japan was experiencing rapid economic growth, and companies were becoming huge. School graduates were expected to become cogs in a relentless machine that required personal sacrifice and forbearance. This social milieu may have been one factor behind the popularity of Takakura's films.

During the Kyōhō era (1716–1735), there was a rapid increase in the number of merchants who adopted names that were passed down from generation to generation.[13] This was no doubt convenient for achieving continuity when a business was inherited. As the conservative system that legislated such arrangements grew stronger, however, ordinary people were pressured to conform. This, too, may have boosted the popularity of chivalrous commoner plays.

The pattern of forbearance followed by sudden, violent action remained viable for centuries until it flowered on the silver screen in the films starring Takakura Ken. Again and again, he played characters who stoically endured unbearable humiliation until they reached the breaking point and uttered the trademark line, "You're going to die." Fans then delighted in seeing Takakura turn around, open his umbrella, and walk out into the rain. At least one source of this "aesthetic of forbearance" can be traced back to *Natsu Matsuri*.

## What's a Woman to Do?

Returning now to the play itself, let's look at what happens after Danshichi kills his father-in-law. Because he's dropped one of his sandals at the scene of the crime, it's only a matter of time before he's arrested. Knowing this, Tokubē pretends to have an affair with Danshichi's wife so the two can divorce.

In this way the murder will no longer be defined as a patricide, enabling Danshichi to avoid the extreme punishment of having his head sawn off. Such scenes of couples having to part against their will are another common pattern of chivalry plays. Often, the husband leaves his wife and children to protect them from the consequences of his actions. This reflects the system of "guilt by association" that prevailed during the Edo period.

Plays featuring the famous chivalrous commoner Banzuiin Chōbē, for example, were staged from the early Edo period. One such play still performed today is *Kiwametsuki Banzui Chōbē*,[14] which contains a deeply moving scene in which Chōbē bids farewell to his wife and child before visiting the home of his enemy, where he knows assassins are awaiting him. The very essence of the chivalry play as a genre resides in a man's valuing his honor even more than family love and unflinchingly facing death.

Japanese culture is said to have homosocial[15] overtones, even today. The chivalry play genre can be considered an example of this tendency. In this context it's worth noting that, in *Natsu Matsuri*, Tokubē's wife Otatsu purposely disfigures her own beautiful face as if in retaliation for the emotional bonds that tie the male characters together more tightly than the bond between husband and wife.

It's also worth noting that profligate heroes such as those described in chapter 2 (which in the case of *Natsu Matsuri* applies to Isonojō) are always secondary characters in chivalry plays. Such characters were given the lead role only in the early days of the Genroku era. Though the character type survived, in later eras it was never again elevated to the status of protagonist.

In the same way that prewar and postwar Japanese society were completely different despite being in the same century, the three centuries of the Edo period were by no means homogeneous. Even within the same historical period, the image of the ideal hero evolved with the changing times. One of the most appealing benefits derived from an understanding of kabuki's history is a deeper sense of the flow of those changes.

CHAPTER SEVEN

# Sanmon Gosan no Kiri

## A Montage of Stage Effects

### Tales of Sedition

Now that kabuki is viewed as a "classical" art form, it's easy to forget that for much of its history audiences expected to see a brand new work with each new production. Plays were written specifically for resident actors who were reshuffled annually among various theaters. This helps to explain why kabuki evolved by incorporating both earlier performance styles and the latest trends as it developed. When creativity flagged, producers turned to the puppet theater and simply transplanted puppet plays in their entirety to the kabuki stage until another brilliant kabuki playwright came along who could inspire a new flowering.

After the chivalrous commoner fad discussed in the previous chapter had run its course, a new genre began to appear in Kyoto and Osaka. The earliest examples are called *muhonnin-geki* (sedition plays) and might be characterized as picaresque adventures. They date to around the 1740s, or just before *Natsu Matsuri* debuted. A typical protagonist in these plays is first introduced as a mere roughneck but is later revealed to be the scion of a famous warrior who was defeated by the present rulers. This motivates him to become a rebel dedicated to overthrowing the current regime.

One early example is the play *Miyoshi Chōkei Sato no Agemaki*,[1] which opens with a comical skit featuring two thieves who turn out to be the Sengoku-period warriors Miyoshi Chōkei and Matsunaga Hisahide. Subsequent plays featured the exploits of many other ex-warriors who were often portrayed in historical accounts as rebels, such as Akechi Mitsuhide and Akamatsu Mitsusuke.[2]

In a typical sedition play, the protagonist reveals his true identity only to discover that his enemy also has a hidden identity. Complicated stories with uncertain outcomes developed from this premise of double deception. Audiences often couldn't quite tell who was the hero and who the villain, and these plays proved to be extremely popular.

Having a ruffian reveal himself to be the son of a famous warrior is similar to the premise in *yatsushi-goto* plays (discussed in chapter 2) featuring stylish, high-born "profligate heroes" who are down on their luck. This type of sudden identity revelation displaced the older, "profligate" trope in plays performed in the western cities of Kyoto and Osaka. Edo, on the other hand, saw a slightly different but related kind of displacement, which I'll discuss in more detail in chapter 9.

What fueled the explosive popularity of complicated storylines featuring the exploits of ruffians? The answer is simple: the emergence of extremely gifted writers. One of them was Namiki Gohei,[3] the author of *Sanmon Gosan no Kiri* (The Temple Gate and the Paulownia Crest),[4] the subject of this chapter. The preeminent master of the genre, however, was Gohei's teacher and mentor, Namiki Shōza.[5]

In my opinion, there have been surprisingly few geniuses in Japanese history. If I had to name one, though, the first person that comes to mind is Namiki Shōza. In an era completely

A Montage of Stage Effects

dominated by the puppet theater, it was the genius of this man that almost singlehandedly brought kabuki back to life.

In this chapter I'll provide a glimpse of the kinds of backstories that were woven into *Sanmon*. In doing so, I may find myself introducing not just the play's author Namiki Gohei, but also the brilliant creativity of his teacher, Namiki Shōza.

## Mystery and Deception

The present-day version of *Sanmon* (the word *sanmon* means "main temple gate") begins with the character Ishikawa Goemon[6] uttering the famous line, "Such a stunning view!" The scene lasts only about 15 minutes, but the incredible backdrop of cherry trees in full bloom, coupled with the lavishly colorful *sanmon* gate that rises on the central trap lift, is a magnificent sight that fully demonstrates kabuki's love of spectacle.

Today, audiences tend to be interested not in the storyline as much as the refined style and splendid costume of the actor portraying Goemon. However, the scene is only one small part of an extremely long play that presents an epic tale full of mystery and deception. Although the scene has a deep significance for the story as a whole and is certainly

Paulownia Crest

important, one would never know that by watching it in isolation. It might be helpful, then, to summarize the overall plot.

The full title, *Sanmon Gosan no Kiri*, means "The Temple Gate and the Paulownia Crest." The paulownia crest in question is the family crest of the great warlord Toyotomi

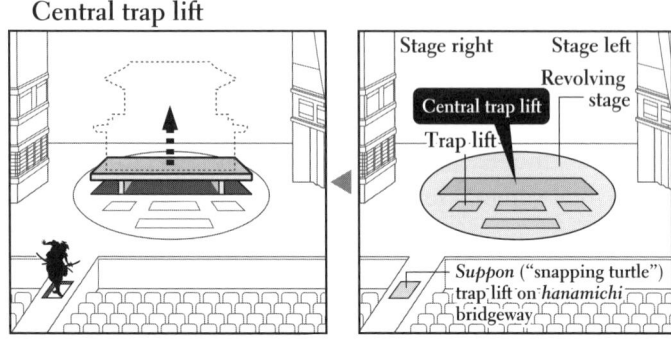

Hideyoshi, whose history is described in his biography, *Taikōki*. Because Hideyoshi had been a rival of the Tokugawa clan, his story could not be told in a positive way during the reign of the Tokugawa shoguns. He was therefore given the name Mashiba Hisayoshi in the play. Other historical figures are also given pseudonyms, with Hideyoshi's liege lord Oda Nobunaga being called Oda Harunaga; Akechi Mitsuhide called Takechi Mitsuhide; and Hideyoshi's nephew Hidetsugu—who historically came to be known as the "Murderous Regent"—called Hisatsugu.[7]

Because Hideyoshi was responsible for building the city of Osaka, many plays about him were written there. This particular play, however, stands out for its grand depiction of the events that followed Hideyoshi's attempts to invade and conquer Korea.

The story begins with generals under the command of Hisayoshi (the character based on Hideyoshi) arriving on a deserted island in the Genkai Sea, where they discover a stone monument after being shipwrecked. The monument bears an inscription that begins, "The first was born a wild orange south of the river, the second a mandarin orange north of the river..." The monument is signed by the Chinese general Sō Sokei. The inscription makes it clear that Sō Sokei had three children. The first was born in China and the other two in Japan to a Japanese mother. These three were bent on overthrowing the leaders of Japan in retaliation for Hisayoshi's invasion of Korea. The play focuses on discovering their true identities.

Hisayoshi's adopted son Hisatsugu (based on the historical Hidetsugu) is a treacherous rascal who refuses to mend his ways despite the admonitions of his faithful retainer Konomura Ōinosuke. Unable to tolerate Hisatsugu's bad behavior any longer, Ōinosuke finally decides to have him killed. However, it becomes clear that Ōinosuke is "actually" Sō Sokei in disguise. Not only that, but Hisatsugu "actually" knows Ōinosuke's true identity and has purposely misbehaved, hoping that his death will expose Sō Sokei for what he truly is: Hisayoshi's enemy.

The play goes on to depict a multifaceted contest of wits and mutual deception that unfolds between those loyal to Hisayoshi and those on the side of Sō Sokei. For example, one of Sō Sokei's trusted retainers "actually" turns out to be Katō Masakiyo (the historical Katō Kiyomasa), who serves Hisayoshi. At every turn, sudden revelations throw the whole story into renewed doubt and suspense, with heroes and villains jumbled together, positions changing, and the balance of power tilting first one way then another. Audiences are fed a dazzling array of mysteries and con games that keep obscuring the truth.

When Ōinosuke is finally forced to reveal his true identity as Sō Sokei, he changes his clothes from traditional Japanese *kamishimo* samurai attire to a colorful Chinese costume. Just before he dies, he writes a letter to his robber ally Ishikawa Goemon, saying he has heard that his China-born son had come to Japan. He asks Goemon to give to that son his final testament, which orders him to take revenge on Japan. That death note is delivered to Goemon by a white-spotted hawk that magically emerges from a famous hanging scroll painted by Chinese Emperor Huizong.[8] Watching the hawk fly off, Sō Sokei curses the Japanese and prays for their eradication with his dying breath.

## Showdown at Nanzen-ji Gate

All of this is the prelude to the *Sanmon* scene in which Ishikawa Goemon proclaims, "Such a stunning view!" as he gazes upon the beautiful spring scenery from atop the main gate of Nanzenji Temple. The hawk arrives bearing Sō Sokei's note, through which Goemon learns that Sō Sokei is dead and that his plot has failed. As Goemon continues to read, however, he learns that Sō Sokei gave each of his sons a piece of fragrant wood taken from Ranjatai—a treasured piece of aloeswood that was sent to Japan from China in the seventh or eighth century. With this revelation, Goemon realizes that he is Sō Sokei's son.

In this play, Ishikawa Goemon is born in China and comes as a young boy to Japan, where he becomes the adopted son of Takechi Mitsuhide (a character based on the historical figure Akechi Mitsuhide) and assumes the name Takechi Samagorō. The *Sanmon* scene, therefore, reveals to the audience for the first time that Hisayoshi is the enemy of both Goemon's foster father Mitsuhide[9] and his birth father Sō Sokei. Precisely at the moment when Goemon perceives this double requirement for revenge and resolves to destroy his enemy, the great gate gradually rises and the audience sees a pilgrim at its base, writing the following graffiti on the gate's pillar: *"Though finite the grains of sand on a riverbank or beach, there is no end in this world to the sprouting of thieves."* Seeing the suspicious figure below, Goemon hurls a *shuriken* blade at him, but the pilgrim catches it with a ladle (see plate 4). The curtain closes as the pilgrim utters the words, "Alms for the pilgrim, please." That's all there is to the scene. This pilgrim, of course, is Goemon's arch enemy Hisayoshi in disguise.

The *Sanmon scene*, then, is the dramatic high point of the entire play depicting both Goemon's determination to strike his enemy and his first face-to-face encounter with his foe. The importance of the scene apparently makes it a difficult challenge for the actor who plays Hisayoshi. Onoe Kikugorō I,[10] who played the role in the premiere production, was panned by critics.[11] A rather subdued portrayal by Ichikawa Danzō,[12] on the other hand, earned a fair amount of praise.[13] Ichikawa Danjūrō VII[14] later reinstated a more colorful and dynamic style, and other famous actors attempted various approaches until the current staging became the norm, with Hisayoshi doing little more than simply appearing.

One of the interesting things about the play are the accusations that Goemon, himself a rascal and a thief, levels at Hisayoshi, the supreme ruler of Japan, when they next meet. Openly challenging the political order, he chides Hisayoshi for spending a fortune to mount military campaigns in foreign lands and to build a great Buddha statue[15] when ordinary people were suffering. At another point, he accuses Hisayoshi of being a far more detestable thief than he was himself because Hisayoshi was just a retainer of Oda Harunaga (based on the historical figure Oda Nobunaga) who had usurped Harunaga's reign.

Goemon's complaints are not completely without basis. Rebels, after all, have their own kind of logic. Many plays were created in western Japan from the middle of the eighteenth century onward that presented mutinous roughnecks not as evil men but as antiestablishment heroes.

After writing many hit plays in Kyoto and Osaka, *Sanmon* author Namiki Gohei moved to Edo, where he introduced many innovations to streamline kabuki there. He thus became a bridge between Edo and western Japan and was incidentally the protagonist of my first novel, *Tōshū Sharakusashi*, as well as a character in *Ichi no Tomi* and other books in the *Namiki Hyōshirō Tanetorichō* series.

## Expanding Dramatic Potential with a Movable Set

As we've seen, the sedition plays that were so popular in the second half of the eighteenth century had complicated storylines with unexpected twists. We should also note that the nature of playwriting underwent a fundamental change through the revolutionary development of stage sets. The *Sanmon* scene, for example, unfolds like a film montage. The protagonist sets his heart on revenge and seems to float upward on the gate, as if he were an image on a screen. Moving sets, in other words, began to play a primary role in telling the story. It was Namiki Gohei's teacher Namiki Shōza who had a decisive influence on the development of large stage props as tools for creating drama.

One of the elements that clearly differentiated kabuki from performance forms such as Shakespearean drama was

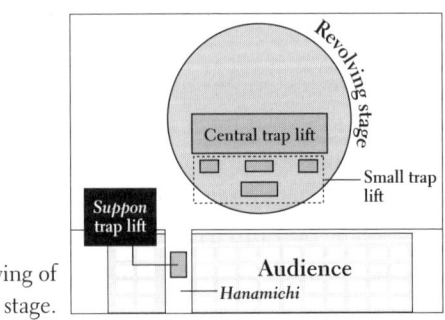

Schematic drawing of a revolving stage.

A MONTAGE OF STAGE EFFECTS

## Revolutionary Moving Set Invented by Namiki Shōza

**Trap Lifts**: Stagehands raise the *suppon* trap lift located near where the *hanamichi* bridgeway connects to the stage. Scholars believe that trap lifts were first used in kabuki in 1753.

**Revolving Stage**: The revolving stage was reputedly inspired by spinning tops. It was first used in the twelfth month of 1758 at the Kado no Shibai Theater in Osaka.

the liberal use of trap lifts and revolving stages[16] that evolved from primitive mechanical beginnings.

Trap lifts themselves were used in kabuki from very early on, but they generally raised just one person at a time. In his play *Keisei Ama no Hagoromo* (A Courtesan and Heaven's Feathered Robe),[17] Shōza had three actors on the second floor and four actors on the first floor raised on trap lifts simultaneously to create an astonishing finale. The use of trap lifts made it possible to instantaneously change dramatic scenes in a way that resembled the montage technique used in film.

Another innovation attributed to Shōza was the large revolving stage. A smaller, earlier version called *bun mawashi* was apparently invented by the Edo-based kabuki playwright Nakamura Denshichi in the 1710s. This consisted of two layers of square panels that could be slid into position. But it was Shōza who succeeded in developing a large revolving mechanism that covered the entire stage. This was a revolutionary invention even by international standards.

## The Synergy of Story and Set

The large revolving stage first appeared in *Sanjikkoku Yofune no Hajimari* (Thirty Bushels of Rice and the Night Boat's Beginning),[18] in which a tatami room scene suddenly gives way to a waterwheel scene on the Yodo River. The revolving mechanism made it possible to create effects similar to cinematic flashbacks.

As a technical achievement, the revolving stage is impressive in itself. But I think it was truly brilliant of Shōza to conceptualize stage dramas with rapid scene changes despite the fact that he never saw a movie. Combined with the surprising twists and turns of concealed identity, his sudden and complete scene changes must have dazzled audiences of the time.

While we're on this topic, I'd like to introduce one more play by Namiki Shōza titled *Kuwanaya Tokuzō Irifune Monogatari* (The Tale of Kuwanaya Tokuzō's Incoming Ship).[19] A young and profligate samurai lord, infatuated with a courtesan in the Yoshiwara licenced district, lingers in Edo despite the fact that he must arrive at his native home in Sanuki in three days. He believes that he is dallying in a nearby restaurant, but in fact he's been deceived by his retainers and is on a ship that's taking him home.

When he learns that he's actually on a huge ship measuring about 220 meters long, the young lord gasps in amazement. In that moment, all the props in the reception room fall flat, the stage revolves, and we suddenly find ourselves on the deck of the ship. The young lord isn't the only one amazed by an astonishing twist that has also fooled the audience.

The development of movable sets had a huge impact on the way plays were written. One play often performed today that uses the revolving stage to particularly good effect is *Tōkaidō Yotsuya Kaidan* (The Ghost Story of Yotsuya), which I discuss in more detail in chapter 9. It depicts two scenes in alternation, with a woman named Oiwa suffering while her husband Iemon trysts with another young woman.

In performance arts like noh where almost no sets are used, scenes are created with mere words spoken by the actors. The drawback of "real" sets is that quick scene changes are difficult. The development of movable sets provided a clever solution to this problem, making it possible to speed up dramatic development and even enabling a play to begin from the climax.

## A Multifaceted Genius

Namiki Shōza began his career as a kabuki playwright, but he also apprenticed for a time in the puppet theater before returning to kabuki. He was strongly influenced by the puppets and loved to create ever more complex stories. Because historical plays formed the backbone of the puppet theater, plays in that genre often highlighted heroes from the past who were brought to the present day through the trick of hidden identity. Shōza delighted in weaving layer upon layer of concealed identities and false leads into a stunning tapestry of mystery and deception.

Portrait of Namiki Shōza from *Namiki Shōza Ichidai Banashi* (Tales of Namiki Shōza I)

A detailed biography of Shōza titled *Namiki Shōza Ichidai Banashi* (Tales of Namiki Shōza I) was published on the thirteenth anniversary of his death. It relates how he was fascinated as a boy by mechanical dolls and developed a talent for mechanical engineering that involved the use of vises and hawsers. His multiple talents extended to the operation of his own production company in addition to his playwriting and directing careers. The halo shown emanating from his head in one portrait we have of him seems to be an appropriate expression of his genius.

As a side business, Shōza operated a two-story restaurant that had a full garden on the second floor. In one corner of

A Montage of Stage Effects

The second floor of Shōza's restaurant featured a dumbwaiter built to look like a water well that was used to lift food up from the kitchen below. (From *Namiki Shōza Ichidai Banashi* [Tales of Namiki Shōza I]).

the garden there was a dumbwaiter built to look like a water well that was used to lift food up from the kitchen below. When he built the revolving stage for *Sanjikkoku Yofune no Hajimari*, he extended his talents even to civil engineering by using the large amounts of dirt excavated from beneath the stage as landfill in front of Hōzenji Temple and Sennichimae Hill.

Namiki Shōza was a Renaissance man who, like many enormously talented people, died at a relatively young age (he was 44). He was a contemporary of another famous polymath, Hiraga Gennai, who was two years older and lived six years longer than Shōza.

Today, there's nothing special about trap lifts and revolving stages. But imagine how shocking these innovations must have been to audiences when they were first introduced. The next time you see a production of *Sanmon*, I urge you to imagine an era when the Japanese displayed a richness of talent and originality that gave birth to something the world had never seen.

CHAPTER EIGHT

# *Tsumoru Koi Yuki no Seki no To*

A Stylish Fairy-Tale Dance

## 1. DANCE REVUE AS THE STARTING POINT

### Song-Dance: The Foundation of Kabuki

In this chapter I'll focus on the piece *Tsumoru Koi Yuki no Seki no To* (Love Story at the Snow-Covered Barrier), which premiered in the second half of the eighteenth century. Before proceeding, however, we should take a close look at one more element that is crucial to an understanding of kabuki: the element of dance. I feel this is needed because I often hear people say they find themselves baffled by dance pieces despite the fact that they make up a significant part of the current repertory.

The traditional Chinese performance art of Beijing opera is said to be made up of four elements: *chàng, niàn, zuò,* and *dǎ*. Chàng is singing, *niàn* is dialogue, *zuò* is acting, and *dǎ* is fighting. If we apply the same categorizing principle to kabuki, we get three elements: *ka* (singing), *bu* (dancing), and *ki* (also pronounced *waza*), or acting.

The *kanji* used to write the word "kabuki" are used phonetically, though, and carry additional nuances that are not

117

connected to the word's original meaning. "Kabuki" is derived from the verb *kabuku*, meaning to lean or tilt. During the early Edo period (1603–1868) people who sported the latest fashions and drew attention to themselves by defying convention were called *kabuki-mono*, or "tilted people." This was the image that people associated with kabuki in its early years as a performance art. In a way, *kabuki-mono* were similar to what the French called *après-guerre* (postwar) artists who appeared on the scene after World War I. In the aftermath of the chaotic and violent Sengoku period (1467–1603), *kabuki-mono* were artists who overflowed with energy and found themselves shut out of an increasingly rigid social system. Kabuki was thus infused with a nonconformist spirit from its very beginning.

Phonetic characters were used to write "kabuki" from an early date, although it took some time for the last character *ki* to be conventionalized. Clearly, the concepts of song and dance (as signified by the characters *ka* and *bu*) were recognized as the most important elements of kabuki from the start. Rather than think of them as separate things, however, it may be more useful to combine them into a concept of "song-dance" for reasons that I hope this chapter will make clear.

## *Mai* and *Odori*: Two Kinds of Dance

Today, Japanese refer to dance with the word *buyō*, but this term came into use only in the modern era. Prior to that, there were two distinct words for different dance types: *mai* and *odori*.

A late Edo-period scholar of ancient Japanese literature and culture named Motoori Uchitō[1] offers a deft analysis of the difference between these two types of dance. In his book *Senjakō* (A Humble Man's Thoughts), he defines *mai* as "dancing based on mimetic movement that conveys meaning," while *odori* is "spontaneous movement through which the dancer forgets himself, with no concern for form." According to Motoori's view, *mai* is a choreographed expression of something specific, while *odori* is a passionate embrace of free-form movement.

More recent scholars have investigated the origins of the word *mai* and concluded that it's related to the word *mawaru*, which means to move in a circle. *Odori*, on the other hand, can also be written with a *kanji* that means "jump," making its fundamental movement a vertical one. Circular motion can also be found in *odori*, though, making a simple distinction problematic. This was pointed out by the folklorist Yanagita Kunio, who also observed that *mai* provides a kind of background music and appeals primarily to the ear, while *odori* is characterized by stylized movements called *te* (hands) whose appeal is primarily visual. Another folklorist, Orikuchi Shinobu, noted that *mai* tends to be placid and quiet, often expressing an aspect of the gods, while *odori* tended to express somewhat rough and vulgar emotions associated with demonic spirits.[2] Of course, it's the inherent vagueness of the images we have for these two types of dance that has given rise to so many different proposed definitions.

One of *odori*'s roots can be traced to the *odori nenbutsu* (danced Buddhist prayer) reputedly invented by the Buddhist monk Kūya[3] of the Heian period (794–1185), which later became popular under the influence of the monk Ippen[4] in the Kamakura period (1185–1333). Beating time on gongs and drums, believers performed a walking dance while reciting prayers in what might be called a primal form of danced religion.

Also during the Kamakura period, there was a dance form called *shirabyōshi no mai*[5] (literally, "white beat" dance) that is mentioned in the military epic *The Tale of the Heike* and other literary sources. This was performed by professional women dancers, so another way to distinguish between *odori* and *mai* is to say that *odori* involved amateur performers while the latter was the domain of professionals. If we go back to the historical roots of *odori nenbutsu* and *shirabyōshi no mai*, it does seem that Motoori's definitions as cited above come close to the mark.

One important feature of *shirabyōshi no mai* is that it's danced by women who wear men's clothing, including a *suikan* court robe, tall *tate eboshi* lacquered hat, and *shiromaki-zaya* white-sheathed sword. Transvestitism of this kind was an aspect of Japanese performance art from ancient times, and such transgendered elements must be considered in any discussion of Japanese dance.

*Shirabyōshi* dances were performed while the dancer sang *imayō*, which were the popular songs of medieval Japan. As we've already seen, *nenbutsu odori* were accompanied by chanted Buddhist prayers. It seems that by the Muromachi period (1336–1573), the latter became firmly entrenched as *bon odori* dances performed in local communities to commemorate deceased kin at midsummer *bon* festivals. Scholars also believe that the dance form was later accompanied by short, lyrical *kouta* (short songs) during the Sengoku period (1467–1603). The beating of gongs and drums, the use of leaping dance movements accompanied by Buddhist chanting, and the addition of popular songs ultimately gave birth to the traditional Japanese dance forms that are still performed today.

## *Bon Odori* as Seen by Lafcadio Hearn

Perhaps one extreme generalization we can make about the difference between *mai* and *odori* is that *mai* tends to be static and *odori* tends to be dynamic. Of course, such distinctions are premised on a relative perspective. For a more objective view of Japanese dance, we can turn to Lafcadio Hearn (1850–1904), the famous author of *Kwaidan*, a collection of Japanese ghost stories.

Hearn's father was Irish and his mother was Greek. Working as a journalist, he went from Europe to the United States at age 19, fell in love with and married an African woman, lived for a time in the islands of the West Indies, and eventually moved permanently to Japan, where he became a naturalized Japanese citizen and adopted the name Koizumi Yakumo. His exposure to and absorption of many different cultures makes it impossible to pigeonhole him as an orientalist. In his book, *Glimpses of Unfamiliar Japan*,[6] he shares his impressions when he first witnessed *bon odori* dancing in the Izumo region. With wonderful expressiveness, he describes the strange attractive power of Japanese dance far better than any native-born Japanese could. Because I also believe that Hearn's description overlaps with the impressions that we today have of Japanese dance, I'll quote his observations at length.

> All together glide the right foot forward one pace, without lifting the sandal from the ground, and extend both hands to the right, with a strange floating motion and a smiling, mysterious obeisance. Then the right foot is drawn back, with a repetition of the waving of hands and the mysterious bow. Then all advance the left foot and repeat the previous movements, half-turning to the left. Then all take two gliding paces forward, with a single simultaneous soft clap of the hands, and the first performance is reiterated, alternately to the right and left; all the sandaled feet gliding together, all the supple hands waving together, all the pliant bodies bowing and swaying together. And so slowly, weirdly, the

processional movement changes into a great round, circling about the moonlit court and around the voiceless crowd of spectators.

And always the white hands sinuously wave together, as if weaving spells, alternately without and within the round, now with palms upward, now with palms downward; and all the elfish sleeves hover duskily together, with a shadowing as of wings; and all the feet poise together with such a rhythm of complex motion, that, in watching it, one feels a sensation of hypnotism—as while striving to watch a flowing and shimmering of water.

And this soporous allurement is intensified by a dead hush. No one speaks, not even a spectator. And, in the long intervals between the soft clapping of hands, one hears only the shrilling of the crickets in the trees, and the shu-shu of sandals, lightly stirring the dust. Unto what, I ask myself, may this be likened? Unto nothing; yet it suggests some fancy of somnambulism—dreamers, who dream themselves flying, dreaming upon their feet.[7]

The *bon odori* that Hearn witnessed in Izumo in the late nineteenth century was apparently very quiet, and it seems reasonable to assume that this was its original form. Even though it was a kind of *odori* and not a *mai*, it struck Hearn as being static, not dynamic.

When Hearn writes about "soporous allurement," many modern Japanese may well find that they have had a similar experience while watching Japanese dance. It's a type of dance that seems to generate alpha waves in spectators' brains,[8] and it seems to me that Hearn fully conveys this attribute in his prose.

Okuni performing a skit in which she pretends to be a man in a brothel (detail from *Okuni Kabuki Figure Screen*). Photo courtesy of Kyoto National Museum.

## A Transgender Revue: The Kabuki of Okuni

In a way, Lafcadio Hearn's encounter with *bon odori* in the Izumo region of Japan might have been the work of fate. I say this because no historical account of kabuki would be complete without mention of a person who hailed from Izumo. Her name was Okuni.

In *Kabuki Jishi* (A Kabuki Primer)[9] and other Edo-period publications about the performing arts, Okuni is always identified as the founder of kabuki. Further examination of documents dating to Okuni's time reveals that she actually did exist, but the stage art she practiced apparently had only a tenuous connection with the kabuki we see today. Her repertory and performance techniques have not survived to the modern age, and it appears that her enthronement as the founder of kabuki is a myth that was concocted by Edo historians.

In the chronicle *Tōdaiki* (A Contemporary Record), which is thought to have been compiled around 1615 (shortly after Okuni was active), mention is made of *kabuki odori* (kabuki dance) that is dated 1603. It says that the performer was a "not especially beautiful" shrine maiden from Izumo named Kuni who brought the dance to Kyoto. This Kuni (who would have been called "Okuni" with an honorific "o") reportedly carried samurai swords, wore men's clothing, pretended to dally with ladies in brothels, and became enormously popular among people of all classes in Kyoto. She was frequently invited to perform at Fushimi Castle, and later kabuki troupes learned from her and went on tour in provinces throughout Japan. It was this entry in *Tōdaiki* that provided the basis for Okuni's reputation as the founder of kabuki.

Another chronicle titled *Nozuchi* (Field Spirits) dated 1621 records that Okuni dressed as a Buddhist monk, beat a gong, and chanted prayers as she performed *nenbutsu odori*. This source goes on to say that "later, she dressed as a man, carried swords at her side, and sang and danced in a manner that came to be popularly called 'kabuki.'"

Like the *Tōdaiki* chronicle, *Nozuchi* states that kabuki originated as a stage art performed by a woman dressed as a man. Some might wonder, then, if it was like the all-female shows produced in modern times by troupes like Takarazuka, but this appears not to be the case. According to the early Edo-period Confucian scholar Hayashi Razan,[10] kabuki was a form of popular entertainment in which men dressed as women, women as men, and performers of both sexes sang and danced.

What sort of singing and dancing was it? A genre of picture scrolls and books called *kabuki sōshi* (kabuki storybook),[11] as well as a genre of screen paintings called *rakuchū rakugai-zu* (scenes in and around the capital)[12] show women and men

A Stylish Fairy-Tale Dance

Panels 2 through 4 of the right screen of a *rakuchū rakugai-zu* (scenes in and around the capital) pair. Panel 3 shows women performing kabuki in a theater in a dry river bed near Shijō Road in Kyoto.

dressed in drag performing comical skits and dances in what appears to be a revue format.

One *kabuki sōshi* depicts a scene in which Okuni calls the spirit of a deceased general named Nagoya Sanza[13] to the stage. This practice of bringing dead spirits to the stage was an important motif in Japanese performance art and often an element in noh theater, in particular.

Okuni is called a *miko* (shrine maiden or shaman) in historical accounts. In her time, there were groups of "walking *miko*" who did not belong to any particular shrine but traveled from place to place offering prayers and soliciting donations for religious institutions on the one hand, while offering

125

Maekawa Kumenosuke was a popular *wakashū* (youth) kabuki actor in the 1670s and 1680s. His *yarō bōshi* (man's hat) and two swords indicate that he was active after *yarō kabuki* (men's kabuki) had developed. From a *kabuki wakashū zu* (youth kabuki illustration).

performances and sexual services on the other. Some scholars believe that Okuni belonged to one of these groups.

After Okuni's time, many similar performance groups sprang up that were collectively grouped under the term *yūjo kabuki* (prostitute kabuki). These entertainment groups were deemed socially harmful and banned by the authorities in 1629, after which women did not return to the public stage for a very long time.

Following the ban, *yūjo kabuki* was replaced by *wakashū kabuki* (youth kabuki), which was probably very similar to the pretty-boy fad we're now experiencing in our own pop culture, except that the young male performers were more overtly the object of homosexual attraction. This in turn sparked numerous incidents of violent death and injury, eventually triggering another ban similar to the first that was imposed in 1652. Entertainers who survived the second ban regrouped, shaved their forelocks (an act that signified adulthood) and continued to perform by adding mimetic, realistic elements to their acts. The important thing to remember, then, is that the stage art we now call kabuki originated primarily as a revue show that focused on singing and dancing.

## Terms Meaning Dance

It seems that remnants of the early revue approach still strongly colored Genroku-era kabuki, as we can easily see from an illustrated synopsis titled *Wankyū Ukiyo Jikkai* (Wankyū's 10 Realms of the Floating World). One of its illustrations shows a finale in which the entire cast crowd the stage and dance together. Such grand finales were called *ō-odori* (large dance) or *sō-odori* (total dance).

Dance scenes were sprinkled liberally in other parts of a play as well. Because the word *buyō* (dance) had not been coined yet, such scenes were referred to by such terms as *shosa-goto* (gestural matters) or *hyōshi-goto* (rhythm matters). Although both of these terms denoted dance, they had slightly different nuances, with the former referring to the use of body language and the latter focusing more on pure movement. Actors praised in critical guidebooks as being *hyōshikiki* (skilled in beats) were no doubt performers who also possessed a good sense of rhythm.

Another important term used in the Genroku era was *onryō-goto* (vengeful spirit matters), which featured dance

*Tsumoru Koi Yuki no Seki no To*

The entire cast dancing the finale in the play *Wankyū Ukiyo Jikkai*.

scenes depicting ghosts or the spirits of living people who have scores to settle. Apparently, these scenes often included acrobatic stunts, such as tightrope walking and tumbling, often performed by men playing *onnagata* female roles. One famous *onnagata* actor named Mizuki Tatsunosuke[14] was particularly skilled at moving like a cat and performing a dance called *nanabake* (seven transformations) that featured seven quick costume changes.

As time passed, new terms were coined to refer to dance, including *furi-goto* (choreographed matters). In western Japan, the term *kei-goto* (view matters) supplanted *shosa-goto* as the term of popular choice. The component *kei* in this last term is the same character as that is used in the word for "scenery." Its usage stems from the fact that travel scenes in the puppet theater tended to feature dancelike elements accompanying text that described scenery passed on a journey.

## The Flowering of *Onnagata* Dancing

Perhaps the most famous kabuki dance piece still performed today that dates back to very early days is *Kyōganoko Musume Dōjōji* (A Maiden at Dōjōji Temple),[15] which premiered in 1753. No dance pieces from the Genroku era survive today; the oldest ones we have date from the Kyōhō through Hōreki eras (1716–1762).

At the risk of digression, I'd like to note that, according to surveys conducted among audiences in the 1960s when kabuki went on tours of the United States, the Soviet Union, and Europe,[16] *Musume Dōjōji* was surprisingly unpopular. Despite being performed by the top *onnagata* actors of the time—Nakamura Utaemon VI[17] and Onoue Baikō VII[18]—Westerners showed little enthusiasm for it. I suggest we keep this in mind as we continue our discussion.

The actor Sadojima Chōgorō[19] was nearing the end of his life when *Musume Dōjōji* premiered. Let's take a look at what he says in the introduction to his work, *Shosa no Hiden* (Secret Teachings of Dance):

> Choreography is rooted in the text. When the words have no particular meaning, you should convey the feeling the text evokes. When there is no text and you are dancing to a long section of instrumental music, focus on the music's rhythm. Because the movements you use in daily life form the basis of your dance, always maintain an awareness of the kind of gestures you use.

This is all quite straightforward advice. Because Chōgorō's work is titled "Secret Teachings," many people try to read more significance into his words than they merit. Teachings of this kind are highly practical and should not be read with the expectation that they contain deep philosophical truths.

Even so, the above passage clearly delineates one of kabuki's great principles: the choreography is based on the words. In this respect, kabuki is quite different from Western classical ballet, which has no words, although there is an underlying story. In kabuki, words are always sung in the background to the dance, although hearing the lyrics doesn't necessarily help in understanding the story. *Musume Dōjōji*, for example, uses motifs from the noh play *Dōjōji*,[20] which is based on the legend of Kiyohime, a young woman who, enraged at being spurned by the young monk Anchin, transforms herself into a great, fire-breathing serpent and kills him. The words actually sung during the kabuki dance version, though, have almost nothing to do with the plot, as any careful listening will reveal. This may be one reason why the piece was unpopular abroad: it proved to be too difficult to understand. And it seems to me that Japanese audiences today also encounter this barrier to comprehension.

Regardless of the type of background singing employed, whether *nagauta, tokiwazu,*[21] *kiyomoto,*[22] or *gidayū*, most modern listeners are hard-pressed to glean the meaning from the words. In many cases, the performers themselves don't fully comprehend what's being sung and are merely dancing as they were taught by their teachers. If subtitles were available to present the text in modern Japanese translation, I'm quite sure that more people would be able to better enjoy kabuki dance.

## Revealing True Feelings through Song

The highlight of *Musume Dōjōji* is a section called the *kudari*, in which a lyrical *nagauta* melody accompanies words that express the long lament of a young girl's tender heart. Since an understanding of the text will greatly affect how a viewer experiences the piece, I'll provide an abridged translation here.

## A Stylish Fairy-Tale Dance

Oh, I redden my lips with rouge, but to whom may I show them? In letters he and I exchanged, we swore we'd be together. Were they all a lie? I know I shouldn't give in to jealousy, but women are weak and wretched! I can't help longing for him. What can he be thinking? Why have I fallen for such a heartless man?

Musically, long laments of this kind are called *kudoki*, and are often considered the highlight of a piece. The word *kudoki* comes from the verb *kudoku*, which interestingly has two meanings: to complain and to seduce. Set to lyrical melodies, *kudoki* are passionate cries from the heart that might be likened to arias in Western opera. Where a prima donna will sing her heart out in an operatic aria, an *onnagata* actor in kabuki will dance with lithesome grace, accompanied by a lyrically chanted lament.

*Kudoki* are not restricted to dance pieces, however. They can often be found in the most dramatic scenes of plays that originated in the puppet theater,[23] such as those I discussed in chapters 3 through 6. In Act VII of *Chūshingura*, for example, a *kudoki* is performed to express the feelings of Okaru after she learns of her lover Kanpei's death. Singing on her behalf, the chanter exposes her somewhat brazen sentiments as she muses on how much Kanpei must have wanted to see her before he died. As these words are being sung, the actor playing Okaru expresses those feelings through dance. Other *kudoki* generally provide glimpses into the true thoughts and emotions of the characters, sometimes with erotic overtones. The words were bold, even shocking in their time, and the fact that they were not used as dialogue but instead provided the background for dances is a prominent characteristic of kabuki. This performance practice may also be in keeping with the hesitation many Japanese feel for expressing themselves with unabashed frankness in everyday conversation.

Onoe Kikugorō VII dances the *Koi no Tenarai* (Lessons of Love) section from *Kyōganoko Musume Dōjōji* (A Maiden at Dōjōji Temple). (Performed at the National Theatre in March, 1985. Photo courtesy of the National Theatre.)

*Musume Dōjōji* makes liberal use of quick costume changes, a fact that's mentioned in *Sadojima Nikki* (Sadojima Diary) by Edo-period actor Sadojima Chōgorō I. Chōgorō complains that actors in his day had taken to wearing many layers of clothing, which they removed one layer at a time by turning their backs to the audience during the dance while the music continued to play. He claims that the original intent behind the rapid costume change was to jolt the audience awake, but that this effect was now dulled or even negated by excessive use.

Chōgorō's claim that costume changes were designed to wake audiences up brings to mind the passage by Lafcadio Hearn I quoted earlier. Who, specifically, were the targets of Chōgorō's criticism? It wouldn't be surprising if they were performers like Segawa Kikunojō I[24] or Nakamura Tomijūrō I, both of whom were star *onnagata* dancers in Chōgorō's time. Tomijūrō was in fact the actor who premiered *Musume Dōjōji*, and Kikunojō had previously performed many dances that were based on the noh play *Dōjōji*. Other actors performed pieces referencing the *Dōjōji* story as well.

## Acrobatic "Stone Bridge" Dances

There's another type of dance that was created about the same time as *Musume Dōjōji* and is still performed. Called *shakkyō-mono* (stone bridge pieces), this genre is also based on a story found in noh, this time the play *Shakkyō* (Stone Bridge). Set in China, it tells the tale of a monk who tries to cross a narrow stone bridge to Shōryōsen Mountain, where he encounters a celestial lion that dances and frolics among peonies. The play ends with a colorful and energetic dance, which was adapted for kabuki with showy choreography performed by an *onnagata* actor. Many varieties of lion dance were created on this theme, including *Aioi-jishi* (Coupled Lions) and *Makura-jishi* (Pillow Lion) by Kikunojō I and *Shūchaku-jishi* (Obsessed Lion) by Tomijūrō I, all of which are still performed.

*Makura-jishi*, while still in the repertory, is actually only rarely performed, having been eclipsed by a variant called *Kagami-jishi* (Mirror Lion).[25] The character who dances the original *Makura-jishi* is a prostitute, and Ichikawa Danjūrō IX changed this premise in the Meiji period, making the dancer a lady-in-waiting at the imperial court to give the piece more respectability. In doing so, he also changed the title to *Kagami-jishi*. Even so, the piece retains the essential form of the *shakkyō-mono* popular in the mid-eighteenth century, with the first half performed by a female character and the second half performed with heroic vigor by the same dancer dressed as a lion.

Another kabuki lion dance called *Ren-jishi* (Pair of Lions)[26] was first performed in 1872. As the title suggests, two lions appear in this piece, both wearing costumes that closely resemble those worn by the *shite* actor[27] in the noh play *Shakkyō*. When the *shakkyō-mono* genre first developed in the mid-eighteenth century, though, the dancer was dressed as a woman with the kimono hem tucked up, wearing a light headdress made of two overlapping fans fitted to a white wig. While there might not have been as much shaking of the head to accentuate the long, flowing wig of the later versions, the lion dances originally created by Kikunojō I and Tomijūrō I were no less dynamic.

Chōgorō makes an interesting comment about this in *Sadojima Nikki*:

> In *Shakkyō* and other pieces, the dancer falls down flat on the stage after the dance and the stage attendants pick him up and bundle him off to the dressing room. Such behavior is wholly nonsensical. For one thing, it's rude to the audience. Also, for that actor to present such vulgarity as a kind of kabuki is an affront to other practitioners of the art and a stain on the Way of Theater.

It seems that the dance performed in Chōgorō's time was so violent that the dancer collapsed at the end of it and had to be carried off stage. Like modern-day rock concerts, where performers may faint from exhaustion, there might have been an element of calculation in such performances. Chōgorō's earnest criticism of it as being rude to the audience and vulgar seems to indicate that the targets of his criticism were the top actors of the day, such as Tomijūrō. Otherwise, such comments would have been unwarranted.

## A Stylish Fairy-Tale Dance

*Sugata no Hana Azuma no Datezome* was performed at the Ichimura-za in Edo in March 1812. Segawa Rokō IV is shown playing the *nochi-jite* role in the *Aioi-jishi* (Coupled Lions) scene. (Artist: Utagawa Toyokuni I). Photo courtesy of Tsubouchi Memorial Theatre Museum, Waseda University.

Although the above pieces *Aioi-jishi*, *Makura-jishi*, and *Shūchaku-jishi* have survived, their choreography has not. If we take into consideration the *onryō-goto* (pieces about vengeful spirits) that were performed earlier in the Genroku era, however, it's not difficult to imagine that the early lion dances were energetic and acrobatic.

## Characteristic Ways to Use the Body

Kabuki in the mid-eighteenth century produced many *onnagata* actors like Kikunojō and Tomijūrō who were extremely skilled dancers. Indeed, dance was considered the domain of the *onnagata*, and the unnatural premise of having a man dance as a woman had a decisive influence on how *onnagata* actors used their bodies.

In *Shosa no Hiden*, Chōgorō says that actors playing female roles should stand with *wani ashi* (alligator feet) and keep the kimono hem open to make the hips appear slimmer. Generally speaking, *wani ashi* simply means that the feet should not be pointed straight ahead. When playing men's roles, the toes should be turned outward (*soto wani*), while in women's roles, the toes should be turned inward (*uchi wani*).

*Onnagata* actors tried various costume strategies to achieve the crucial task of making a male body appear feminine. According to *Kabuki Jishi*, it was the famous onnagata Ogino Sawanojō[28] who first widened the women's *obi* (broad sash) to the size used today. If that's true, it's fascinating to think that Sawanojō's onstage innovation to accentuate the feminine look had an impact on how women dressed in the real world. The pigeon-toed walk customarily used by women

*Uchiwani* (In-turned) and *Sotowani* (Out-turned) Feet Positions

in kimono might also be traced to the *uchi wani* stance developed by *onnagata* actors. Many other examples could be cited showing how kabuki influenced women's fashion during the Edo period, but perhaps it's best for us to return now to the topic of dance.

At the end of *Shosa no Hiden*, Chōgorō observes that "Dance is an art using the eyes. Dance is like the human body, and eyes are like the soul." The importance of the eyes to kabuki dance cannot be overstated. This is a characteristic that applies to all traditional Asian dance forms, including *kathakali* dance drama from India.[29]

The location of the body's center of gravity is another important and universal element of dance. Western ballet, for example, strives for a high center of gravity, as if the dancer longs to rise to heaven. In contrast, Japanese dance has a low center of gravity, with performers keeping their feet on the ground and stamping on the earth, thereby creating a sense of oneness with nature.

Dance was monopolized by *onnagata* actors when Segawa Kikunojō I and II and Nakamura Tomijūrō were active. That changed, however, with the emergence of Nakamura Nakazō (1736–1790), a gifted dancer who played male roles. Nakazō ushered in an era of full-fledged dance dramas featuring both male and female characters, beginning with the piece that is the main topic of this chapter: *Tsumoru Koi Yuki no Seki no To* (Love Story at the Snow-Covered Barrier), commonly called *Seki no To*.

Nakazō was an extraordinary actor who faced many challenges as he worked his way up from the ranks of a utility actor to become a top-tier star. My historical novel *Nakazō Kyōran* (Nakazō's Frenzy) was based on his autobiography. Segawa Kikunojō III, an actor who shared the stage with Nakazō, also appears in my first novel. I chose to focus on these two actors in my fiction because of the tremendous appeal exerted by the dance piece *Seki no To*, which has survived to the present day.

## 2. A DANCE DRAMA MASTERPIECE

### Drawing on Heian-Era Literature

*Seki no To* was originally part of a longer play called *Jūnihitoe Komachi Zakura* (Komachi and the Cherry Tree) that premiered in 1784. Although the full script has not survived, guidebooks and a summary discovered in the early twentieth century give us the general story. Because it was performed as a *kaomise* (face showing) piece, as described in chapter 1, the first half featured a *Shibaraku* scene that was apparently quite entertaining. The *uke* villain in that scene was the ghost of Tachibana no Hayanari.[30] When the *Shibaraku* hero forces the *uke* to look into a mirror called Yakoe no Meikyō (Mirror of Eight Voices), he loses all of his hair to reveal his original form as a white skeleton.

*Kaomise* pieces always have a scene either before or after *Shibaraku* called *danmari* (pantomime) in which the main characters are shown scrambling in the dark fighting over some important object that provides the starting point for the story. In this case, that important object is the Seal of Kangō.[31] The last person to take the Seal of Kangō drops half of a *wappu* insignia tablet.[32] All of these items—the mirror, the seal, and the insignia—appear in *Seki no To* and would theoretically clarify the plot, but because the play as a whole is no longer performed, their significance verges on the incomprehensible.

Three characters appear in the dance piece: the early Heian-era court poet Ono no Komachi,[33] her lover Yoshimine no Munesada,[34] and Sekibē, the guardian of Ōsaka Barrier

Gate. In the second half of the piece, Sekibē's true identity is revealed as the rebellious nobleman Ōtomo no Kuronushi (830?–923?),[35] who plots to usurp the throne. In the premiere performance, Segawa Kikunojō III played the role of Komachi, and Nakamura Nakazō played Kuronushi.

Yoshimine no Munesada was a nobleman famous for the following poem that is included in a poetry anthology called *Hyakunin Isshu* (One Hundred Poems by One Hundred Poets):

Oh, winds of heaven
Blow closed the cloud paths
So that this celestial maiden
Might linger yet awhile

He is better known in his later years as the Buddhist high priest Henjō who, along with Komachi and Kuronushi, is one of the "Six Immortal Poets"[36] mentioned in the Preface of the *Kokin Wakashū* (Collection of Ancient and Modern Poems) compiled in the early tenth century. As I discussed in Chapter 2, Edo-period kabuki audiences were fascinated by ancient Heian culture, and this piece directly depicts characters from that time while cleverly weaving their poetry and other attributes into the text.

For example, the play opens with Kuronushi (disguised as Sekibē) entering dressed as a woodcutter. Presumably, this entrance refers to a comment found in the Preface of the *Kokin Wakashū* concerning Kuronushi's poetry, which states that his style is coarse, like a mountain peasant resting under cherry blossoms with a load of firewood on his back. From this allusion we can see that Heian-period literature provided an important educational foundation for Edo-period writers. The fact that the Ōsaka Barrier Gate was chosen as the setting can also be explained by another poem in the *Hyakunin Isshu* identifying it as an appropriate location for people to meet ("Ōsaka"—not to be confused with the city of that name—can be translated literally as "Meeting Hill").

> It is here, where people come and go
> Following their parted ways
> Friend or stranger, all must meet
> Here at Ōsaka Barrier Gate, the "Meeting Hill."

Let's look now at some of the highlights one encounters as this piece unfolds on stage.

## Gestures as Puns

The curtain opens with a musical prelude called *oki*. The opening words, *Mukashi, mukashi* (once upon a time), prepare the audience for a fairy tale, with a large, impressive cherry tree standing at the center of the stage. According to the story, the blossoms of this tree had grown especially rich in color because of a poem composed by Komachi, which is why it came to be known as the Komachi Cherry. Later, however, all of its blossoms turn black when it mourns the death of Emperor Ninmyō.[37] The tree onstage has pale pink blossoms in full bloom against a snowy background that suggests the tree is blooming out of season. Perhaps because *kaomise* pieces were customarily performed in the winter, the last scenes were always set in snow. The juxtaposition of cherry blossoms and wintery snow has a visually jarring effect.

A brushwood fence and gate placed in front of the tree represent the Ōsaka Barrier Gate. Ono no Komachi enters along the *hanamichi* bridgeway, dancing to a short travel song. When she tries to pass through the gate, she's stopped and interrogated by Sekibē, the gate's guardian. Sekibē's first highlight scene is performed to words with the following general meaning:

## A Stylish Fairy-Tale Dance

You are peerless in beauty, better far than the blossoms. Any man, whether a nobleman or warrior, would surely stop you on sight, yet you insist I let you pass. Only a hopeless country bumpkin or insensitive, pampered idiot would let you go. It mystifies me why men of the world do not try to stop you with a joke or to seduce you. It's completely beyond my comprehension!

While these words are being sung by the narrator, Sekibē performs a dance in imitation of Komachi. This type of dance, in which an obviously ill-bred man intentionally dances like a woman in a comical and offensive manner, is called *warumi* or *warimi* (literally, "bad self") and is one of kabuki's distinctive dance forms. As I've already noted, Japanese dance has always had a strong transgender tendency, and it was quite common to see a performer dance both male and female parts in a single piece. *Warumi* can be considered an example of this.

As we've seen, kabuki choreography is closely keyed to the text, and we're treated to a very clever example of this in the movement that accompanies the phrase "hopeless country bumpkin or insensitive, pampered idiot." As the following illustration shows, each syllable in the text is associated with a homophonic pun that is acted out in the dance. Thus *kiyabo*, the word for "country bumpkin," is broken down into its three constituent syllables and each syllable provides the basis for a pun (*ki*=tree, *ya*=arrow, *bo*=stick) that is acted out. Similarly, *usudon*, the word for "idiot," is broken down into *usu*=mortar and *don*=bang. *Jōnashi*, the word for "insensitive," becomes "without padlock," and *kunashi*, the word for "pampered," becomes "having nothing to eat." The entire sequence can thus be enjoyed as a clever game of charades.

If one watches kabuki dancing on television with the sound off, its pantomimic nature and close association to the text become vividly clear. For this reason, though, overly

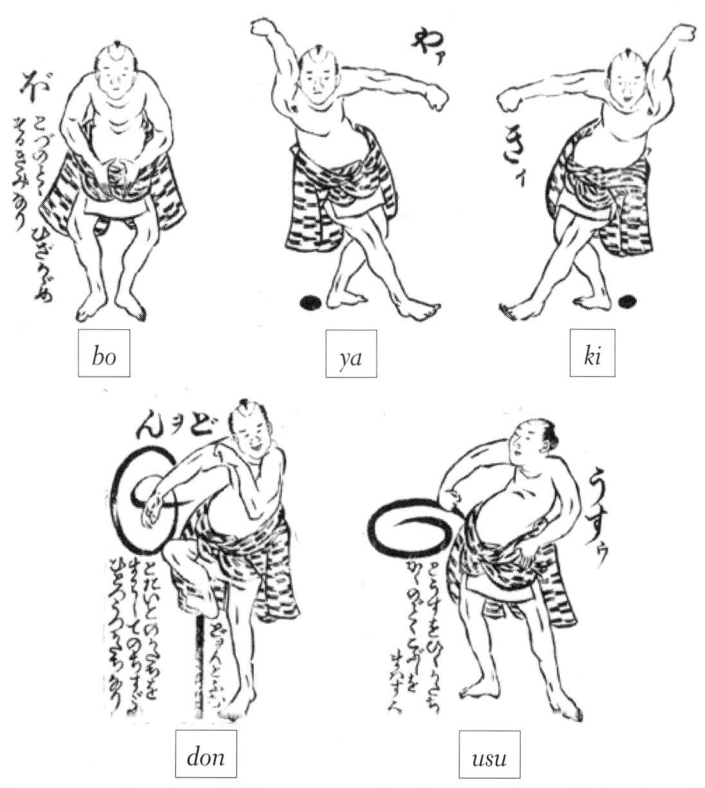

Gestures are timed to syllables to create visual puns as shown for *kiyobo* and *usudon* in *Hitori Odori Geiko* by Katsushika Hokusai.

obvious gestures are avoided as being unsophisticated. In this piece, Nakazō managed to emphasize the overall meaning of "country bumpkin" through light-hearted puns on individual syllables, thereby avoiding the trap of obviousness. Although Nishikawa Senzō II is credited with choreographing the overall piece, it's safe to assume that Nakazō, who had experience himself as a choreographer, added many of his own touches to the part he danced. The choreography for Sekibē includes forward leaning and swaying that reflect his physical habits and have come to be known as "Nakazō style" dancing.

## The Joy of Hand-Dancing

The next highlight after Sekibē's comic dance is a love scene between Komachi and Munesada. Komachi tries to pass through the barrier gate in order to make a pilgrimage to the temple Miidera;[38] Munesada is there to pray for the soul of deceased Emperor Ninmyō. The two lovers meet after a long separation and reminisce about how they fell in love at the "Temple at Furu."[39] That temple is identified in *Gosen Wakashū* (Later Collection of Japanese Poems), an imperial poetry anthology published in 951, as the place where Komachi and Munesada first met (although in that source Munesada is identified by his later name, Henjō). The mention of the temple shows that playwright Takarada Jurai[40] was making full use of his classical education.

The lovers' first meeting at Furu is recounted, when Munesada was reading a sutra for the repose of Emperor Ninmyō's soul and Komachi was on a prayer retreat to ease the afterlife of her mother. Falling in love at first sight, they forget all about their prayers and sleep together with "pillows side by side." This unabashed abandonment of emperor and parent for the sake of carnal pleasure is precisely the kind of plot development one would expect from kabuki.

This scene is followed by Komachi's *kudoki*, which as we've seen is a kind of set piece that expresses unadorned passion in words that accompany an erotically charged dance.

Sekibē then intrudes, stating that, as the person responsible for the two lovers being reunited, he wants to help them get married. As he says this, however, two objects fall accidentally from the breast of his kimono. One is the Seal of Kangō, and the other is half of a *wappu* insignia. These objects raise suspicions about Sekibē's identity in the minds of Komachi and Munesada, foreshadowing dramatic developments. In the climax of the first half of the piece, the three characters dance together, each concealing their private thoughts.

They all perform the same choreography in an up-tempo dance that is so lively and vibrant as to make the audience forget their questions about the objects that fell out of Sekibē's kimono. Sections like this are called *te-odori* (hand-dancing) and are reminiscent of kabuki's earlier appeal, as presented in *wakashū* (youth) kabuki and the *ō-odori* (large dance) sections performed in the Genroku era.

After the *te-odori*, the piece quickly takes a dramatic turn. Sekibē exits, and during his absence a hawk glides down to the remaining two characters, delivering a white sleeve that has the words "two brothers, one boat" written in blood. The words are a quote from a Chinese poem composed by a prince of the ancient Kingdom of Wey[41] who sacrificed himself so that his older brother could live. From this, Munesada understands that his younger brother Yasusada has made a similar sacrifice and is now dead. Of course, in the full-length play *Jūnihitoe Komachi Zakura*, there was a scene showing Yasusada committing ritual suicide and writing the words on the sleeve with his own blood.

Munesada places the sleeve on a stepping stone in a garden and the blood magically causes a rooster carved on the back of the Mirror of Eight Voices to crow. Hearing it, Munesada digs beneath the stone and finds the mirror. Having now seen the Seal of Kangō, half of the *wappu* insignia, and now the Mirror of Eight Voices, the two lovers are convinced there's something more to Sekibē than meets the eye. Komachi leaves to get help, and Munesada hides the bloodstained sleeve inside his *koto* (a long Japanese zither). Sekibē reappears and pretends to be dead drunk from the saké that was served to celebrate the lovers' nuptials; Munesada quickly departs.

A Stylish Fairy-Tale Dance

Lady Komachi and Sekibē, guardian of Ōsaka Gate (from the print *Tsumoru Koi no Yuki no Seki no To* by Toyohara Chikayoshi.

## The Decisive Moment of Sedition

After Munesada leaves, Sekibē reaches for another drink. Suddenly a drum beats ominously offstage, and a board in the shape of a black cloud descends from the ceiling, adorned with an image of the Big Dipper, and Sekibē sees the constellation reflected in the saké that fills his oversized cup and realizes that the time is precisely the hour of the tiger (about four o'clock in the morning). It should be noted that the black cloud with the Big Dipper is a prop used in other plays as well. Called *hoshiguri*, it symbolizes the moment a character gains an insight and resolves to act. Its use became so common that the prop's name also became the name of the scene in which the prop appears.

The stars reveal to Sekibē that if he chops down the old cherry tree at that very moment and then burns the wood and offers prayers before the grave of Hanzoku Taishi,[42] he can become the supreme ruler of Japan. He sharpens his axe and tests it by chopping the *koto* in half, revealing the bloodstained sleeve. Meanwhile, the Seal of Kangō flies out of his kimono and lodges itself in a branch of the cherry tree. Though he tries to cut down the tree as quickly as possible, some magical power prevents him. Befuddled, he sees a mysterious woman emerge from an opening in the tree trunk. She identifies herself as a courtesan named Sumizome from the famous Shumoku-machi pleasure district. With abrupt frankness, she says she has come just to see him and begs him to become her lover. Shumoku-machi was located in the Fushimi area of Kyoto, and Sumizome is portrayed in the manner of a courtesan from the Yoshiwara district in Edo. In fact, the scene is accompanied by a shamisen melody called *Sugagaki*, which is closely associated with Yoshiwara. There's something quintessentially kabuki-like about this sudden time-space warp from the Ōsaka Barrier Gate in the Heian period to the Yoshiwara district in Edo.

Sekibē and Sumizome perform a long dance duet that imitates first a procession of courtesans and then an erotic dalliance between a prostitute and her lover. Eventually Sumizome accuses Sekibē of infidelity, arbitrarily identifying the bloodstained sleeve as a passionate love letter sent to him by another woman. Caught in a one-sided lovers' quarrel, Sekibē begins to suspect there's something unnatural about Sumizome's obsession with the sleeve. The argument escalates until each demands to know the other's true identity. For the first time, Sekibē reveals who he really is, declaring: "What have I to hide? I am Ōtomo no Kuronushi, scion of Counselor Yakamochi, and I seek lordship over all of Japan."

The historical Ōtomo no Kuronushi was neither a rebel nor a villain. His name did have dark connotations because if its similarity to the names of such renegades as Ōtomo no Ōji[43] of the Jinshin War and Tomo no Yoshio[44] of the Ōtenmon Incident, which might help explain why he's depicted as an evil man. It's also worth noting that Ōtomo no Yakamochi[45] is mentioned only because of his fame as a poet and had no real-life connection to Kuronushi whatsoever. This is the kind of play on words that appealed to Edo-period authors.

## An Electrifying Ending

After announcing his true identity, Kuronushi removes his hood to reveal a punkish hairstyle called *ōji katsura* (prince wig). He executes a quick *bukkaeri* costume change that clothes him in the robes of a court noble. The ax he holds is also suddenly transformed into a giant broadax about three times its former size. The broadax has a mirror set in it, which the actor uses onstage to apply dynamic make-up that symbolizes his new role as an evil nobleman. These quick-change techniques performed onstage instantly achieve a radical transformation.

Sumizome also reveals her true identity, declaring: "I'm the insentient spirit of the cherry tree, born into the human world of seven emotions, where I exchanged vows of love with Lord Yasusada." Thus we discover that she's the lover of Munesada's dead younger brother. In the full-length play, Yasusada had a human courtesan for a lover, but she had been killed. The cherry spirit transformed herself into human form to take her place. As we learned in chapter 4, kabuki often presents fairy-tale scenarios in which the spirit of an animal or plant interacts with humans. After announcing her true identity, Sumizome also executes a *bukkaeri* quick costume change and, shaking her head, loosens the hair of her wig to spine-chilling effect.

No ordinary mortal she, this spirit-master of karmic law who flits and dances, light as cherry petals in storm-driven snow. Concealed by mist and the haze of night, she glimmers untouchable, moonlight on water, seen, not seen, then seen again. Now liberated, she breaks free of human transmigration, the endless cycle of birth and death, returning to her roots. "Watch for the sign!" she calls as her form fades, leaving nothing but her voice. Once again becoming a cherry tree revisited by blossoms each spring, she makes her way through trampled snow, water flowing clear with her return. And so the fame of the Komachi Cherry Tree has spread far and wide, her tale passed down in written words.

This text is set to an extremely fast and lively melody. Kuronushi is now garbed in black, aristocratic clothing and wields his giant battleax; Sumizome, now dressed in a pale pink kimono, holds a flowering cherry branch. They circle around and around the cherry tree in a vigorous battle dance. Kuronushi performs a swaggering *roppō* (six directions) sequence in *aragoto* style; Sumizome in turn performs an *ebizori* backbend. Both characters execute flashy choreography in breathless, tension-filled sequences, building to a great climax that ends the piece (see plate 5). This type of ending is called *chirashi* (scattering) and corresponds to the *kyū* (rapid) section in the traditional aesthetic concept of *jo-ha-kyū* (slow beginning–development–rapid climax) that informs many Japanese arts. The true identity of the woman as the spirit of a cherry tree has a fairy-tale quality one can also find in Western ballet. In that context, I suppose the final scene corresponds to the coda of a *grand pas de deux*.⁴⁶

## A Taste for Playfulness

In a classical *grand pas de deux*, the male dancer is normally there to lift the prima ballerina and provide her with constant support that symbolizes his love for her. In *Seki no To*, however, the man and woman are engaged in a fierce battle. I find this distinctively Japanese approach quite fascinating. Just before the final dance, Sumizome and Sekibē have a lovers' quarrel, and it's important to note that this quarrel is extended and enlarged after the characters reveal their true identities.

As I discussed in Chapter 2, the quarrel between Yūgiri and Izaemon is one of the highlights of the play *Kuruwa Bunshō*. Such quarrels between couples (called *kuzetsu-goto*) were an indispensable element in early-modern Japanese performance and literary arts. In fact, courtesans in Edo's Yoshiwara district received training in how to pick coquettish fights with their clients. There's also a popular saying that can be translated as "Not even dogs will eat a marital spat," which means that tiffs between couples are so commonplace that not even dogs, which are otherwise always on the lookout for food, bother to pay attention. Perhaps because lovers' quarrels were felt to be a backhanded expression of love, many works of light fiction written in the Edo period feature them. One extreme example is a book called *Sekai no Makunashi* (The World Goes On),⁴⁷ which focuses exclusively on the quarrel of a married couple on New Year's Day.

It seems that even today, many Japanese are too embarrassed to say "I love you" directly to a lover's face. Instead, we seem to prefer to tease and quarrel with each other as a roundabout strategy for achieving a good relationship. This is the ethnic temperament that gave rise to our "quarrel culture."

Before the climactic dance, Sumizome and Sekibē give the audience a full dose of the kind of repartee one might expect between a prostitute and her patron. That quarrel gradually takes on delusional overtones until it develops into a full-fledged, over-the-top battle set in ancient Japan. This is where the true charm of *Seki no To* lies, and it fully reflects the playfulness so prized by playwrights in old Edo.

## A Gaudy Flower with No Fruit

The original play *Jūnihitoe Komachi Zakura* apparently had more stories to tell, but we surmise that this showy dance scene was probably the finale. However that may be, the dance piece now titled *Tsumoru Koi Yuki no Seki no To* is all that remains. Without the context of the entire play, it's difficult to understand the plot as it now stands, but the piece is still popular because it conveys an idea of what kabuki was like when the piece was created.

This being so, it might be useful to add a little historical information here about the year 1784, when the play premiered. A great famine[48] had already begun in northeastern Japan, and Mount Asama had just had a major volcanic eruption. People found it difficult to make ends meet, and social unrest was on the rise. Tanuma Okitsugu,[49] a senior counselor to the shogun, had become the target of deep resentment; when his son was assassinated in Edo Castle, the people cheered. Just three years later, there were large-scale riots in Edo and Osaka that threatened the very existence of the Tokugawa shogunate. Chief Senior Counselor Matsudaira Sadanobu[50] stepped in and implemented a new financial policy known as the Kansei Reforms. Previous to that, the commodity economy had revived under the Tanuma administration, energizing the merchant class in the large cities at the expense of rural communities. This created an economic bubble that enabled playwrights in western Japan, such as Namiki Shōza and Namiki Gohei, to invest in expensive stage props and create their spectacular, large-scale plays.

Tanuma Okitsugu was a self-made man who worked his way to the top of the Tokugawa government. In his time, actors like Nakamura Nakazō I and Segawa Kikunojō III were also rising from the bottom ranks to stardom without the advantages of hereditary connections. The fact that they were able to reach the pinnacle of the kabuki world is highly suggestive of the tenor of the times.

The Kansei Reforms ushered in a period of severe austerity and pessimism, naturally making it impossible for kabuki producers to continue operating on such a grand scale. Another economic bubble that occurred in the early nineteenth century fueled a revival, but kabuki's late eighteenth-century flowering during the Tanuma years must be considered one of the art form's historical peaks. *Seki no To*, which premiered during that time, was truly a gaudy flower that, madly blooming as it did at the height of a bubble economy, bore no fruit.

Subsequent kabuki dance pieces showed little further development within the context of complicated storylines. Instead, they became independent works divorced from dramatic elements. In the early nineteenth century, the actors Nakamura Utaemon III and Bandō Mitsugorō III[51] tried to outdo each other performing *henge-mono* (transformation pieces), a genre of dance in which a single actor plays many roles by making quick costume changes. This was not a new development, however. Its roots can be traced back to the Genroku era and the *nanabake* (seven transformations) pieces performed by Mizuki Tatsunosuke. Being short, *henge-mono* are relatively easy to perform. Many of the pieces that are considered the epitome of Japanese dance today started out as *henge-mono* segments, including *Sagi Musume* (Heron Maiden),[52] *Fuji Musume* (Wisteria Maiden),[53] *Shiokumi* (Salt Maidens),[54] *Echigo Jishi* (Echigo Lion),[55] and *Tomo Yakko* (The Footman Attendant).[56]

Many other dance pieces were composed with no connection to dramatic plays at all. Some depicted festivals or annual ceremonies; others were sketches of daily life, including the doings of vendors and street performers. No doubt the original appeal of these pieces lay to some degree in their fidelity to real life, but today not even many kabuki performers know to what extent they are a faithful depiction of past reality and to what extent they are idealized expression. This is precisely where the limitations of this type of dance become evident.

*Seki no To* is without question a masterpiece linked to kabuki's development as a theater art that mixed drama and dance. As is true in all places and times, however, dance depends heavily on the talent and appeal of individual performers. The excellence of this piece, then, is not necessarily evident when performed by merely average dancers.

CHAPTER NINE

# Tōkaidō Yotsuya Kaidan

## Queen of Japanese Horror

### Japan's Scariest Ghost

Tōkaidō Yotsuya Kaidan (The Ghost Story of Yotsuya), which is usually referred to by the shortened name *Yotsuya Kaidan*, is very famous in Japan. Still, it might be useful to give a quick summary of the plot here.

An impoverished ronin (masterless samurai) named Tamiya Iemon is reproached by his father-in-law for a past transgression, and his wife Oiwa has been recalled to her family home. Enraged, Iemon kills his father-in-law but hopes to win Oiwa back by convincing her that the murder was committed by someone else and that he will avenge the crime. Meanwhile, Iemon has caught the amorous eye of Oume, the daughter of a wealthy samurai family. Oume's grandfather, Itō Kihē, is also fond of Iemon and wants him for a grandson-in-law. Although Iemon and Oiwa are eventually reunited, Oiwa fails to recover her health after giving birth, and Iemon gradually tires of her and her wan appearance. To make matters worse, the Itō family sends Oiwa poisoned medicine that

153

grotesquely disfigures her face. Iemon, who hates his poverty, agrees to marry Oume, despite knowing that the Itōs have poisoned Oiwa. Made aware of Iemon's betrayal and the malice of the Itōs, Oiwa dies bearing a bitter grudge. Her ghost comes back to haunt them, and people begin to die. . . .

Besides the tale of Iemon and Oiwa, *Yotsuya Kaidan* also tells a parallel story about Oiwa's younger sister Osode and her illicit affair with Naosuke Gonbē. In this chapter, however, I'll focus on Iemon and Oiwa.

*Yotsuya Kaidan* is probably the best-known play in the entire kabuki repertory. Even people who are unfamiliar with works like *Chūshingura* or *Kanjinchō*[1] have no trouble identifying *Yotsuya Kaidan* as the "play about Oiwa." Before the character Sadako[2] came on the scene in *The Ring*, Oiwa was unmistakably the queen of Japanese horror.

## A Character That Terrified Fellow Performers

There are three key people who must be mentioned in any discussion of *Yotsuya Kaidan*. The first is Onoe Kikugorō III,[3] who was the first to perform the role of Oiwa.

Records show that Kikugorō performed in nine productions of the play in his lifetime, with the second production following immediately after the premiere run. Today the kabuki repertory is fairly fixed, and the same plays are performed repeatedly, so it's not unusual for an actor to reprise a role many times. This was not the case in 1825, however, when *Yotsuya Kaidan* premiered. During the Edo period, it was customary to present a new play with each new production. Although an actor might play roles that were very similar to ones he had done before, it was rare for him to repeat the same role. The fact that Kikugorō performed

Oiwa in nine productions without even changing the name of the play indicates the tremendous success he achieved with it.

Kikugorō was reputedly a very handsome man. Born the son of a cabinetmaker, he was adopted and trained by kabuki actor Onoe Matsusuke I. One anecdote relates how he stood in front of a mirror and muttered to himself, "What a fine man," and people around him agreed.[4]

Various stories have also been handed down about how terrifying Kikugorō was as Oiwa. Ichikawa Danjūrō VII, the actor who first played Iemon, was reportedly afraid to look Oiwa in the face onstage and was reprimanded for it. In the fourth production of the play, Iemon was played by Seki Sanjūrō II,[5] who was so frightened that he became ill and had to take time off.[6]

One time in the dressing room, Kikugorō asked his disciple Onokura if his (Kikugorō's) Oiwa was scary, to which Onokura replied, "Not really, since I see it every day." Kikugorō later hid in the shadows and sprang out at Onokura, who was so terrified that he fainted.[7] Kikugorō probably felt compelled to startle his apprentice because being told he wasn't terrifying made his job more difficult onstage. The quality of fear was a basic and indispensable element in the portrayal of the Oiwa role.

The Japanese language has two words for ghost: *obake* and *yūrei*. When asked the difference between these two, Kikugorō said that the former should be performed with a carefree heart, and the latter with a heart full of pain.[8] He went on to say that an actor must "be careful to fully retain the resentment and malice felt at the moment of death." Oiwa was treated cruelly and died harboring deep hatred. The very foundation of this role is the expression of that resentment and the terror it inspires.

## Amazing Stage Effects

The second key person in any discussion of *Yotsuya Kaidan* is Kikugorō's foster father, Onoe Matsusuke I.⁹ Matsusuke was a master of special stage effects, the kind of tricks and grand illusions one might expect from David Copperfield or Princess Tenko today. Matsusuke was adept at creating spectacles, such as transforming skeletons into human beings or showing underwater quick costume changes onstage. The former, called *kotsuyose* (bringing bones together), is still used in kabuki today.¹⁰

In the Edo period, large kabuki theaters were closed during the summer, when most actors took a vacation. However, some young and lesser known actors used the summer season to stage experimental works and engage in "battle of the bands" type performance events. Even today, younger actors often take center stage during February and August—the two months that tend to have the smallest audiences. According to the lunar calendar, the height of summer came in the sixth month, which was when actors usually took a break. But Matsusuke achieved tremendous box-office success by presenting *Tenjiku Tokubē Ikokubanashi* (India Tokubē's Foreign Tales)¹¹ in midsummer.

This play was full of special effects that included a toad transforming into a human, diving into a tank of water, performing a quick costume change, and then suddenly entering down the *hanamichi* bridgeway as if by magic. As I discussed in chapter 6, kabuki featured tricks involving real water from early on, but Matsusuke enhanced these with an element of magical illusion. Another one of his innovations was a realistic portrayal of head hair.

> ## Kabuki Design
>
> *Toita gaeshi* (Door Reversal)
> Iemon goes to a canal to fish and finds a door covered by a woven mat that he recognizes. He pulls the door to shore and removes the mat to reveal the corpse of Oiwa attached to the door. Horrified, he turns the door over, only to find the corpse of Kohei on the other side. Both corpses are played by one actor who does a quick costume change.

"Canal of Hidden Death," part of the print series *Tōkaidō Yotsuya Kaidan* by Ōju Kunisada. Performed in August 1831 at the Ichimura-za in Edo.

Iemon (top) played by Seki Sanjūrō II; Oiwa (left) and Kohei (right) played by Onoe Kikugorō III.

A book called *Okyōgen Gakuya Honsetsu* (Backstage Stories of Kabuki)[12] published in the mid-nineteenth century contains detailed explanations of how these stage effects are achieved. Among other things, it includes illustrated descriptions of the tricks used in *Yotsuya Kaidan*, including the hair combing scene (in which massive amounts of Oiwa's hair fall out as she combs it), the door scene (in which Iemon sees the ghosts of his wife Oiwa and his servant Kohei [whom he has also murdered] lashed to two sides of a door that bobs up in a canal), and the lantern projection scene (in which Oiwa's face seems to emerge from a paper lantern). Other effects explained in the book include *rokuro kubi* (flying head) and *renri biki*, in which a ghost reaches out as if grabbing the scruff of an escaping person's neck and magically pulls him back to the stage without physical contact. One of the most impressive tricks is *kaen kubi* (burning head), in which the actor's head, visible through a face hole cut in a burning wheel, revolves as the wheel turns. The fact that this book was published suggests that such stage illusions were extremely popular in their day. Many of them were pioneered by Onoe Matsusuke I, and it seems safe to assume that he passed on their secrets to his foster son Kikugorō III, who continued the tradition.

Elements like special stage effects might seem incongruous if kabuki is classified as a "classical" stage art in the Western sense. By the nineteenth century, "classical" theater forms in the West had no room for such foolish antics. They were expected to be more refined and sophisticated than kabuki could ever be. On the other hand, the willingness of kabuki artists to indiscriminately adopt and hand down virtually any element deemed entertaining is what makes their art so fascinating. In Japan, a certain playfulness was considered essential to performance art.

*Kaen kubi* ("burning head," right), and its mechanism (left). The actor squats inside the wheel with his hands on the axle and shows his face through a cut-out hole while a stage assistant turns the wheel by pulling on rope handles. From *Okyōgen Gakuya Honsetsu* (Backstage Stories of Kabuki).

The third key person associated with *Yotsuya Kaidan* was the popular kabuki playwright Tsuruya Nanboku IV,[13] who wrote the script in collaboration with Onoe Matsusuke I. Nanboku had a long period of apprenticeship and only gradually gained prominence as a writer. His first big break came when he partnered with Matsusuke to create *Tenjiku Tokubē Ikokubanashi*, mentioned above. Later, he worked with such famous actors as Matsumoto Kōshirō V[14] and Iwai Hanshirō V[15] to produce many hit plays. Nanboku was an old man when he wrote *Yotsuya Kaidan* for performance by Matsusuke's adopted son, Kikugorō III.

One legend connected with Nanboku tells us that the stage effects in *Tenjiku Tokubē Ikokubanashi* were so astonishing that they were rumored to be the sorcery of Catholic priests, resulting in Nanboku being investigated by town magistrates. Of course, he was cleared of all suspicion, but the scandal further boosted the play's notoriety, and it appears that Nanboku engineered the whole affair as a publicity stunt. Although we can't be sure, another legend claims that prior to the premiere of *Yotsuya Kaidan*, a kite bearing a woman's freshly severed head holding a long-sleeved kimono in its teeth was flown from the roof of the theater. Apparently Nanboku was an advertising genius as well as a great innovator in the world of Edo-period kabuki.

## A Connection to *Chūshingura*

In its premiere production, *Yotsuya Kaidan* was performed on a double bill with *Chūshingura* over the course of two days. On the first day, *Chūshingura* was performed through Act VI (Kanpei's suicide), followed by the first three acts of *Yotsuya Kaidan*. On the second day, *Chūshingura* resumed from Act VII through the final vendetta scene, followed by the second half of *Yotsuya Kaidan*. Thus audiences were given only half of each play at a time.

For this reason, *Yotsuya Kaidan* is written as if it were a spinoff of *Chūshingura*. In fact, the character Tamiya Iemon is a ronin because his master was En'ya Hangan, whose death sparked the vendetta in *Chūshingura*. *Yotsuya Kaidan* ends with Iemon being killed by Satō Yomoshichi, the husband of Oiwa's younger sister, Osode. Yomoshichi is modeled on Yatō Emoshichi,[16] one of the 47 ronin. The final scene is set in falling snow, which echoes *Chūshingura*'s vendetta scene.

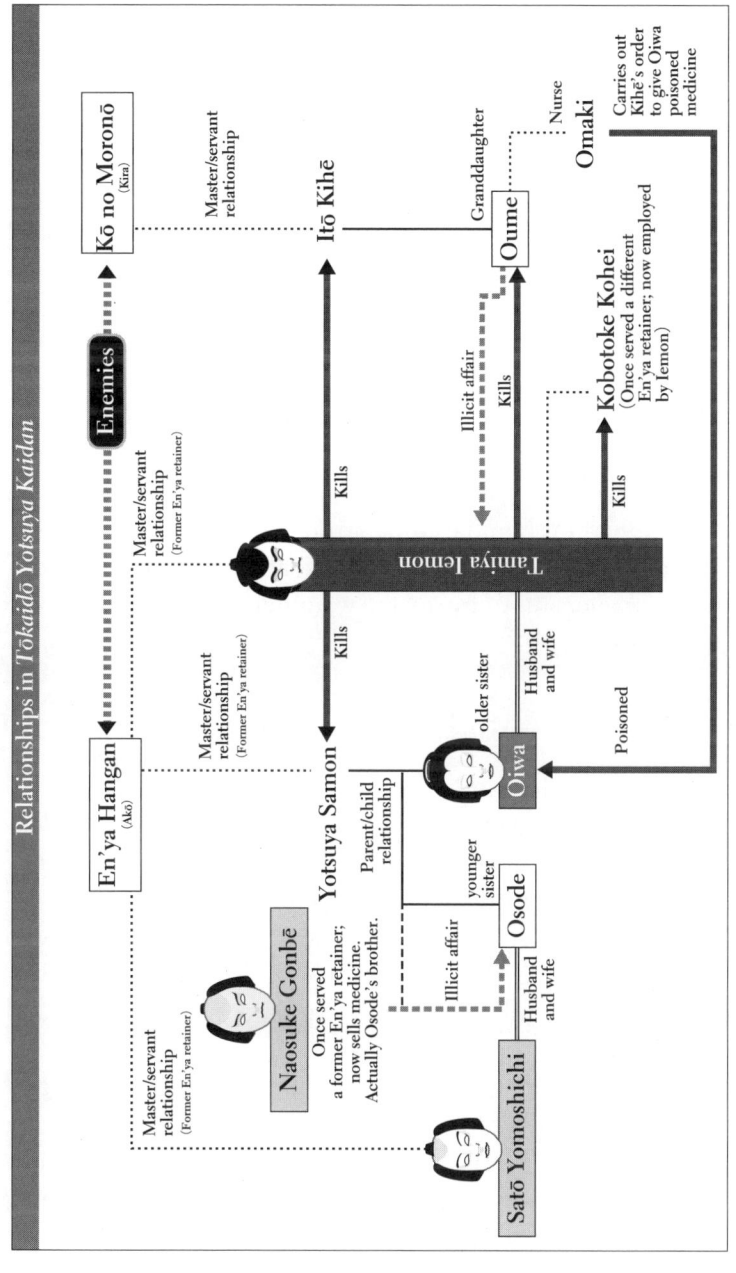

In chapter 5, I discussed how *Chūshingura* took an actual Edo-period incident involving a samurai named Asano Naganori and set it in the "world" of the *Taiheiki* (Chronicle of Grand Pacification), changing the name of the doomed lord to En'ya Hangan in the process.

As a denizen of the *Chūshingura* world, Iemon is cast as a ronin of the dead Hangan, while Itō Kihei, the grandfather who poisons Oiwa, is seen as a retainer who serves Hangan's enemy, Kō no Moronō. In other words, the story of *Yotsuya Kaidan* as a whole is woven into the larger tale of *Chūshingura*.

This aspect of these plays might be difficult for modern-day audiences to understand, given the fact that not even *Chūshingura* is familiar to everyone today. But in Edo times, viewers apparently found it easier to appreciate stories featuring characters they already knew, rather than those that were newly invented.

## Leaps in Time and Space

Nanboku wrote another play called *Nazo no Obi Chotto Tokubē* that predates and closely resembles *Yotsuya Kaidan*. However, its background world is not *Chūshingura* but *Natsu Matsuri Naniwa Kagami* (see chapter 6). The Iemon character in that play is named Danshichi, and his wife, who corresponds to Oiwa, is named Okaji. While Okaji doesn't become a vengeful ghost, her husband does kill her father and treat her cruelly.

As we've seen, the practice of taking an Edo-era story and setting it in another time and place arose in part because performers wanted to avoid censorship. But they probably also did it simply because they enjoyed it. Nanboku was certainly not the only playwright who indulged in it. The practice was a notable feature from a very early time, particularly in kabuki performed in Edo.

A play titled *Chūjō Hime Kyō Biina* (Princess Chūjō, the Doll of Kyoto)[17] premiered in 1708 and features Princess Chūjō, a character of ancient legend who is also known in Japan today for lending her name to a medicine for gynecological disorders. The princess is sold into servitude and becomes the character Oshichi, who works for a greengrocer. The interesting thing is that there actually was a greengrocer named Oshichi[18] who committed arson in Edo in the seventeenth century. Thus a character dating from sometime around the eighth century is whisked through a time warp to the early Edo period.

Similarly, Ichikawa Danjūrō II (mentioned in chapter 1) took the Edo-period double-suicide play *Agemaki Sukeroku* (Agemaki and Sukeroku), which was popular in Kyoto and Osaka, and embedded the story in the twelfth-century world of the Soga brothers. This was the original form of *Sukeroku*,[19] which is still performed.

Danjūrō II also combined another play called *Kaibyaku Genbuku Soga* (The Soga Brothers' Coming of Age) with Chikamatsu Monzaemon's *Sonezaki Shinjū* (The Love Suicides at Sonezaki) to create *Sogazaki Shinjū* (The Love Suicides at Sogazaki). The new play's title is nearly identical to that of Chikamatsu's work, the only difference being that *Sonezaki* has been changed to incorporate the name of the Soga brothers. The protagonist, Hiranoya Tokubē, is in fact the younger brother Soga no Gorō in disguise. Danjūrō II thus recast an Edo-period domestic drama typical of western Japan into the twelfth-century world of the Soga brothers. This suggests that time warping was already quite common in Edo by the early seventeenth century.

In some of the early Edo-style kabuki scripts that have survived, we find instances where a slight similarity between the names of two totally unrelated characters is enough to prompt authors to weave the two together. A simple play on words is all it takes to suggest a connection. This can be considered a subtle variant of the "character-in-disguise" trope we examined in chapter 7 with respect to kabuki performed in western Japan. Edo-style kabuki also made liberal use of the trope, but in Edo, the connection between the different identities was often no more substantial than a tenuous verbal pun.

Edo-style kabuki in its early days had a strong revue element. Perhaps this helps to explain why authors in later years didn't hesitate to move their characters through space and time. Revues focus on presenting memorable characters rather than telling a coherent story. Since a rich variety of characters unquestionably makes the revue format more interesting, authors were probably encouraged to make liberal use of time and space warps.

## Entwining Different Stories

In Edo-style kabuki, playwrights freely mixed different stories together in plays that had strong revue elements. But it was Namiki Gohei, the author of the play *Sanmon* discussed in chapter 7, who introduced writing techniques from his native western Japan to Edo productions. After Gohei moved east, realism and logic began playing a more prominent role in Edo-based plays.

An author named Sakurada Jisuke,[20] who traveled from Edo to western Japan to study playwriting, experimented with various combinations of "story" and "world" elements, and eventually succeeded in creating dramatically interesting plays after he returned to Edo. He pioneered a particular writing technique that was later perfected by his disciple, Tsuruya Nanboku IV. That technique is called *naimaze* (entwining).

The idea behind *naimaze* is to take two or more story lines and braid them together like strands in a rope, with all the strands visible at the same time. Nanboku was especially adept at this and wrote many complex plays that wove together multiple worlds.

One of his masterpieces still performed today is called *Sakura Hime Azuma Bunshō* (The Story of Princess Sakura).[21] It combines two worlds: that of the Sumida River legend about a mother whose child is abducted and killed by slave traders; and that of the legend of the priest Seigen, who is ruined because of his obsession with the beautiful Princess Sakura.

One could say that Nanboku also wrote *Yotsuya Kaidan* using the *naimaze* technique. Iemon and Oiwa were the names of a couple who actually lived in the early Edo period and were familiar to Edo audiences. Rumor had it that Oiwa went mad and died because of her husband's infidelity and maliciously haunted his household. We can view the play, then, as an entwining of this urban legend with the world of *Chūshingura*.

## A Life-Size Ghost

Let's return now to the story of *Yotsuya Kaidan*. I've thought about why this play was so terrifying to the audiences who saw the premiere back in 1825, and I've reached the conclusion that it had something to do with its everyday realism. Consider, for example, *The Ring*—the blockbuster novel and film that I briefly mentioned at the beginning of this chapter. Surely the horror engendered by the character Sadako is connected in some way to the fact that she emerges from a television screen. The concept of having a ghost emerge from an everyday object like a TV or video screen was radically unsettling.

Oiwa's role is most terrifying in the hair-combing scene. Having realized that she's been poisoned and that her husband has been taken from her, she goes mad with rage and decides to confront her enemies. Despite her horribly deformed face, she is still woman enough to want to look her best, so she applies tooth blackening and decides to comb her hair. Traditional wisdom discouraged new mothers from washing their hair because it tends to fall out, but Oiwa is determined to comb it anyway, holding her baby in her arms. As one might expect (this being kabuki), her hair falls out in great clumps (see plate 6). The realism of this scene is truly heart-wrenching.

An earlier play called *Ōakinai Hirugakojima*[22] by Sakurada Jisuke also has a hair-combing scene. This was the first play in which the famous song *Kurokami* (Black Hair)[23] was played as accompaniment. It was followed by Nanboku's *Okuni Gozen Keshō no Sugatami* (Okuni Gozen Putting on Her Makeup),[24] which is considered the direct antecedent of Oiwa's hair-combing scene. The character Okuni Gozen is a concubine in the home domain of a daimyo lord whose legal wife lives in Edo. She is overcome by jealousy and great clumps of her hair fall out when she combs it. It's interesting to note that the terror generated by Sadako in *The Ring* is also amplified by her long, black hair. I suspect that Sadako's appearance was influenced by Oiwa as portrayed in her hair-combing scene.

In *Yotsuya Kaidan*, Iemon and Oiwa are so poor that they are forced to pawn even their mosquito net. Oiwa becomes ill after giving birth and suffers her husband's domestic abuse. Their newborn baby cries constantly, and because their net is gone the house is hazy with smoke from burning mosquito coils. Oiwa's mental state quickly deteriorates under these miserable conditions. Meanwhile, Iemon's growing frustration with his impoverished life is portrayed with crushing realism. His plight as a masterless samurai, reduced to making umbrellas for a living, was a recognizable situation for many members of the audience.

Perhaps this play was so intensely frightening precisely because it was so deeply rooted in the realities of day-to-day life in Edo. Nanboku pioneered this realistic approach to drama by highlighting the destitution and corrupt social conditions of the time. Today, this type of play is called *kizewa-mono* (raw domestic pieces).

Kabuki has portrayed many ghosts since the Genroku era, but the early ones were probably not as frightening. It seems safe to say that *Yotsuya Kaidan* was the first play that approached our modern conception of horror, because it was the first to feature a ghost that felt life-sized to the audience. The stark realism of the play provided the basis for a true sense of fear.

After its initial success, *Yotsuya Kaidan* was mounted many more times while undergoing revisions that further intensified the fear factor. The story proved so popular that it was adapted to other stage genres as well as film, earning it a place as the starting point for Japanese horror.

CHAPTER TEN

# Sannin Kichisa Kuruwa no Hatsugai

## BONNIE AND CLYDE, JAPANESE STYLE

### On the Road to Destruction

I'd like to introduce one more playwright, someone who came after *Yotsuya Kaidan* author Tsuruya Nanboku. Active in the second half of the nineteenth century, his name was Kawatake Mokuami.[1] Although he was known for most of his life as Kawatake Shinshichi and adopted the name Mokuami only after the Meiji period began in 1868, I'll refer to him throughout this chapter as Mokuami.

As we've already seen, kabuki didn't start out as a "classical" performance form. It evolved with the times, incorporating the fashions of the day and constantly generating new plays. Mokuami might be considered the last great playwright who participated in that process.

The author and critic Tsubouchi Shōyō[2] characterized Mokuami not only as a playwright but also as the "great wholesaler of Edo theater" who acquired encyclopedic knowledge of past theatrical practices and ultimately codified them.[3] Mokuami created many masterpieces in the mid-Meiji period and had a tremendous influence on modern-day kabuki. Let's

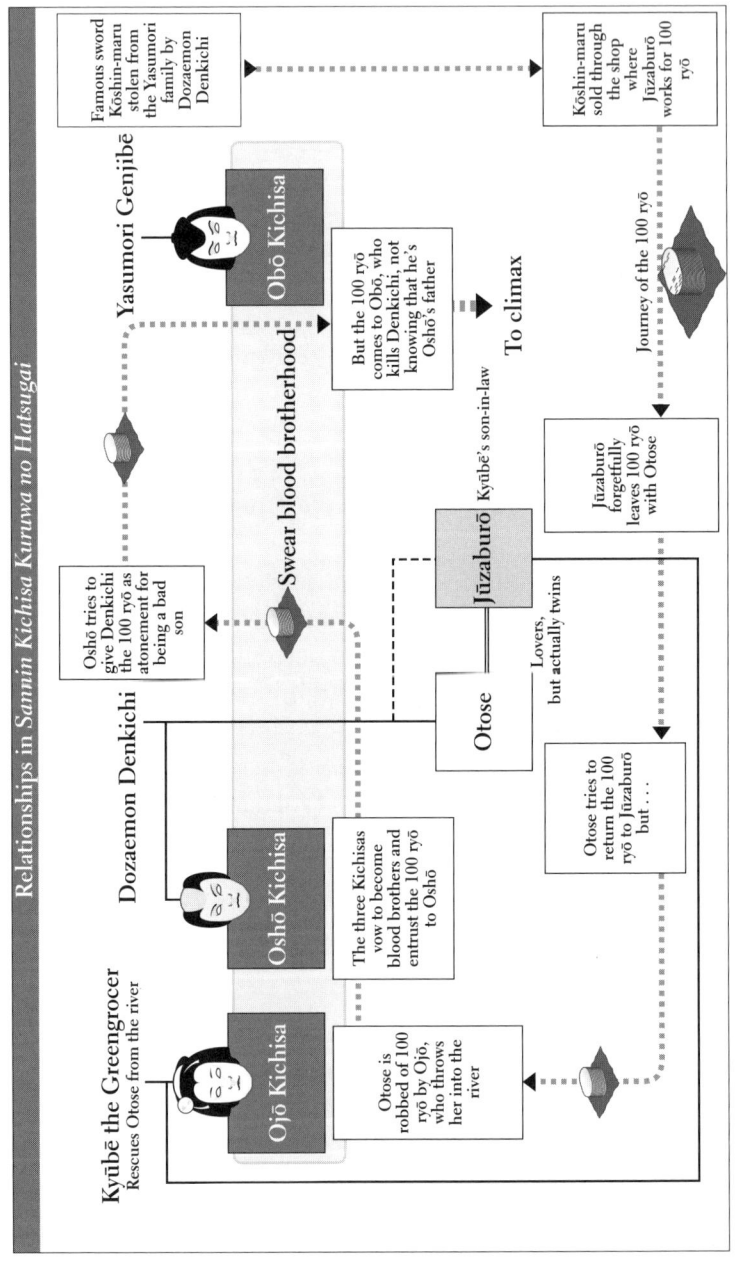

take a look at the story of one of his best-known works, *Sannin Kichisa Kuruwa no Hatsugai* (Three Men Named Kichisa), commonly called *Sannin Kichisa*.

At 45, Mokuami was in his prime when he wrote this play and said he always found it to be "the most heart-wringing" of all. Known for its famous lines that begin, "The spring sky blurs both the moon /And the whitefish fishing fires in mist . . . ," it tells the story of three thieves, all of whom are named Kichisa.

When the curtain opens, a streetwalker named Otose enters with the honest intention of returning the sum of 100 ryō that one of her clients has absentmindedly left behind. As she walks on the banks of the Ōkawa River, a woman stops her to ask directions, and when Otose kindly obliges, she suddenly finds herself thrown into the water. The woman she thought she was helping is actually the thief Ojō Kichisa, who commits his robberies disguised as a woman. Having taken the 100 ryō and thrown Otose into the water, Ojō pauses to recite the famous "spring sky" lines. His actions are witnessed, however, by the degenerate ronin Obō Kichisa, who orders Ojō to hand over the money. The two scuffle, only to be stopped by Oshō Kichisa, a reprobate priest. Ojō and Obō are deeply impressed by Oshō's fearlessness and take a liking to him. They decide to give him the money and the three of them pledge to become blood brothers (see plate 7).

Otose is rescued from the water and returns home, where she finds Jūzaburō, the client who forgot the 100 ryō. Because the money belonged to his master, Jūzaburō feels compelled to commit suicide, but Otose prevails on her father Dozaemon Denkichi to come to his aid. It becomes apparent that Otose and Jūzaburō have secretly fallen in love, but the cruel truth is later revealed: they are twins who were separated at birth.

Denkichi also happens to be the father of Oshō the thief. Oshō gives Denkichi the stolen money, but then Obō, not knowing that Denkichi and Oshō are father and son, kills Denkichi and steals it again. Obō had once been a samurai, but his family was ruined by Denkichi, who was a thief himself and had stolen a priceless heirloom from them: the famous sword Kōshin-maru. Although Obō is a murderer and thief, he feels deep remorse for killing Denkichi without knowing that he was Oshō's father. Now pursued by the authorities, he decides to commit suicide with Ojō, but the pair's plans are interrupted once again by Oshō, who tells them that he has killed his own sister Otose and her brother/lover Jūzaburō (who were guilty of incest) and passed their bodies off as those of Obō and Oshō. In the end, however, their efforts prove futile and all three meet a tragic fate.

One of the interesting aspects of this play is the 100 ryō, which passes through the hands of many characters as the story unfolds. As the money makes its rounds, the complex personal relationships gradually become clear, a process that is in itself the structure of the piece. All of the characters are trapped in the circle of money and apparently lack the ability to step outside it. In this sense the play has an extremely claustrophobic feeling. When the three main characters finally do attempt to escape the money trap, they end up stabbing each other to death. That heartrending last scene is impressive for a strange sense of release that reminds me of that New Hollywood masterpiece, *Bonnie and Clyde*.[4] Ever since I realized the similarity, I've characterized *Sannin Kichisa* as the *Bonnie and Clyde* of the late Edo period.

## Petty Scoundrels in Lead Roles

*Sannin Kichisa* premiered in 1860, the year the senior shogunal official Ii Naosuke was assassinated in the Sakuradamon Incident.[5] The part of Oshō was played by Ichikawa Kodanji

IV,[5] who was rather small in stature and not especially impressive in his bearing but famous for his acting skill. Seven years earlier,[6] Mokuami had mounted his first work *Miyakodori Nagare no Shiranami* (The Bandit Courtesan and the Family Seal)[7] in collaboration with Kodanji. *Sannin Kichisa* was one of the high points of their long collaborative careers.

After entering the theater world, Mokuami earned a reputation as a serious and reliable man who didn't drink much and always met his deadlines. This staid man was writing stories about petty thieves and blackmailers at a time when the Tokugawa shogunate was collapsing. Such plays were called *shiranami-mono* (white wave plays).

The term *shiranami* meaning "bandit" was coined in reference to a band of bandits called the White Wave Gang, who were the remnants of the Yellow Turban rebels[8] depicted in Luo Guanzhong's historical novel *Romance of the Three Kingdoms*. *Sannin Kichisa* is one of Mokuami's best known plays in this genre, but he wrote many others, including *Shiranami Gonin Otoko* (Five Men of the White Waves,[9] also known as *Aoto Zōshi Hana no Nishiki-e*), which is often performed today and depicts the exploits of the thief Benten Kozō and his ruffian friends. Mokuami's strong association with the genre earned him the nickname "White Wave Author."

The nineteenth-century storyteller Shōrin Hakuen II,[10] a contemporary of Mokuami, was so successful at telling tales of thieves and scoundrels that he was known as "Bandit Hakuen." Popular stories he told included *Tenpō Rokkasen* (Six Great Men of the Tenpō Period)[11] and *Nezumi Kozō* (The Rat Kid).[12] Mokuami recast these and other narrative pieces as kabuki plays.

The tremendous popularity of plays and stories featuring thieves reflects the corruption and sense of frailty that characterized the closing days of the Tokugawa shogunate. After more than 250 years of dominance, the feudalistic system had finally reached an impasse. Uncertainty about the future was no longer restricted to the learned class; it had spread to the common man, and the claustrophobic atmosphere of *Sannin Kichisa* felt familiar to audience members of the day.

## Depicting the Moment of Corruption

Of Mokuami's many works, the prologue of *Fune e Uchikomu Hashima no Shiranami* (Stowaway Thieves Between Bridges), a play more commonly called *Ikakematsu* (Matsugorō the Tinker), is to my mind an extremely potent depiction of the social conditions that prevailed in the final days of the Edo period. The protagonist is an itinerant tinker named Matsugorō, who travels a circuit repairing pots and pans. Tradesmen like him were found in towns throughout Japan at the time.

In the prologue, three samurai bullies are picking fights and extorting money from townspeople on the main street in Ryōgoku. In my work as a historical novelist, I study the diaries of townsfolk who lived in those times, and from what I can tell, this depiction in *Ikakematsu* is true to life: there really were a large number of malicious, low-ranking samurai. Matsugorō appears on Ryōgoku Bridge (in the play it's called Hanamizu Bridge) and laments the current state of the world, saying that high prices are killing the poor and, though he knows he sounds like an old codger saying so, wishing that the good old days would return. His companion, a scrap-paper peddler, agrees that the world was a better place when he was a child, since people now seem so small when viewed through the lens of the past.

This play was performed in 1866. The fourteenth shogun Tokugawa Iemochi had passed away, followed in death by Emperor Kōmei. A proposed marital link between the shogunate and the imperial family had failed to materialize, and Japanese history was at a major turning point. It's no wonder that Matsugorō's conversation with his friend resonated so deeply with audiences of the time.

The highlight of the play comes in the next scene, when Matsugorō reaches a turning point in his personal life as well. As he crosses Ryōgoku Bridge, he sees a pleasure boat on the Sumida River below carrying well-to-do revelers who are obviously enjoying themselves. Matsugorō thinks, "They must have made a killing down in Yokohama," referring to the city where trade with foreigners was flourishing. Japan had just been forced to open its doors to the West, so Matsugorōs comment might be translated today as the envy some feel toward the nouveau riche who are benefitting from globalization. Watching the raucous merrymakers float by, Matsugorō murmurs "one life's as good as another" and throws his tinker tools into the river. In that moment the seeds of evil are planted, and Matsugorō becomes a bandit.

This kind of sudden character transformation is seen in another famous play by Mokuami still performed called *Satomoyō Azami no Ironui*, commonly called *Izayoi Seishin* (The Love of Izayoi and Seishin).[13] After failing in his attempt to commit double suicide with his prostitute lover, Seishin the disgraced priest demands money from a passerby and inadvertently kills him. Filled with remorse, he decides once again to kill himself. But then, as with Matsugorō, he hears a pleasure boat filled with revelers float by and says to himself, "But wait. With money comes pleasure. All things being equal, I'd rather live like them." At that moment he completely abandons the world of respectability and turns to crime.

Mokuami captures the moment when a previously honest and hard-working person has an experience that causes him to abandon the straight and narrow. Had this happened to the characters of Namiki Shōza or Namiki Gohei in the middle of the eighteenth century (see chapter 7), they would have transformed into great renegades bent on ruling Japan. But in the works of Mokuami at the end of the Edo period, no such grand stories and great villains appear. Instead we see realistic, life-size commoners who are down on their luck and, unable to see a way forward, decide to become petty crooks.

Kabuki has traditionally specialized in evil protagonists, starting with the fallen playboys of the earliest plays and including larger-than-life renegades and chivalrous commoners who stoically endure humiliation until exacting deadly revenge. Even though such stories usually end with good prevailing over evil, the most appealing characters have always been the villains who are ostracized from proper society.

In the waning days of the Tokugawa shogunate, Mokuami struck gold with his nihilistic anti-heroes. In a modern context, his plays were equivalent to television dramas featuring temporary employees who lose their jobs. Mokuami enjoyed tremendous success precisely because audiences of his time could sympathize with people who had nowhere to go.

## The Era of Meiji Enlightenment

The Edo period (1603–1868) gave way to the Meiji period (1868–1912), and with that momentous transition there was a strong expectation that theater should point the way to the future. Mokuami responded with modern plays called *zangiri-mono* (cropped-hair plays). "Cropped hair" was the new male hairstyle in the Meiji era, signifying a break with the top-knots of the past. As one saying put it, "Knock on a cropped-hair head, and you'll hear the sound of civilization and enlightenment." *Zangiri-mono*, then, were domestic dramas that actively incorporated the mores of the new era.

One of Mokuami's *zangiri-mono* was *Suitengū Megumi no Fukagawa* (The Grace of Suitengū Shrine in Fukugawa), which premiered in 1885. Also known by the name *Fudeya Kōbē* or just *Fudekō* (Kōbē the Brush Seller), it tells the story of a samurai who is ruined by the Meiji Restoration. Inept as a businessman, he ekes out a living for himself and his family by selling calligraphy brushes but becomes depressed because of the pressures of poverty and decides to leap to his death. He is rescued, however, and regains his mental stability through the compassion of others. The man who prevents Kōbē's suicide is a rickshaw runner, and Kōbē also benefits from the persuasive remonstrations of a policeman. Both of these were new professions at the time, and they are portrayed in an idealized light.

Through *zangiri-mono*, Mokuami tried to find a way forward for kabuki by reflecting the changing times. However, the emergence of *shinpa* (new school drama)[14] made it more and more difficult for kabuki to stay on the cutting edge of theater. In the end, kabuki artists began looking backward instead of forward, and Mokuami set about editing and compiling the many plays he had already written, endeavoring to establish kabuki as a "classical" performance art.

## The Pros and Cons of Seven-Five

Japanese poetry is traditionally set in patterns of seven and five syllables, and the seven-five meter of Mokuami's spoken lines is one of their most appealing attributes. Take, for example, the famous monologue delivered by Ojō Kichisa after he steals Otose's money and throws her into the river.

*Tsu-ki-mo-o-bo-ro-ni*      *shi-ra-u-o-no*
*Ka-ga-ri-mo-ka-su-mu*      *ha-ru-no-so-ra*
*Tsu-me-te-e-ka-ze-mo*      *ho-ro-yo-i-ni*

*Sannin Kichisa Kuruwa no Hatsugai*

*Ko-ko-ro-mo-chi-yo-ku*  *u-ka-u-ka-to*
*U-ka-re-ga-ra-su-no*  *ta-da-i-chi-wa*
*Ne-gu-ra-e-ka-e-ru*  *ka-wa-ba-ta-de*
*Sa-o-no-shi-zu-ku-ka*  *nu-re-te-de-a-wa*
*O-mo-i-ga-ke-na-ku*  *te-ni-ha-i-ru-hya-ku-ryo-o*
*Ho-n-ni-ko-n-ya-wa*  *se-tsu-bu-n-ka*
*Ni-shi-no-u-mi-yo-ri*  *ka-wa-no-na-ka*
*O-chi-ta-yo-ta-ka-wa*  *ya-ku-o-to-shi*
*Ma-me-da-ku-sa-n-no*  *i-chi-mo-n-no*
*Ze-ni-to-chi-ga-tte*  *ka-ne-tsu-tsu-mi*
*Ko-i-tsa-a-ha-ru-ka-ra*  *e-n-gi-ga-i-i-wa-e*

*The spring sky blurs both the moon*
*And the whitefish fishing fires in mist*
*I'm tipsy; how delightful the cool, wayward wind!*
*A wayward libertine am I, a single crow*
*Returning in solitude to a riverbank roost*
*See how easy!*
*Like droplets running down a fishing pole to wet my hands,*
*Easy profits have come my way*
*An unexpected hundred ryō!*
*Could tonight be winter's end?*
*A "night hawk" (prostitute) fallen in the river*
*Has banished all evil to the Western Sea (hell)*
*Not just a single coin, but a bundle of gold*
*Plentiful as the beans thrown on spring's first day*
*To exorcise demons!*
*Surely this is spring's good luck omen to me!*

Even if the meaning of the passage is somewhat obscure, it has a pleasant lilting quality that's easy on the ears. I suppose many people today have the impression that all kabuki plays are written in seven-five meter, and it's certainly true that, as efforts were made to establish kabuki as a classical art, many scripts were rewritten after Mokuami's day to fit that mold. But if we look at the original works of earlier authors such as Nanboku, the text is not cast in beautiful seven-five verse nearly as often as it is in Mokuami's work. The vast majority of lines found in earlier plays have a realistic tone that's much more akin to daily speech.

Japan's first great playwright Chikamatsu Monzaemon was quite critical of seven-five meter, saying that it resulted in the use of unnecessary grammatical particles and caused dialogue to sound unnatural.[15] Although seven-five meter does have a pleasant lilt, it runs the risk of obscuring crucial content. With what I believe to be remarkable shrewdness, Chikamatsu recognized this danger from a very early date.

Noted translator Matsuoka Kazuko once made an interesting observation about why Shakespeare so often uses blank verse in his plays. She noted that, although it isn't rhymed, blank verse's carefully constructed meter helps actors remember their lines.

The same principle might apply to kabuki with regard to seven-five meter. Mokuami wrote his plays following the principle of "the three kindnesses": kindness to the head of the theater troupe, the actors, and the audience. We can reasonably infer that seven-five meter was a kindness for the actors, helping them to memorize the lines. And that advantage was probably magnified still further by the fact that, amid rapidly changing times, forgetful actors were finding it increasingly difficult to improvise dialogue in a style of speech that was quickly becoming archaic.

Despite the aesthetic appeal of lines cast in seven-five meter, one can't help regret the loss of a sense of realistic content. From Mokuami's time onward, kabuki dialogue definitely ceased to be realistic, and declamation gradually evolved away from ordinary speech toward song.

Listening to early twentieth-century recordings of such great actors as Ichimura Uzaemon XV[16] and Onoe Kikugorō VI,[17] one is struck by how much more realistic their delivery was then than that used by kabuki actors today. The tempo was also surprisingly fast. While *geza* (offstage) music conventionally accompanies dialogue cast in seven-five meter, these earlier actors skillfully manipulated it with their varied pacing so that the content of the words clearly reached the ear. The recordings prove that the actors thoroughly knew the meaning of the text and conveyed it in a way that the audience could understand. This tells us that even in the past half century, kabuki has undergone significant changes.

## The Joy of Audience Participation

The pleasant lilt of seven-five meter often entices audience members to recite the lines for their own enjoyment. Ojō's monologue quoted above, for example, is often recorded and included in modern introductory guides to kabuki. It seems that this impulse to learn and recite lines from kabuki plays goes all the way back to the late seventeenth century, as evidenced by published collections of kabuki dialogue. Apparently it was a popular pastime among fans to imitate the vocal inflections of the actors as well. By the late eighteenth century, publications of this kind had come to be called *Ōmu ishi* ("parrot rocks," so named because they were likened to rock formations that produced clear echoes). When Mokuami was beginning his career, these had become lavish, multi-colored books that included actor portraits. Seven-five meter had permeated the audience and sparked a mode of enjoyment analogous to karaoke today. It can be credited with encouraging audience participation as a form of entertainment, which is another distinctive feature of Japanese performance art.

*Yakusha hyōbanki* (actors' guidebooks) contain precious historical material that I've frequently quoted in this book. Full of drama criticism, they were published almost every year for about 200 years. In the early nineteenth century, the humorist Shikitei Sanba published a parody of these collections titled *Kyakusha Hyōbanki* (Audience Guidebook),[18] which divides kabuki patrons into various categories and offers explanations of each type. At the top of Sanba's list are *hiiki no jōren*, or diehard fans who are devoted to particular actors. I believe this category is relevant as the largest, most mainstream group of kabuki aficionados even today. Next come the *shibai-zuki*, or drama fans, who love to see plays regardless of who the actors are and will attend shows at any theater. Other categories include *migōsha* (discerning viewers who watch with a critical eye); *shibai-tsū* (fans intimately familiar with what goes on backstage); participatory categories like *miburi-zuki* (fans who imitate actors' gestures) and *kowairo-zuki* (fans who imitate actors' voices); and narcissistic *yakusha kidori* (those pretentious enough to think they're actors themselves). Perhaps the strangest type are the *sajiki-hari* (gallery watchers), groups of unsavory men who come not to see the play but to check out the female spectators sitting in the gallery seats.

Sanba's *Audience Guidebook* teaches us that there are many ways to enjoy kabuki. The same holds true today. There's no "correct" way to watch it; people are free to enjoy it any way they choose.

Even so, if we're talking about enjoyment stemming from a deep knowledge of kabuki, I believe it's difficult to learn all there is to know simply by watching the plays and reading books about it. For example, why is the opening of *Sanmon* set at Nanzenji Temple? The answer lies in the peace negotiations that followed Toyotomi Hideyoshi's ill-fated invasion of Korea. Hideyoshi appointed Genpo Reisan, the head priest of Nanzenji, to act as his envoy (called Reizan Kokushi in the play). The choice of locale, then, cannot be fully understood unless one knows the historical facts upon which the author was drawing. Conversely, if one watches kabuki and begins to wonder why something is a certain way, it can be truly delightful to discover things one never knew about Japan before.

In these pages we've looked at 10 famous plays in the current kabuki repertory. Presented in chronological order, they offer a glimpse of what appealed to audiences at the time they premiered and help us to define a distinctly Japanese approach to entertainment. This, too, is one way to enjoy kabuki, and I would be delighted if it can help many more readers enjoy it in ways of their own choosing.

# Notes

### INTRODUCTION

1. Examples include: *kuromaku* (literally, "black curtain," which refers to a behind-the-scenes power broker); *sashigane* (literally, "carpenter's square," but denoting a bamboo pole used in kabuki by black-clad stage assistants to invisibly manipulate butterflies and other flying objects on stage, and referring by extension to a political fixer or mastermind); and *dondengaeshi* (a complete reversal of circumstances or a plot twist). These and many other terms have entered the Japanese lexicon from kabuki, indicating just how powerful its cultural influence has been.

### CHAPTER ONE

1. The *kurumabin* (wheel spoke) hairstyle is one of about 20 different hairstyles used by *tachiyaku* (male) roles. Five large, hardened spikes of hair jut out sharply from either side of the head to create a ferocious appearance that's used exclusively for *aragoto* (bravura) style acting.
2. The oil-based makeup applied in swirling lines and gradated colors to indicate role types is called *kumadori*. Generally

speaking, red denotes vigor, blue indicates malice and wickedness, and black is used for demons and evil ghosts. Sujiguma, which is one of more than 10 conventional kumadori patterns, features dynamic red swirls that start at the outer edges of the eyelids and create a symmetrical pattern up and down the entire face. It symbolizes great physical strength.

3. A *suō* is a crested linen costume worn by low-ranking samurai on ceremonial occasions, consisting of a long-sleeved, light jacket worn with long divided skirts that trail out behind the wearer.

4. Invented by a chanter named Izumi Dayū in the Meireki era (1655–1658), the *Kinpira jōruri* puppet play genre became very popular in Edo in the 1660's. It's named after Sakata no Kinpira the son of Sakata no Kintoki, who is the hero of a number of military tales associated with the legend of Shuten Dōji, the wine-drinking demon of Mt. Ōe.

5. Quoted from *Geijutsu kigyōron* (The Art Entrepreneurship Theory) by Murakami Takashi.

6. The word *kyōgen* (literally, "mad words") typically refers to the medieval comedic plays that developed alongside noh drama during the Muromachi period (1392–1568). However, it can also refer to scripts and performances of kabuki plays. *E-iri kyōgen bon* were illustrated books containing synopses of kabuki hits. More than 200 such books published in Edo, Kyoto, and Osaka are extant today.

7. Yamanaka Heikurō (1642–1724) was a famous Edo actor active primarily during the Genroku period (1688–1704). He was unsurpassed in playing villain roles (both nobles and commoners), as well as vengeful ghosts and demons.

8. For about 200 years beginning in the second half of the seventeenth century until the end of the Edo period, *yakusha hyōbanki* guidebooks were generally published at the beginning of each lunar calendar year. Contributing writers

included Ejima Kiseki, an author of *ukiyozōshi* popular fiction (books of the floating world), and other men of letters who had theater connections.

9. Quoted from the 1715 New Year's edition of *Yakusha Futokoro Zetai* (Intimate Glimpses of Actors at Home).
10. *Sekai* (world) is a technical term used in the kabuki and *jōruri* puppet theaters to indicate the historical era or incident that provides the backdrop for a play. Even when the storyline is essentially the same, a change of "world" will naturally generate variations because the characters will be different. Already by the middle of the eighteenth century, people connected with a new production would gather to determine what world the new play would be based on in a meeting called *sekai sadame* (deciding the world).
11. From an illustration of the play *Banmin Daifuku Chō* (The People's Ledger) found in *Yakusha Futokoro Zetai* (Intimate Glimpses of Actors at Home).
12. *Yakusha Shokugataki* (Actors in Competition).
13. *Yakusha Tanaoroshi* (Inventory of Actors).
14. *Shibai Kinmō Zui* (Encyclopedia of Theater) was written by Shikitei Sanba (1776–1822), the author of such famous comic works as *Ukiyoburo* (The Bathhouse of the Floating World) and *Ukiyodoko* (The Barbershop of the Floating World). Patterned after other encyclopedias of the time but comical in tone, it is an illustrated compendium of kabuki published in 1803 that defines the theater as a "Nation of Plays" and explains play content, performance techniques, actors and audience members by comparing and contrasting them with their counterparts in the real world.
15. *Shitennō Ubuyu no Tamagawa* (The Four Guardian Kings at the Ubuyu and Tama Rivers) was performed in a *kaomise* program at the Tamagawa Theater in Edo in 1818. It presented a highly unusual version of the *Shibaraku* vignette during the second act (the act usually reserved for realistic

stories centered on everyday life) instead of in its customary place at the beginning. Because of the everyday nature of the typical second act, the scenes are set in Ichikawa Danjūrō's home and in a theater restaurant. The act begins with a visitor to Danjūrō's home who brings with him a picture of Danjūrō dressed in his *Shibaraku* costume. When the visitor complains that the Danjūrō he meets at home looks nothing like the Danjūrō depicted onstage, Danjūrō immediately changes into his costume and performs *Shibaraku* at the restaurant.

16. The female version of *Shibaraku* was first performed by the *onnagata* actor Yoshizawa Ayame II in 1745. It was only after a performance of the role by Iwai Hanshirō IV in 1791, however, that this variation came to be performed occasionally by energetic actors. Since then, the content has been more or less fixed, with the female warrior Tomoe Gozen portrayed as the heroine instead of Kamakura Gongorō Kagemasa, and Kabanokaja Noriyori portrayed as the villainous lord instead of Kiyohara no Takehira. Also since Hanshirō IV's time, the implicit aesthetic goal has been to infuse all aspects of the lead role with a ladylike shyness.

17. *Ehon Shibai Nenjū Kagami* (Illustrated Compendium of Annual Theater Practices) provides explanations of all the annual ceremonies related to kabuki that were held from the first performance of the year to the last, as well as costumes and props. Authored by Takamura Chikuri, it contains illustrations by Utagawa Toyokuni I, a woodblock print artist famous for his portraits of actors. Published in 1803, this work is a precious resource for understanding kabuki as it was performed in the late eighteenth century, especially when consulted in conjunction with the encyclopedic *Shibai Kinmō Zui* (see note 14) published the same year.

CHAPTER TWO

1. Yūgiri (1653?–1678) was a courtesan of the early Edo period. She worked at the Ōgiya brothel in the Shimabara district of Kyoto, which transferred her to another establishment it operated in Osaka's Shinmachi district. Her beauty and talent brought her great fame, but she died young. Her contemporary, the popular writer Ihara Saikaku, frequently referred to her in his debut work of fiction *Kōshoku Ichidai Otoko* (The Life of an Amorous Man).
2. Ihara Saikaku (1642–1693) was a writer of *ukiyozōshi* (books of the floating world) and a *haikai* linked-verse poet. Born into an Osaka merchant family, he began his career as a *haikai* poet but turned to prose fiction at the age of 41 with the publication of *Kōshoku Ichidai Otoko*. He went on to write many amorous tales and stories about the lives of townspeople and samurai based on his trenchant observations of human nature. His main works also include *Kōshoku Gonin Onna* (Five Women Who Loved Love), *Kōshoku Ichidai Onna* (The Life of an Amorous Woman), *Shoen Ōkagami* (The Great Mirror of Beauties), *Nippon Eitaigura* (The Eternal Storehouse of Japan), *Seken Munesan'yō* (This Scheming World), *Budō Denraiki* (Transmission of the Martial Arts), *Saikaku Shokoku Banashi* (Saikaku's Tales from the Provinces), and *Honchō Nijū Fukō* (Twenty Cases of Unfilial Children).
3. Sakata Tōjūrō I (1647–1709) was an actor during the Genroku era in western Japan based in Kyoto. In 1678, immediately after the death of the courtesan Yūgiri, his performance of the character Fujiya Izaemon in the play *Yūgiri Nagori no Shōgatsu* (Yūgiri's Farewell New Year) was a huge hit that boosted his popularity. He excelled in *yatsushi-goto*, *nure-goto* (love scenes), and *kuzetsu-goto* (lovers' quarrels fueled

by jealousy). Through clever dialogue, he originated the *wagoto* (gentle) style of acting associated with western Japan, as contrasted with the *aragoto* (bravura) style of Edo.

4. Chikamatsu Monzaemon (1653–1724) was a writer of *jōruri* puppet and kabuki plays. Born to a samurai family that served the Fukui domain, he was raised in Kyoto. He partnered with the chanter Takemoto Gidayū on his first play, *Shusse Kagekiyo* (Kagekiyo Victorious), and continued that collaboration to create many new plays for the puppet theater. His influence was so decisive that anything preceding him is called "old *jōruri*." He also wrote many kabuki plays for Sakata Tōjūrō I, including *Keisei Hotoke no Hara* (The Courtesan on Buddha Plain), which contributed to the full flowering of Genroku kabuki in western Japan. Returning to the puppet theater at the beginning of the eighteenth century, he went on to author many more masterpieces. Famous works include *Sonezaki Shinjū* (The Love Suicides at Sonezaki), *Meido no Hikyaku* (The Courier for Hell), *Shinjū Ten no Amijima* (The Love Suicides of Amijima), and *Kokusen'ya Kassen* (The Battles of Coxinga).

5. *Saikaku Okimiyage* (Saikaku's Parting Gift) was a work published posthumously in 1693. The preface contains the famous death poem: "Moon of the floating world / I have gazed at you / Two years too long." The 15 stories included in this work all depict the vicissitudes of men who were ruined by amorous adventures.

6. Published in 1682, *Kōshoku Ichidai Otoko* (The Life of an Amorous Man) was Saikaku's first work of fiction. It describes the life of Yonosuke, the son of a profligate big spender and a courtesan, who is sexually awakened at age 7 and spends the next 53 years pursuing sensual pleasure. In the end, he makes a final voyage to the legendary Isle of Nyogo, which is inhabited only by women. His debauchery as described by Saikaku is prodigious, including liaisons with 3,742 women and 725 boys.

7. *Nippon Eitaigura* (The Eternal Storehouse of Japan), along with *Seken Munesan'yō* (This Scheming World), is Saikaku's representative work about townspeople. Published in 1688, it comprises 30 short stories that highlight the rise and fall of merchants in Japan's urban areas (primarily Edo, Kyoto, and Osaka) and extol the virtues of the common man.
8. This anecdote is found in the New Year's edition of the magazine *Yakusha Itchō Tsuzumi* (The Drum of an Actor), published in 1702.
9. As the term implies, *ikyōgen* (sitting kyōgen) is performed by an actor who simply sits on stage and tells long stories. Although gestures are used, the performer does not move around on stage.
10. Located stage right, the *geza* area is surrounded by black partitions with black bamboo blinds on a window facing the audience. This is where the *nagauta* singers, three-stringed shamisen players, and *hayashi* (flute and percussion) musicians provide background music for the play.
11. *Nagauta* (long song) is representative of the more melodious song genres that are accompanied by the shamisen. In addition to the thin-necked shamisen, it might also incorporate other instruments, including those borrowed from noh drama (*nōkan* flute, *kotsuzumi* shoulder drum, *ōtsuzumi* hip drum, and *taiko* stick drum), depending on the piece. In general, *nagauta* songs tend to be quite lively and rhythmical.
12. *Bungo-bushi* is a genre of *jōruri* singing invented by Miyakoji Bungo-no-Jō (1660(?)–1740). Charming, gentle, and slightly risqué, it enjoyed tremendous popularity and gave birth to such other genres as *tokiwazu-bushi* and *kiyomoto-bushi*.
13. Known for his skill in dancing, Ichimura Uzaemon IX (1725–1785) was the head of the Ichimura-za, one of the three main kabuki theaters in Edo. He often performed in western Japan during the Hōreki era (1751–1764). In Kyoto he performed a piece about the courtesan Yūgiri titled *Kotobuki Yūgiri Soga*

(Auspicious Encounter of Yūgiri and the Soga Brothers) that featured *bungo-bushi* singing.

14. Nakamura Tomijūrō I (1721–1786) was a leading *onnagata* actor of the An'ei and Temmei eras (1772–1789). Born in Kyoto, trained in Osaka, and given the stage name of Tomijūrō in Edo, he was popular in all three centers of kabuki performance. A handsome and gifted dancer, he gained fame as the original performer of the play *Kyōganoko Musume Dōjōji* (A Maiden at Dōjōji Temple).

15. Segawa Kikunojō III (1751–1810) was a popular and talented *onnagata* actor in Edo during the Bunka and Bunsei eras (1804–1830). Born the second son of Osaka-based choreographer Ichiyama Shichijūrō, he moved to Edo and became an apprentice of Segawa Kikunojō II. He was adopted and granted the name Segawa Kikunoj III in accordance with his teacher's dying request. Enormously popular, he held concurrent positions at two theaters one year, during which he earned the handsome sum of 1,850 ryō. He also served as the head of his troupe, which was unusual for an *onnagata*.

16. Nakamura Utaemon III (1778–1838) was a famous actor in Osaka during the Bunka and Bunsei eras (1804–1830). His versatility ranged from male leads to villains, women's roles, and dance, all characterized by a skillful performance style that earned him overwhelming popularity in Kyoto, Osaka, and Edo. His talents as an all-around kabuki master extended to directing and playwriting.

17. For a more detailed account, see the author's *Shijō "Butai Kanshō" Kuruwa Bunshō* ("Watching a Play" in a Magazine: *Love Letters from the Licensed Quarter*), included in the *Kabuki Sōken* section of the special edition of the journal *Kokubungaku*, Vol. 37, No. 6.

18. Quoted from the New Year's issue of *Yakusha Toshikoshigusa* (Actors' Wheat) published in 1762.

19. Orikuchi Shinobu (1887–1953) was a literary scholar, folklorist, and poet who wrote under the pen name Shaku Chōkū. He was best known as a scholar of the ancient *Man'yōshū* (Collection of Ten Thousand Leaves) poetry collection, producing such works as *Kōyaku Man'yōshū* (Man'yōshū in Colloquial Translation) and *Manyōshū Jiten* (Man'yōshū Dictionary). He was also deeply influenced by the folklorist Yanagita Kunio and pursued folkloric research related to Japanese literature, writing *Kodai Kenkyū* (Study of Ancient Times) on the basis of surveys conducted on the islands of Okinawa, Miyakojima, and Yaeyama. As a literary writer, he published the *tanka* poetry collections *Umi Yama no Aida* (Between the Sea and the Mountains) and *Haru no Kotobure* (Harbinger of Spring); the poetry collection *Kodai Kan'ai Shū* (Collection of Ancient Feelings of Love); and the novel *Shisha no Sho* (The Book of the Dead), among others.
20. *Keisei Hotoke no Hara* (The Courtesan on Buddha Plain) is a play about contested family succession rights set in Echizen (now Fukui Prefecture). Chikamatsu, who was born in Fukui, borrowed his title from the noh play *Hotoke no Hara* (Buddha Plain), which is set in Kaga, not far from Echizen. For the performance in 1987, the script was written by Kinoshita Junji with revision and supplementation by myself; Takechi Tetsuji was the director; and the lead role was played by Nakamura Senjaku (now Sakata Tōjūrō IV). It drew attention as a revival of a play that had not been performed for 290 years.
21. Kinoshita Junji (1914–2000) was a leading playwright and critic in postwar Japan. His representative works include *Hikoichi no Hanashi* (A Story of Hikoichi) and *Yūzuru* (Twilight Crane), which are based on Japanese folktales, and *Ottō to Yobareru Nihonjin* (A Japanese Called Otto), which dealt with the Sorge Incident (about a Russian spy arrested in

Japan during World War II). His *Shigosen no Matsuri* (The Meridian Rite) incorporated performance techniques from the traditional Japanese stage arts of kabuki, noh, and kyōgen and is known as an avant-garde piece that utilized collective declamation.

22. *Kogetsushō* (Moon on the Lake Commentary) is an annotated edition of *The Tale of Genji* in 60 volumes. First published in 1673, it was popular throughout the Edo period and into the Meiji period (1868–1912).
23. Hasegawa Mariko (b. 1952) is an anthropologist and professor at the Graduate University for Advanced Studies. She researches and writes about human behavioral proclivities and sexual selection from the perspective of socio- and evolutionary biology. Her publications include *Kagaku no Me, Kagaku no Kokoro* (Eyes of Science, Heart of Science) and *Dōbutsu no Kōdō to Seitai* (The Behavior and Ecology of Animals).
24. This anecdote is found in *Kengaishū* (Collection Beyond Wisdom), which is included in *Yakusha Banashi* (Discussion of Actors) published in 1776.
25. Found in *Saikaku Okimiyage* (Saikaku's Parting Gift).
26. Found in *Kengaishū* (Collection Beyond Wisdom).

CHAPTER THREE

1. *Sugawara Denju Tenarai Kagami* (Sugawara and the Secrets of Calligraphy) premiered at Takemoto-za in Osaka in 1746. It was written jointly by Takeda Izumo, Namiki Senryū, and Miyoshi Shōraku. The play is based on the story of Sugawara no Michizane (Kan Shōjō), the Minister of the Right, who lost his standing at court and was banished from the capital. It paints his rival, Minister of the Left Fujiwara no Shihei, as a ruthless villain. Triplet brothers were added to the plot to incorporate the sensational news of the birth of triplets

around the time the play was written. The oldest brother, Umeō-maru (Plum), served as Kan Shōjō's personal valet; the second, Matsuō-maru (Pine), served Shihei; and the youngest, Sakura-maru (Cherry), served Prince Tokiyo, the emperor's younger brother. The immediate cause of Kan Shōjō's banishment was a romance between his adopted daughter Kariya and Prince Tokiyo, which was considered taboo because Kariya was a commoner. Sakura-maru feels responsible for the banishment since he was the one who arranged for the lovers to meet. He and his two brothers have a rare reunion at their family home to celebrate the seventieth birthday of their father, but wracked with guilt, Sakura commits ritual suicide at the gathering. The suicide scene, called *Ga no Iwai* (Longevity Celebration), ranks with *Terakoya* as one of the climactic scenes of the full-length play.

2. *Kōyō Gunkan* (Military Exploits of the Takeda Clan) is a treatise on the military tactics employed by the Takeda family, which held sway in Kai Province (now Yamanashi Prefecture) in the fifteenth and sixteenth centuries. It was probably completed in the early seventeenth century by Obata Kagenori, the founder of Kōshū-ryū Gungaku, an academy dedicated to the study of the art of war. Focusing on battles fought by the feudal lord Takeda Shingen and his generals, it was widely read because it went beyond the usual framework of military science to include strategy and mental preparedness.

3. *Ningyō jōruri* is a stage art consisting of *jōruri* style chant, shamisen accompaniment, and puppets. It originated early in the Edo period and reached full flower after Takemoto Gidayū (the originator of *gidayū-bushi* style chanting) established the Takemoto-za in Osaka in 1684, with Chikamatsu Monzaemon writing new plays. These developments also had a strong impact on kabuki. Throughout the Edo period, the genre was known as *ayatsuri jōruri* (manipulated *jōruri*),

and it wasn't until the Meiji period (1868–1912) that the term *ningyō jōruri* came into use. The term *bunraku* that is used today to denote the puppet theater comes from Bunraku-za, established by producer Uemura Bunrakuken in 1805, which remained in operation after rival theaters like Takemoto-za went out of business.

4. Quoted from *Takemoto Toyotake Jōrurifu* (Records of *jōruri* at the Takemoto and Toyotake Theaters).

5. Known as a master of realism and chiaroscuro, the Dutch painter Rembrandt (1606–69) is considered one of the most important artists in the history of Western painting. However, a significant percentage of the 650 paintings attributed to him were actually painted by apprentices who had mastered his techniques. The master and his students are known collectively as the "Rembrandt school."

6. Quoted from *Shimbun Zasshi* (Newpaper Magazine), page 40, published in April 1872 and compiled in *Shimbun Shūsei Meiji Hennenshi Daiikkan* (Newspaper Collection, Meiji Chronicle, Vol. 1).

7. See *Engei Gahō* (Illustrated Journal of Theater), Vol. 23, No. 6.

8. *Nibelungenlied* (The Song of the Nibelungs) is a German epic poem dating to the early thirteenth century. Prince Siegfried of Xanten cleverly helps King Gunther of Burgundy woo and wed Queen Brünhild of Iceland, thereby winning the hand of Gunther's younger sister Kriemhild for himself. Later, Brünhild discovers that she had been tricked into marrying Gunther under false pretenses and orders her vassal Hagen to kill Siegfried in revenge. Siegfried's widow Kriemhild gets remarried to King Etzel of the Huns (Attila the Hun), but seeks to avenge Siegfried's death. A battle ensues between the Burgundians and the Huns, and all are killed. Kriemhild achieves her revenge by cutting off Hagen's head, but loses her own life.

NOTES

9. Max Reinhardt (1873–1943) was an Austrian director known for his fantastical, expressionist style. In 1929 he established the Max Reinhardt Seminar, an acting school in Vienna. He fled to the United States in 1933 when the Nazis came to power in Germany.
10. See Sang-Kyong Lee, *Tōzai Engeki no Deai: Nō, Kabuki no Seiyō e no Eikyō* (The Meeting of East and West: The Influence of Noh and Kabuki on Western Theater), edited by Nishi Kazuyoshi and translated by Tanaka Tokukazu.
11. Nitobe Inazō (1862–1933) was an educator who, in his book *Bushidō: The Soul of Japan* (1899), attempted to link traditional Japanese virtues like honor, courage, and charity to the universal values of Christianity. Originally written in English, the book was later translated into Japanese.
12. Bandō Jusaburō III (1886–1954) was a kabuki actor based in Osaka. He was the third actor to adopt this professional name, which was first used by the late-Edo, early Meiji star who eventually came to be called Nakamura Nakazō IV (1855–1916). Born in Osaka, he worked in Tokyo for a while with the troupe of Ichikawa Sadanji II but returned to Osaka after the Great Kantō Earthquake of 1923. In 1929 he started the Daiichi Gekijo (First Theater), which included performers active in *shinpa* (new school) theater and film. They presented new works by Tanizaki Jun'ichirō and others, but the theater closed after only a year. With his modern sensibilities, Bandō Jusaburō III was particularly skilled at performing new kabuki and in his later years achieved great success with his stage partner Ichikawa Sumizō VI (later called Ichikawa Jukai III).
13. *Shingeki* (new theater) is a distinctive modern type of theater that is neither kabuki nor *shinpa*. It started with the founding of Tsukiji Shōgekijō (Tsukiji Little Theater) in 1924 as a noncommercial theater linked with left-wing causes. *Shingeki* performances were suppressed during World War II but made a comeback in the postwar period, primarily through

the activity of three troupes: Bungaku-za, Haiyū-za, and Gekidan Mingei.
14. The *shingeki* version (with the title written in the *katakana* syllabary instead of the usual Chinese *kanji* characters) was directed by Aoyama Sugisaku and featured Tomoda Kyōsuke as Matsuō and Higashiyama Chieko as Chiiyo.
15. See *Engei Gahō* (Illustrated Journal of Theater), Vol. 23, No. 10.
16. Of unknown authorship, the play is called *Nakamitsu* by the Kanze school of noh but *Manjū* by the Hōshō, Kongō, and Kita schools. In a full, five-play noh program, it would usually be placed fourth. Fourth-category plays, known as "miscellaneous," cover a wide variety of topics that do not fit into any of the other categories, such as tales of mothers separated from their children, jealous women, and minstrel-monks. They tend to be relatively dramatic in nature, focusing on human emotions and interpersonal conflict.
17. *Kōwakamai* is a narrative form that incorporates simple dance movements and is accompanied by drums and flute. After going through many stylistic changes, it became a performance form for three men who take turns singing but are not assigned specific character roles.
18. *Kojōruri* (old *jōruri*) refers to any *jōruri* form that came before *gidayū-bushi*, the chanting style invented by Takemoto Gidayū. *Jōruri* is thought to have originated in the fourteenth century when the love story *Jōruri Hime* (Princess Jōruri), a tale about Minamoto no Yoshitsune, was set to music and chanted. Later, the three-stringed shamisen entered Japan and was added as an accompanying instrument. Various *jōruri* chanting styles emerged, including *kinpira-bushi* and *ōzatsuma-bushi*. *Gidayū-bushi*, which appeared at the end of the seventeenth century, overshadowed rival forms because of its fresh delivery and emotional resonance, so that anything predating it came to be called "old."

19. Premiered in 1681, *Higashiyama-dono Ne no Hi no Asobi* (Collecting Herbs at the Silver Pavilion on the Day of the Rat) features a plot line similar to *Manjū*. A princess who has incurred the wrath of the shogun Ashikaga Yoshimasa is taken in by the feudal lord Hatakeyama Mochikuni. Because of a nefarious plot, Mochikuni is ordered to kill the princess. Cornered by circumstances, he mutters, "In this world of sadness, woe unto them who serve the rulers of the land."
20. *Chūshin Migawari Monogatari* (The Tale of Loyal Self-Sacrifice) premiered in 1689. It's essentially a reworking of *Manjū*, but here again Chikamatsu writes the "Woe unto them" line for the character Wada Tamemune, who is forced to sacrifice his own child.
21. Yanagita Kunio (1875–1962) is the father of Japanese folklore studies. He entered the civil service after graduating from Tokyo Imperial University and also pursued a literary career. He often traveled to give lectures in outlying areas of the country, and this exposure to the realities of rural Japan awakened in him a strong interest in regional research. This led to his founding of the field of folk history, which focuses on folkloric, linguistic, and cognitive transmission that is not dependent on the written word.
22. "Imo no Chikara" (The Power of Women) focuses on the religious power that women exert on the men who surround them. The following passage is relevant to the discussion here: ". . . it seems to me that people have generally become gentler, particularly when it comes to customs pertaining to the care of children. In earlier days, children were left to fend for themselves, so that only those who could survive without care grew up. But such inattentive parents have declined in number. . . ." (From "Imo no Chikara," published in October 1925.)
23. The formal title of *Chimorai* (Seeking Milk) is *Hana to Yuki Koi no Te Kagami* (Flower and Moon: A Tale of Love). Written

by Nishizawa Ippō and Kanazawa Ryūgyoku (Nakamura Utaemon III), it premiered at the Kitagawa no Shibai Theater in Kyoto in March of 1833. Considered a foremost example of kabuki comedy as performed in western Japan, it tells the story of a painter named Kanō Shirōjirō, who is ruined by debauchery and forces himself on his fiancée without realizing who she is. He fosters the resulting child without knowing he's the father, and finally meets and reconciles with his fiancée while seeking milk for the baby.

CHAPTER 4

1. *Yoshitsune Senbonzakura* was first performed at the Takemoto-za in Osaka in 1747.
2. *Kokusen'ya Kassen* tells a rather complicated tale. Tei Shiryū, the grand tutor of the Ming emperor, is banished from China and flees to Bizen in Japan, where as Rō Ikkan he marries a local woman who bears him a son named Watōnai. Hearing that China faces destruction at the hands of the invading Tatars, Rō Ikkan, his wife, and their son Watōnai sail there to help and ask General Kanki, the husband of Rō Ikkan's daughter Kinshōjo, to join forces with them. Kanki agrees to be their ally, but insists that his beloved Kinshōjo be killed, since it would be shameful for the world to think that a great general such as himself was acting only at her behest. Understanding this dilemma, Kinshōjo commits suicide, thereby paving the way for Kanki to join forces with Rō Ikkan. Watōnai is renamed Coxinga and goes to war side-by-side with Kanki and General Go Sankei, who are victorious. They succeed in expelling the Tatar king, enthroning Emperor Eiryaku, and bringing peace to the realm.
3. Satō Tadanobu (1161–1186) was a samurai from Mutsu, a feudal domain in north-central Honshū. Originally a

retainer of Fujiwara no Hidehira, the lord of Hiraizumi, he was ordered by Hidehira to serve Minamoto no Yoshitsune, under whose command he distinguished himself in the Genpei War between the Taira and Minamoto clans. Tadanobu parted from Yoshitsune in Yoshino, after which Yoshitsune made his way to Hiraizumi to evade his brother Yoritomo's troops. Tadanobu hid in Kyoto but was discovered by Yoritomo's forces and forced to commit suicide. He was the younger brother of Satō Tsugunobu, who in the Battle of Yashima died shielding Yoshitsune from an arrow shot by the great archer Taira no Noritsune.

4. The author of the noh play *Tenko* (The Heavenly Drum) is unknown. The play with that title written by Chikamatsu Monzaemon for the *jōruri* puppets premiered at the Takemoto-za in Osaka in 1701.

5. The Heiji Rebellion (1159) was instigated by Minamoto no Yoshitomo and Fujiwara no Nobuyori in an effort to unseat Taira no Kiyomori, who had seized power in league with Fujiwara no Shinzei in the Hogen Rebellion of 1156. The failure of the Heiji Rebellion ushered in a period of absolute ascendency for the Taira clan.

6. *Utsubo-zaru* (The Monkey-Skin Quiver) features a *kyōgen* actor who wears a mask and a monkey suit. The monkey role is often the first role a child actor performs. In the play, a daimyo lord out on a hunt demands that a monkey trainer kill his pet in order to provide a skin for a quiver of arrows. The trainer refuses at first but is finally forced to accede under the daimyo's threats. He prepares to kill his monkey, but its innocent playfulness is so touching that the daimyo relents and allows it to live. The delighted trainer makes the monkey dance, and the play ends with the daimyo merrily dancing along.

7. Comprising 27 volumes, *Konjaku Monogatari Shū* (Tales of Times Now Past) contains over a thousand stories about

ghosts, demons, and other strange creatures. Foxes figure in five tales, including one in which a fox transforms into a woman, and another in which a fox repays a kindness.

8. Shikitei Sanba (1776–1822 ) was a late Edo-period light fiction (*gesaku*) writer who started out as an apprentice to a bookseller and made a living on the side as a pharmacist while pursuing a literary career. He began writing comic fiction at an early age and made his public debut as an author at age 19 with *Tendō Ukiyo no Dezukai* (Emerging Stars on the Heavenly Path of the Floating World). His most famous works include *Ukiyoburo* (The Bathhouse of the Floating World) and *Ukiyodoko* (The Barbershop of the Floating World), both of which vividly portray the quirks and all-too-human emotions of ordinary townsfolk. Known as a theater connoisseur, he also published such works as *Shibai Kinmō Zui* (Encyclopedia of Theater) and *Kyakusha Hyōbanki* (Spectators' Guide).

9. Matsuoka Kazuko (b. 1942) is a translator and theater critic who graduated from the Department of Literature and Culture in English of Tokyo Woman's Christian University. A self-avowed "publicist for Shakespeare," she is currently translating all of Shakespeare's plays. Her books include *Subete no Kisetsu no Sheikusupia* (Shakespeare for All Seasons) and *Sheikusupia "Mono" Gatari* (Shakespeare Speaks of "Things").

10. Originally a puppet play written jointly by Namiki Sōsuke (Senryū), Asada Itchō, Namioka Geiji, and Namiki Shōza, *Ichinotani Futaba Gunki* (A Chronicle of the Battle of Ichinotani) premiered at the Toyotake-za in Osaka in 1751. A dramatization of the Battle of Ichinotani as described in the *Heike Monogatari* (The Tale of the Heike), the third act of this work, *Kumagai Jin'ya* (Kumagai's Encampment), proved especially popular and premiered as an independent kabuki play in 1752. The story is based on the premise that

the young warrior Taira no Atsumori was in fact the illegitimate son of Emperor Goshirakawa. Atsumori's purported enemy, Minamoto no Yoshitsune, thus secretly orders his retainer Kamagai to spare him. The order comes in the form of a poem left near a cherry tree which says, "To cut one branch, one finger must also be cut." The cruel meaning of this verse is that Kumagai must sacrifice his own son so that the emperor's son might live. As in the *Heike Monogatari*, Kumagai kills Atsumori in a battle on Suma Bay, but unlike the original story, the victim is actually Kumagai's son, Kojirō. This scene is called *Dantoku-sen* (Mt. Dantoku) and is particularly effective when Atsumori's riderless white horse gallops away along the shore, having lost its master. In the next scene, *Kumagai Jin'ya* (Kumagai's Encampment), the truth about Kojirō's death is revealed. His mother Sagami is grief-stricken, and Kumagai, pained by the transience of life, becomes a Buddhist monk.

11. In ancient Japan, Buddhist precepts were publicly orated at temples in a style that commoners could easily understand. During the medieval period, this form of declamation was secularized, set to chant, and performed on street corners accompanied by a rattle-like instrument called a *sasara*. This form of public entertainment was called *sekkyō-bushi* (sermon-ballad chanting). By the seventeenth century, shamisen accompaniment had also been added, but in the eighteenth century the form was eclipsed by *gidayū-bushi* and eventually died out.

12. *Ashiya Dōman Ōuchi Kagami* (Sorcerer Ashiya Dōman at the Palace) was originally a puppet play written by Takeda Izumo that premiered at the Takemoto-za in Osaka in 1734. It can be considered a compilation based on the tradition of the famous tale of marriage between a human husband and a fox wife, *Shinoda-zuma* (The Fox Wife of Shinoda). The plot centers on a dispute between Abe no Yasuna and

Ashiya no Dōman over ownership of a book of divination called *Kin'u Gyokuto Shū* (Collection of the Golden Crow [sun] and Jeweled Hare [moon]). Abe no Yasuna marries a princess named Kuzunoha, but she is actually a white fox in disguise who gives birth to the great sorcerer Abe no Seimei. The kabuki premier was staged in 1735 by the Nakamura Tomijūrō troupe in Kyoto. As in the original puppet play, the climax of this popular work is the scene when the fox mother, whose true identity has been revealed, writes a parting poem to her son on a *shōji* screen and returns to the woods of Shinoda.

13. Abe no Seimei (921–1005) learned the arts of divination and astrology from Kamo no Takayuki and his son Kamo no Yasunori and often read the stars and conducted rituals for the court, thereby earning the deep trust of the imperial family and other nobility.

## Chapter 5

1. *Gishi Meimei Den* is a large compendium of stories related to the Akō Incident that consists of three sub-collections: *Hon Den* (Main Accounts), which describe events leading up to the vendetta; *Meimei Den* (Individualized Accounts), which present episodes in the lives of each of the 47 loyal retainers; and *Gai Den* (External Accounts), which treat a broader range of people, including Kira Yoshinaka, the model for the villain Moronō in the play. The collection was so important that it led to a popular saying: "Professional storytellers live off *Gishi* in the winter and ghost stories in the summer."
2. Tōchūken Kumoemon (1873–1916) had a stirring vocal delivery that won the hearts of a generation of listeners in the early twentieth century. Finding it difficult to make headway as an entertainer in his early years, he found himself relegated to distant Kyūshū, where he accepted a young political

activist named Miyazaki Tōten as his student. Through Tōten, Kumoemon gained the support of the Black Ocean Society and completed *Gishiden* (Legend of the Loyal Retainers) in 1903. His *Bushidō Kobu* (Exhortation to Follow the Way of the Samurai) met with success in Kyūshū, leading to further popular triumphs at the Naka-za in Osaka and the Hongyō-za in Tokyo in 1907.

3. I remember seeing *Salaryman Chūshingura* as a child, which was part of the *Company President Series* produced by Toho and starred Morishige Hisaya. Another childhood favorite was the animated children's film *Bow Wow Chūshingura* produced by Toei, which featured a puppy that avenged the death of its mother. These and other rather unusual versions underline just how universal the story had become and how deeply it had penetrated the hearts of the Japanese.

4. *Akō Rōshi* (Forty-Seven Ronin) was broadcast from January through December 1964. Hasegawa Kazuo made his television debut in this series in the role of Ōishi Kuranosuke, and the star power of other actors in the cast contributed to the program's great popularity. Viewer ratings for the vendetta episode exceeded 50%. Ōish's trademark *ono ono gata* (a polite form of the plural pronoun "you") became a popular catchphrase.

5. In 1979, Ezra F. Vogel, a sociology professor and the director of the East Asia Research Center at Harvard University, published *Japan as Number One*, in which he explores the reasons for the Japanese economy's brilliant success and counsels readers to learn from Japan. The book became a worldwide bestseller.

6. Maruya Saiichi (1925–2012) was an author and critic who gained recognition as the co-translator of James Joyce's *Ulysses* published in 1964. In 1968 he won the Akutagawa Prize for his short story collection, *Toshi no Nokori* (The Rest of the Year), setting the stage for his continued success

as a leading writer. Deeply knowledgeable about classical Japanese literature, he published many thought-provoking critical essays, including *Nihon Bungakushi Hayawakari* (Quick Guide to Japanese Literary History). His *Chūshingura to wa Nanika* (What Is *Chūshingura*?) was published in 1984.

7. Yoshinaka's official title was *kōke* (master of ceremonies). He oversaw matters of protocol for the Tokugawa shogunate, including ceremonies and rituals. From the Muromachi period (1333–1568) the office was customarily held by someone from a leading clan who was a direct vassal of the shogun. The Kira family traced its lineage back to the Ashikaga clan (the line of shoguns that governed the Muromachi period) and traditionally held the post of *kōke no kimoiri* (director of *kōke*).

8. *Kanadehon Chūshingura* was written jointly by Takeda Izumo, Miyoshi Shōraku, and Namiki Senryū. It premiered as a puppet play in August 1748 at the Takemoto-za in Osaka. Four months later in December, a kabuki adaptation was presented at the Naka-za, also in Osaka. In February 1749 the kabuki version was produced first by the Morita-za and then in three-way competition with the Nakamura-za and Ichimura-za in Edo.

9. En'ya Hangan (?–1341), whose real name was En'ya Takasada ("Hangan" is a rank title), was a military commander during the turbulent Nanbokuchō period (1334–1392). He served Emperor Go-Daigo first and later Ashikaga Takauji, the founder of the Muromachi shogunate. He was forced to commit suicide because of the slanderous machinations of Kō no Moronō.

10. Kō no Moronō (?–1351) was a military commander during the Nanbokuchō era. He served Ashikaga Takauji and was appointed steward when Takauji established the Muromachi shogunate in 1336. Defeated in a battle fought against

Takauji's younger brother Ashikaga Tadayoshi, he was assassinated as he was returning to the capital.
11. There is a play on words here. The Japanese term for "shallow" is *asai*, which is a component in the name A*sa*no Naganori, the lord of the Akō domain who was the model for the En'ya Hangan character.
12. Takarai Kikaku (1661–1707) was a haiku poet regarded as the leading disciple of Bashō. After Bashō's death, Kikaku's sophisticated, urban style became a potent influence in the world of haiku. He is sometimes portrayed in *Chūshingura*-related plays as a character who witnesses the vendetta.
13. Chikamatsu's *Keisei Mitsu no Kuruma* (Three Courtesan Carriages) premiered in 1703. It depicts a favorite theme in the Edo period: the family squabbles of a daimyo clan. The main focus is on the young lord Nuinosuke, who was betrothed to the daughter of the Yamazaki clan but also had a romantic liaison with a courtesan. An argument in a brothel leads to a murder, and this incident develops in complex ways to the somewhat outlandish point of a vendetta. At the climax, a crowd of spear-bearing men dressed in white storm a mansion and kill their enemy. In the final scene, they form a line with their enemy's head held aloft. The illustrated synopsis of the play quotes the last line as: "Surely this is an admirable example of the way of the warrior." Some scholars detect a hint of the Akō Incident in this work.
14. *Kenkō Hōshi Monomi Guruma* (The Sightseeing Carriage of Priest Kenkō) premiered at the Takemoto-za in Osaka in 1706. Its sequel, *Goban Taiheiki* (Chronicle of Grand Pacification Played on a Chessboard), premiered at the same theater in 1710.
15. The son of a sweets shop proprietor in Osaka, Ki no Kaion (1663–1742) became a Buddhist monk at a young age but later returned to secular life. Active as a *haikai* poet, he began

working at the Toyotake-za as a *jōruri* puppet playwright and became a rival of Chikamatsu Monzaemon, the resident playwright for the Takamoto-za. Ki no Kaion's plays are justly appreciated for their skillful composition.

16. *Onikage Musashi Abumi* (Stirrups of Musashi's Demon Horse) opened at the Toyotake-za in Osaka in 1710 (see Yuda Yoshio's *Kanadehon Chūshingura Seiritsushi* [Formative History of *Kanadehon Chūshingura*]). Earlier the same year, a kabuki play with the same title by Azuma Sanpachi also premiered in Osaka and enjoyed an exceptionally long run.

17. The legendary character Oguri Hangan has been featured in various performing arts such as *sekkyō-bushi*, *jōruri*, and kabuki since medieval times. Banished to Hitachi Province (now Ibaragi Prefecture), he meets and marries the beautiful Terute-hime. But he is poisoned by the treacherous Lord Yokoyama, who is Terute-hime's father and acting military governor of Sagami Province. Hangan's spirit goes to hell, but he's pardoned by hell's overlord, Enma, and allowed to return to the land of the living as a zombie-like creature that cannot see, hear, or speak. Eventually he is reunited with Terute-hime and restored to his former self.

18. Namiki Senryū (1695–1751) (also known as Namiki Sōsuke) was a playwright who wrote both *jōruri* puppet plays and kabuki plays. He is best known for being the co-author of three major works: *Sugawara Denju Tenarai Kagami* (Sugawara and the Secrets of Calligraphy), *Yoshitsune Senbonzakura* (Yoshitsune and the Thousand Cherry Trees), and *Kanadehon Chūshingura* (The Treasury of Loyal Retainers). The Namiki line of playwrights originated with him.

19. *Chūshin Kogane no Tanzaku* (The Golden Cards of Loyal Retainers) premiered in 1732 at the Toyotake-za in Osaka. In this version of the story, Rikiya falls in love with a Shimabara courtesan named Kokonoe, but Kokonoe's birth father is a retainer of Rikiya's enemy, Lord Yokoyama (that is, Kira). For

the sake of his daughter, the father intentionally allows himself to be killed. He dies in a scene in which he describes the layout of Yokoyama's mansion. In this play, the character based on the historical Ōishi Kuranosuke is named Ōgishi Yuranosuke.

20. Published in 1803, *Jippensha Ikku's Chūshingura Okame Hyōban* (A Bystander's Look at *Chūshingura*) contains anecdotes he had gathered during his many years of involvement in the Osaka theater world.

21. The term *takemoto* refers to performers who provide chanted narration in the *takemoto gidayū* style. In puppet plays, the entire story is presented by the chanter, but in kabuki most of the lines are delivered by the actors onstage. The *takemoto* in this case chants the narrated sections, as well as parts of the dialogue that are set to music.

22. *Kagamiyama Kokyō no Nishikie* (The Color Prints of Kagamiyama), often simply called *Kagamiyama*, is a puppet play written by Yō Yōtai. It premiered in 1782 at the Satsuma Geki-za in Edo. The kabuki version premiered in 1873 at the Morita-za in Edo. The play embellishes on a true story about Omichi, a concubine of Governor Matsudaira of the Suō domain, who mistakenly wore the sandals of a lady-in-waiting. The lady-in-waiting humiliated Omichi for her error, and Omichi committed suicide. Her servant Osatsu then took revenge by stabbing the lady-in-waiting to death.

23. Nakamura Nakazō I (1736–1790) was born the son of a masterless samurai. He started his acting career as a low-ranking actor but worked his way up to stardom through the power of his acting style. The character Sadakurō was his signature role, but he was also a famous dancer in such roles as Sekibē in the dance drama *Seki no To* (Love Story at the Snow-Covered Barrier, see chapter 8). Matsui Kesako's historical novel *Nakazō Kyōran* (Nakazō's Frenzy) depicts the life and times of this actor.

24. Onoe Kikugorō V (1844–1903) was a leading actor of the Meiji period (1868–1912). He became the head of the Ichimura-za troupe at age 8 under the name Ichimura Uzaemon XIII. When he was 18 he premiered the role of Benten Kozō, which became his lifelong signature role. He changed his name to Onoe Kikugorō V in the Meiji period and, along with Ichikawa Danjūrō IX, created a golden era of kabuki known as the "Dan-Kiku Age." Though capable of brilliantly performing the full range of historical plays, domestic plays, and dance dramas, he was most often cast in domestic dramas. Known for assiduously crafting his art and engaging in research, he actively developed new kabuki works that incorporated the new mores of the Meiji era.
25. Sawamura Sōjūrō I (1685–1756) was a leading kabuki actor who started out on the touring circuit and assumed the name of Sōjūrō when he moved to Edo from western Japan. Using the soft *wagoto* style popular in Kyoto and Osaka to good effect, he developed a distinctive artistic style and achieved a popularity in Edo comparable to that of Ichikawa Danjūrō II.
26. *Ōyakazu Shijūshichi Hon* (Launching of 47 Great Arrows) premiered in June 1747 in Kyoto. The incorporation of Yuranosuke's entrance scene into Act VII of *Kanadehon Chūshingura* is noted in several critical works of the time.
27. Many people believed that a pilgrimage to Ise in the year following the renewed installation of the deity at the Ise Shrine brought good fortune. When *Chūshingura* was performed in Edo, the travel scene in Act VIII was often altered to include accompanying music sung in the *tokiwazu-bushi* or *kiyomoto-bushi* styles. One of the versions created in this way was called the *Okage Mairi* (Pilgrimage to Ise) travel scene. First performed at the Namakmura-za in Edo in 1830, it features a lively pilgrimage dance performed while Tonase and Konami are on the road.

28. Chikamatsu Hanji (1725–1783) was apprenticed to Takeda Izumo II and became a resident writer for the Takemoto-za. It's said that he adopted the family name "Chikamatsu" because of his admiration for Chikamatsu Monzaemon, who was a close friend of his father, the Confucianist Hozumi Ikan. Hanji authored many fine works at a time when the *jōruri* puppet genre was in eclipse. He was particularly adept at writing historical plays but also penned the vendetta play *Igagoe Dōchū Sugoroku* (Revenge at Igagoe) and the domestic drama *Shinpan Utazaimon* (The Love of Osome and Hisamatsu), both of which were masterpieces often performed on the kabuki stage. Hanji was considered unrivaled in the grand scale and intricate plots of his plays.

29. *Honchō Nijūshi Kō* (Twenty-four Models of Japanese Filial Piety) was first performed as a puppet play in January 1766 at the Takemoto-za in Osaka. It premiered as a kabuki play in May of that year at the Naka no Shibai Theater, also in Osaka. Set against the backdrop of war between the daimyo lords Takeda Shingen and Uesugi Kenshin, the play is composed of five acts, of which the scenes *Jushukō* (Jushukō Incense) and *Okuniwa* (Inner Garden) in Act IV of the kabuki version are still popular today. In *Jushukō* , Princess Yaegaki-hime of the Uesugi clan is betrothed to Takeda Katsuyori, but she learns that Katsuyori has been killed, so she burns incense before his image as a memorial offering. However, it was really an imposter of Katsuyori who died, and the real Katsuyori has infiltrated the Uesugi mansion in the company of the imposter's lover, Nureginu. Seeing the disguised Katsuyori and realizing that he looks just like the image on her altar, Yaegaki-hime urges Nureginu to steal a helmet that is a family heirloom of the Takeda clan. Meanwhile, Uesugi Kenshin realizes that Katsuyori is still alive and tries to assassinate him. Yaegaki-hime wants to

save her beloved Katsuyori and discovers that the heirloom helmet gives her magical powers.
30. *Imoseyama Onna Teikin* (An Example of Noble Womanhood) premiered as a puppet play in January 1771 at the Takemoto-za in Osaka and as a kabuki play in August of that year at the Naka no Shibai Theater, also in Osaka. Focusing on the conflict between Soga no Iruka, who seeks to usurp the imperial throne, and Fujiwara Kamatari, the play unfolds on a large scale involving legends from the ancient Yamato region of Japan. In the kabuki version, frequently acted scenes include: the *Yoshinogawa* (Yoshino River) scene of Act III, where Iruka causes young lovers to die in a Japanese version of *Romeo and Juliet*; The *Koi no Odamaki* (Love's Columbine) travel scene in Act IV, a danced depiction of the love triangle between Kamatari's son, Iruka's younger sister, and Omiwa, a girl from the provinces; and the *Mikasayama Goten* (Palace of Mikasa Mountain) scene that immediately follows, in which Omiwa is sacrificed in order to destroy Iruka.

## Chapter 6

1. In 1811, sixty-five years after the premiere of *Natsu Matsuri*, a play called *Nazo no Obi Chotto Tokubē* was performed with the character Issun Tokubē as the protagonist. Authored jointly by Tsuruya Nanboku IV and Fukumori Kyūsuke, the play was based on a true incident that occurred in Edo.
2. Kataoka Nizaemon I was almost exactly the same age as Chikamatsu Monzaemon. He started his career as a shamisen player but moved to Kyoto in his mid-thirties, at which time he adopted the name Nizaemon. Later he headed a kabuki troupe for many years in Osaka. Famous for his large frame and piercing eyes, he was nicknamed the "Boss of the Villains."

3. One of the earliest examples of this is *Namazegawa no Amagoroshi* (Nun's Murder at Namazegawa River), which premiered at the Ōnishi Shibai Theater in Osaka in 1684. It was based on a historical incident in which a pregnant nun was murdered by a monk.
4. Anekawa Shinshirō I (1685–1749) was an actor in a touring troupe in his youth and began working for the Daishibai Theater in Osaka in his late 20s. Though not very tall, he was surprisingly adept at playing chivalrous commoner roles. Just as Sakata Tōjūrō in the Genroku era established the paper kimono as a symbol of the down-and-out playboy, Shinshirō established the *nagezukin* squared-off hood as the trademark image for the Kurofune character.
5. *Yakusha Ukeburumai*, published in the third month of 1723.
6. Ichikawa Kon's take on the *Chūhingura* story, based on a novel by Ikemiya Shōichirō with the same Japanese title, came out in 1994 with Nishimura Kō in the role of Kira Yoshinaka. In a departure from usual treatments, it depicts the initial assault in Edo Castle largely from the perspective of the Yonezawa domain.
7. *Yakusha Wakaebisu*, published in 1721.
8. Chikamatsu's puppet play *Sonezaki Shinjū* (The Love Suicides at Sonezaki) premiered at the Takemoto-za in Osaka in 1703. It depicts the love between Tokubē, a clerk at the Hiranoya soy sauce shop, and his betrothed Ohatsu, a prostitute at the Tenmaya brothel. The shop proprietor (and Tokubē's uncle) wants the hard-working Tokubē to marry his daughter and forces him to accept a dowry payment. Tokubē tries to refuse the proposal and intends to return the money, but his good friend Kuheiji comes to him begging for a loan, and Tokubē complies. Kuheiji not only fails to return the money but slanders Tokubē and attacks him in the precincts of the Ikutama Shrine. That night, Tokubē visits Ohatsu and

tells her that, since he can't return the dowry and has been shamed in public, he is determined to commit suicide as the only way to restore his honor. Ohatsu sympathizes with him and decides to join Tokubē in death. The couple steal away in the dead of night and commit double suicide in the woods of Sonezaki.

9. The term *dorobune* originally referred to a box used by plasterers to mix wall clay. In the early years of kabuki, the mud box was installed in an open space created by taking out one of the front-row box seats. Now it's placed on the stage itself.

10. *Mizu karakuri*, also called *mizugei* (water art), included acrobatic stunts and magic tricks that involved the use of water. These arts evolved from *Takemoto karakuri shibai* (Takemoto magic shows), which were simple skits dating from the early Edo period (1603–1868) performed with dolls and toy animals skillfully crafted to spout water in various ways.

11. *Ise Ondo Koi no Netaba* (The Vengeful Sword at Ise), by Chikamatsu Tokuzō (1751 or 1752–1810), is usually simply called *Ise Ondo*. A play in four acts, it premiered at the Kado no Shibai Theater in 1796. The third act, titled *Aburaya* (The Aburaya Brothel), culminates in horrifying bloodshed and is often performed as an independent piece. A low-ranking shrine official from Ise named Fukuoka Mitsugi has been searching for the valuable but cursed Shimosaka sword on behalf of Imada Manjirō, the son of Mitsugi's benefactor. Although he finally obtains the sword, he must still find its certificate of authenticity to complete his mission. Mitsugi goes to visit his lover Okon, a prostitute who works at Aburaya in Furuichi. She keeps him waiting, and when she finally appears she humiliates him in front of other guests by telling him she doesn't love him anymore. Mitsugi doesn't know that Okon's behavior is all an act so that she can get the certificate back from a guest whom she knows has it

in his possession. Enraged by Okon's behavior, Mitsugi unsheathes the cursed Shimosaka sword and a bloodbath ensues.
12. Ruth Benedict (1887–1948) was an American cultural anthropologist who authored *The Chrysanthemum and the Sword* in 1946, immediately after World War II. That book was the most systematic and thoughtful study of the Japanese and their culture to be written by a Western author up to that time. In it, she observes that Japan has a "culture of shame" in which people "take no account of internal sanctions for proper behavior" and place emphasis on "the importance of shame rather than on the importance of guilt."
13. See Inui Hiromi's *Naniwa Osaka Kikuyamachi*.
14. *Kiwametsuki Banzui Chōbē* (The Last Days of Chōbē of Banzui), popularly known as *Yudono no Chōbē* (Chōbē in the Bath), by Kawatake Mokuami premiered at the Haruki-za in Tokyo in 1881. It focuses on the bad blood between Shiratsuka-gumi, a group of shogunal vassals led by Mizuno Jurōzaemon, and a band of townsmen led by Banzuiin Chōbē. One day, one of Jurōzaemon's retainers rudely interrupts the performance of a play Chōbē is watching. Chōbē confronts the rowdy samurai and sees him off, but this action draws the ire of Jurōzaemon. Intent on revenge, Jurōzaemon invites Chōbē to dinner and Chōbē, knowing it's a trap and ignoring the warnings of his underlings and apprentices, accepts the invitation and departs after bidding his wife and son a final farewell. At Jurōzaemon's banquet, a servant intentionally spills saké on Chōbē's kimono and Chōbē is urged to take a bath and change his clothes. Vulnerable in the bath without clothes or weapons, he's beset by a host of Jurōzaemon's henchmen. Though he fights them off valiantly, he's ultimately speared to death by Jurōzaemon himself.

15. I define "homosocial" as an ethos prevailing among closed social groups such as student athletic teams that places heavy emphasis on strong male bonds.

## Chapter 7

1. Authored by Matsuya Raisuke and Namiki Eisuke, *Miyoshi Chōkei Sato no Agemaki* premiered at the Ōnishi Shibai Theater in Osaka in 1742. The title role was played to popular acclaim by Nakayama Shinkurō I, who excelled in portraying warm, open-hearted characters. The historical Miyoshi Chōkei was a general who lived during the Sengoku period (1467–1603) and expelled the twelfth Ashikaga shogun, Yoshiharu, from the capital city of Kyoto. Matsunaga Hisahide attacked the thirteenth Ashikaga shogun, Yoshiteru, and forced him to commit suicide.
2. Akamatsu Mitsusuke (1381–1441) was a general who bore a grudge against the Ashikaga shoguns. He invited the sixth shogun, Yoshinori, to his manor and murdered him there. Assailed in retribution by shogunal forces, he was forced to commit suicide.
3. Kabuki author Namiki Gohei (1747–1808) was born in Doshōmachi, Osaka. After apprenticing with Namiki Shōza, he began working at age 23 as a resident writer for the Hama Shibai Theater. He won acclaim for his masterpiece *Kinmon Gosan no Kiri*, moved to Edo in 1794, and authored another popular hit there called *Godairiki Koi no Fūjime* (Five Great Powers: The Seal of Love). Gohei died in Edo at age 62.
4. Namiki Gohei's *Sanmon Gosan no Kiri* premiered at the Kado no Shibai Theater in Osaka in 1778. Its original title was *Kinmon Gosan no Kiri*, but this was changed to the current title when the play premiered in Edo in 1800. The play is commonly referred to by the shortened name *Sanmon*.

5. Namiki Shōza (1730–1773) was born into a family that owned a theater/teahouse in Dōtonbori, Osaka. At age 19 he completed his first play, *Kajiya no Musume Teoi no Uwasa*. He became a disciple of the puppet playwright Namiki Senryū at age 20 and assumed the professional name Namiki Shōza, by which he's now known. After Senryū's death, Shōza returned to kabuki in 1753 and wrote some 90 kabuki plays over the next 20 years. His *Yadonashi Danshichi Shigure no Karakasa* (Homeless Danshichi in a Drizzle with His Paper Umbrella), in which the author himself is one of the characters, is still performed today.
6. Ishikawa Goemon was a thief who lived in the late sixteenth century. Although his birth and death dates are unknown, he's believed to have been the thief who was boiled in a pot at Sanjō-Kawaramachi in Kyoto in the eight month of 1594.
7. Toyotomi Hideyoshi's nephew and adopted heir Toyotomi Hidetsugu (1568–1595) succeeded Hideyoshi as imperial regent, but then Hideyoshi had a son (Hideyori) who became his rival. Desperate to retain his position, Hidetsugu started killing people indiscriminately and was finally forced to commit ritual suicide at Hideyoshi's order.
8. Huizong (1082–1135) was the eighth emperor of China's Northern Song dynasty (960–1127). Though an incompetent ruler whose policies weakened the state, he was a superb poet and artist famous for perfecting the Song Academy Style of painting, which was noted for its delicate and highly detailed depictions of flowers and birds. Paintings in that style were highly prized by the Japanese from an early date.
9. In 1582, Akechi Mitsuhide was defeated by Hideyoshi in the Battle of Yamazaki, ending his extremely brief rule as the sovereign of Japan.
10. Onoe Kikugorō I (1717–1783) was born in Kyoto. He apprenticed with Onoe Samon and went from playing young men's

roles to women's roles. In 1742 he shared the stage in a production of *Narukami* with Ichikawa Danjūrō II, who was a guest performer in Osaka at the time. That association later brought Kikugorō to Edo, where he prospered as a versatile actor. Roles he played included Ōboshi Yuranosuke in *Chūshingura*.

11. See *Yakusha Ōyakazu*, published in the fifth month of 1778.
12. Ichikawa Danzō (1788–1845) was a talented actor who could play almost any role, with the exception perhaps of young princesses and daughters. He preferred realistic costumes and had a low-key acting style that earned him the sobriquet, *Shibudan* (Understated Dan).
13. See the New Year edition of *Yakusha Chūshigura*, published in 1827.
14. See the New Year edition of *Yakusha Genkindana*, published in 1835.
15. For six years starting in 1588, Toyotomi Hideyoshi undertook a project to construct a huge Buddha statue measuring 18 meters high (the Great Buddha at Tōdaiji Temple in Nara is 15 meters high) in the foothills of Kyoto's Higashiyama, as well as a hall to enclose it. Called the Great Buddha of Hōkōji Temple, it was destroyed in a large earthquake in 1596, just before it was to be consecrated.
16. In contrast to the square *bun mawashi*, Shōza's revolving stage spun like a top around an axle set in the stage basement. The circular revolving portion covered the entire stage area and turned above the stage floor. Soon after, the stage boards were cut in the shape of a circle so that the stage itself could be revolved by stage hands turning the axle below. This is the same basic design used today.
17. *Keisei Ama no Hagoromo* (A Courtesan and Heaven's Feathered Robe) premiered at the Ōnishi Shibai Theater in Osaka in 1753. A sedition play, it depicts a descendent of Ashikaga Yoshimi named Kitagawa Sōemon joining forces with a descendent of Akamatsu Mitsusuke named Akamatsu

Shirō to overthrow the regime of Ashikaga Yoshihisa. The name "Kitagawa Sōemon" was taken from a talisman that was used to ward off an epidemic at around the time of the premiere in Osaka. The talisman also contained nonsense syllables (*ki no ni no ya no ha no mo no*) that were used by the two conspirators in the play as a secret password. In the final scene, Sōemon, one of his retainers, and the retainer's wife commit suicide on the second floor, and their blood trickles down to the first floor, where it's drunk by an Ashikaga princess whose illness is thereby cured. The three people upstairs plus four people downstairs (the princess, Akamatsu Shirō, a samurai lord loyal to the shogun named Hosokawa Katsumoto, and one of Katsumoto's retainers) are all revealed to the audience simultaneously as they are raised on trap lifts.

18. *Sanjikkoku Yofune no Hajimari* (Thirty Bushels of Rice and the Night Boat's Beginning) premiered in 1758 at the Kado no Shibai Theater in Osaka. Set against the backdrop of flood control operations on the Yodogawa River, it depicts an attack by and ritual suicide of a samurai named Hanamitsu Zaemon, and the travails of his retainer and his family until they avenge their lord. The high point of the play is the revolving stage scene when the enemy is struck down. The villain Kawaura Riuken is an evil recasting of the historical riparian engineer Kawamura Zuiken, who was famous for developing new channels for the Yodogawa River and excavating the Ajigawa River. The character's "true" identity is Saitō Kuranosuke, a retainer of Akechi Mitsuhide.

19. *Kuwanaya Tokuzō Irifune Monogatari* (The Tale of Kuwanaya Tokuzō's Incoming Ship) premiered at the Naka no Shibai Theater in Osaka in 1770. The plot combines: the story of the bold sailor Kuwanaya Tokuzō, who routs the giant Dainyūdō in a clash at sea; and a succession dispute in the Sanuki Takamaru clan that involves the worship of Konpira, the guardian deity of seafaring.

CHAPTER 8

1. Motoori Uchitō (1792–1855) was born in Nagoya and later served the Tokugawa clan in Kishū (a domain spanning present-day Wakayama and southern Mie Prefectures). He compiled *Kii Zoku Fudoki* (Continuation of Ancient Records of Kishū).
2. See Orikuchi's essay, *Mai to Odori to* (*Mai* and *Odori*).
3. Kūya Shōnin (903–972) was a Buddhist ascetic who traveled throughout Japan reciting the Pure Land mantra *namu Amida Butsu* (Hail to Amida Buddha). He also engaged in civil engineering projects and contributed to the construction of Buddhist images and temples. His success in propagating the Pure Land teachings earned him the popular names Ichi no Hijiri (Holy Man of the Marketplace) and Amida Hijiri (Holy Man of Amida Buddha). Kūya reputedly beat a gong and danced while reciting the mantra as a means of attracting crowds and winning converts.
4. Ippen Shōnin (1239–1289) became a Buddhist monk as a child. After receiving temple training, he went to Kumano on a prayer retreat and experienced a mystical vision that conferred upon him the name Ippen (literally, "all at once"), after which he traveled throughout Japan distributing prayer tablets. Because he spent his life wandering without affiliation to any temple, he was popularly known as Sute Hijiri (Discarded Holy Man) and Yugyō Shōnin (Wandering Holy Man). Taking his cue from Kūya, he began performing *odori nenbutsu* during a visit to Shinano (in present-day Nagano Prefecture and part of Gifu Prefecture) and continued the practice in his travels to other regions.
5. This song and dance genre became popular late in the twelfth century. The term *shirabyōshi* refers both to the genre and to the women who performed it. According to the *Tale of the Heike*, the form was invented during the reign of Emperor Toba (1103–1156) by two female performers: Shima no Senzai

and Waka no Mai. Beautiful *shirabyōshi* dancers figure in many tales from that era, including Taira no Kiyomori's lover Giō and Minamoto no Yoshitsune's lover Shizuka Gozen.

6. Published in the United States in 1894, *Glimpses of Unfamiliar Japan* was Hearn's first book of observations about his adopted country. Containing his intense impressions of Japan as a Far Eastern nation, it includes a detailed account of his first sensations on his first day: "Elfish everything seems; for everything as well as everybody is small, and queer, and mysterious."
7. Lafcadio Hearn, *Glimpses of Unfamiliar Japan*.
8. Alpha waves are known to be generated in greater quantities when the subject is relaxed, with eyes closed.
9. *Kabuki Jishi* was published in five volumes in Kyoto in 1762. It covers a wide variety of topics, including kabuki's origins, records of plays, annual ceremonies, actors who performed from the 1620s through the 1750s, and notes on authors.
10. Hayashi Razan (1583–1657) was born in Kyoto. As a young man he lent his talents to Tokugawa Ieyasu, the founder of the Tokugawa shogunate. He went on to serve four generations of shoguns, acting as a consultant in the formulation of various Confucian systems and ceremonies. His comments on kabuki are found in Book 56 in the Miscellaneous section of *Hayashi Razan Bunshū* (Collected Documents of Hayashi Razan). He writes: "Women dress as men, and men as women; women cut their hair like men and carry swords at their sides; they engage in vulgar speech, ill-mannered dance, raucous lewdness and noisy confusion; they croak like frogs and chirp like cicadas; men and women mix together singing and dancing; this is the state of kabuki today."
11. *Kabuki sōshi* with titles such as *Okuni Kabuki* (Okuni's Kabuki) were hand-written pamphlets with colorful pictures that accompanied text describing kabuki in its early days.

12. Popular in the sixteenth and seventeenth centuries, *rakuchū rakugai-zu* were usually configured as a pair of folding screens with six panels each. In addition to aerial street views of buildings, they featured detailed pictures of people, making them valuable as historical materials for understanding the manners and customs of the times.
13. Nagoya Sanza (also called Nagoya Sanzaburō) (?–1603) was a military commander in the late Sengoku period famous for his extraordinary skill with a spear. A very handsome man, he was also a playboy noted for his "kabuki" (unorthodox) fashion. Because Okuni summoned his spirit onstage, a legend arose that she was his lover.
14. Mizuki Tatsunosuke (1673–1745) was a top *onnagata* actor in Kyoto and Osaka during the Genroku era. A skilled dancer, he introduced many innovations, such as dancing with a spear and making seven quick costume changes, that brought him popular success. Recognized as a skillful actor as well, he was considered the equal of Yoshizawa Ayame I, the most celebrated *onnagata* actor of the time.
15. Based on the noh play *Dōjōji* (see Note 20 below), *Kyōganoko Musume Dōjōji* (A Maiden at Dōjōji Temple) premiered at the Nakamura-za in Edo in 1753. A *shirabyōshi* dancer (see Note 5 above) appears at a dedication ceremony for a bell newly installed at Dōjōji Temple. During her dance, she suddenly leaps up into the bell, where she's transformed into a giant serpent. Although the kabuki version retains plot elements from the original play, they have been drastically altered to highlight the *onnagata* actor's challenging solo dance, which features many quick costume changes, expresses varied facets of love, and takes nearly an hour to perform.
16. The survey results are found in *Hikaku Engeki Gaku* (Comparative Theater Studies) by Kawatake Toshio.
17. Nakamura Utaemon VI (1917–2001) was a leading kabuki actor in the postwar era. Born the second son of Nakamura

Utaemon V, he had several stage names (Kotarō, Fukusuke, and Shikan) before assuming the name Nakamura Utaemon VI at a naming ceremony held in the reconstructed Kabuki-za in Tokyo in 1951. Devoting his whole life to his acting career, he was a pillar of the kabuki world and delivered sterling performances of difficult princess and courtesan roles, achieving the very pinnacle of *onnagata* art.

18. Onoe Baikō VII (1915–1995) was the adopted son of Onoe Kikugorō VI and assumed his stage name in 1948. A leading *onnagata* actor of the postwar period, he was considered the equal of Nakamura Utaemon VII. With his supple and refreshing acting style, he excelled in domestic dramas and actively promoted new play development, including *Genji Monogatari* (The Tale of Genji).

19. Sadojima Chōgorō (1700–1757) was a kabuki actor active in Kyoto and Osaka. Although he specialized in male roles, he was also known for his dancing skill. *Shosa no Hiden* (Secret Teachings of Dance) is included in *Sadojima Nikki* (Sadojima Diary), which appears in *Yakusha Banashi* (Discussion of Actors) published in 1776.

20. The legend of Kiyohime, her spurned love for Anchin, and her burning of the bell with Anchin inside was passed down in the Kishū domain. Another tale picks up the story some 400 years later, when a new bell is being dedicated to replace the burned one at Dōjōji Temple. In that sequel, the ghost of Kiyohime appears as a *shirabyōshi* dancer, transforms into a monster serpent, and brings the bell crashing down. The noh play is based on this second story. It is a demanding play to perform, with highlights that include a *ranbyōshi* (erratic rhythm) section featuring tension-filled interaction between the *shite* (main actor) and *kotsuzumi* (shoulder drum) drummer, and the *kane-iri* (bell entry) scene, in which the *shite* jumps up into the bell as it comes crashing down.

21. *Tokiwazu* is one type of *jōruri* narrative music used in kabuki. It developed out of an earlier musical style called *bungo-bushi* in the mid-eighteenth century and flourished during the heyday of kabuki in Edo. Known for its superb balancing of narrated sections and song as well as its natural voice production, it became an indispensable element in kabuki dance accompaniment. Representative *tokiwazu* pieces include *Seki no To* (Love Story at the Snow-Covered Barrier), *Modori Kago* (The Returning Palanquin), and *Masakado*.
22. *Kiyomoto* is a type of *jōruri* narrative music that developed out of *bungo-bushi* in early nineteenth-century Edo. Though essentially a narrative form, it was heavily influenced by the more lyrical *nagauta* song genre and features high-pitched vocalizing with unrestrained melodic embellishment. Representative pieces include *Yasuna*, *Kasane*, and *Kisen*.
23. Plays that originated in the puppet theater and were adapted to the kabuki stage are called *maruhon-mono*, which refers to the bound scripts (*maruhon*) used by the *gidayū* chanters. Such plays can also be called *gidayū kyōgen* or *maruhon kabuki*. They feature chanted narrative in the *takemoto* style.
24. Segawa Kikunojō I (1693–1749) was an *onnagata* actor who excelled in dance and enjoyed great success with his kabuki dance adaptations of noh plays, such as *Dōjōji* and *Shakkyō*. He maintained his tremendous popularity after moving from western Japan to Edo, a triumph that earned him the sobriquet, "Foremost *Onnagata* of the Three Capitals" (that is, Kyoto, Osaka, and Edo). He also authored *Onnagata Hiden* (Secret Teachings of *Onnagata* Acting).
25. The full name of this piece is *Shunkyō Kagami-jishi* (The Mirror Lion's Enjoyment of Spring). It was premiered in 1893 by Ichikawa Danjūrō IX at the Kabuki-za in Tokyo. Set in the inner palace of Edo Castle at a rice-cake cutting ceremony marking the New Year, the first half features a young serving woman named Yayoi who performs a series of dances,

first with just her hands, then while holding a fan. She picks up a lion's mask set on an altar which, as if possessed by a spirit, begins chasing butterflies and drags Yayoi off behind the stage curtain. A dance interlude follows performed by two butterfly spirits, after which the second half of the piece begins, featuring the spirit of a *shishi* lion wearing a long white wig. Part of the piece's appeal is the contrast between the girlish dance of the first half and the dynamic lion dance in the second half, both of which are performed by the same dancer. The lively shaking and spinning of the lion's wig is another favorite highlight.

26. The kabuki version of *Ren-jishi* premiered in 1872 at the Nakamura-za in Tokyo. A variant of the *shakkyō-mono* motif, it draws on the parable of the parent lion throwing its child off the bridge into the gorge below as a challenge for the cub. In the first half, two actors dance with lion hand puppets; in the second, parent and child lions dance, climaxing with synchronized wig spinning.

27. The main actor in a noh play is called the *shite* (pronounced "shtay"). In two-act noh plays, the main actor is called *mae-jite* in the first act and *nochi-jite* in the second act. Usually the same actor performs both roles, with an offstage costume change in between.

28. After achieving success as an *onnagata* actor in western Japan, Ogino Sawanojō (1656–1704) moved to Edo, where he worked with Ichikawa Danjūrō I.

29. *Kathakali* is a classical dance form that developed primarily in the South Indian state of Kerala. A narrative form that uses such epic Sanskrit poems as the *Ramayana* and *Mahabharata* as its source material, it is known for its delicate hand gestures and expressive power achieved through partial muscle movement.

30. Tachibana no Hayanari (?–842) was an early Heian author and government official who plotted a rebellion immediately

after the death of Emperor Saga. He was banished to Izu, where he grew ill and died in exile.

31. Originally, the Seal of Kangō served as certification issued to trade ships by Ming China from the end of the fourteenth century to the early sixteenth century indicating that they were engaged in officially sanctioned international trade. In this play, however, it is treated as a sacred treasure that confers political authority on its owner.

32. Made of wood or bamboo, *wappu* insignia tablets bear a written character or other mark. They are broken in half, with each half going to a different person for identification purposes.

33. Little is known about the historical Ono no Komachi, but she was reputedly an astonishingly beautiful woman. She figures in local legends throughout Japan and has been the subject of many performance pieces and literary works. In the Preface of the *Kokin Wakashū*, her poetry is likened to a "beautiful woman suffering from an illness."

34. Yoshimine no Munesada (816–890) is better known as the Buddhist priest and poet Henjō. The grandson of Emperor Kanmu, he served Emperor Ninmyō (see Note 37 below) until the latter's death, at which time he entered the priesthood. After completing his Buddhist training, Henjō built the temple Kazan Gankei-ji, became the head of the temple Unrin'in in Murasakino, and was eventually elevated to the rank of high priest in 885. He was also called Kazan Sōjō, or "High Priest of Kazan."

35. Ōtomo no Kuronushi's dates of birth and death are unknown, but it's believed that he was from Ōtomo Village in the province of Ōmi. His poetry appears in the *Kokin Wakashū* and other poetry anthologies.

36. The Six Immortal Poets (*rokkasen*) are identified by Ki no Tsurayuki, the author of the Preface of the *Kokin Wakashū*, as being poets "whose names have become well-known in recent times." They include Henjō, Ariwara no Narihira,

Fun'ya no Yasuhide, Priest Kisen, Ono no Komachi, and Ōtomo no Kuronushi. The appellation *rokkasen* was conferred upon this group at a later time.
37. Emperor Ninmyō (810–850) is counted as Japan's fifty-fourth emperor. He reigned from 833 to 850.
38. Located in Ōtsu in Shiga Prefecture, Miidera is the head temple of the Tendai Jimonshū Buddhist sect. Its formal name is Nagara San'onjō-ji, and it was reputedly founded by the tomo clan in the seventh century. A temple of considerable fame, it is mentioned in the *Tale of the Heike* and other classical literary works.
39. "Furu" is another name for Isonokami (meaning "above a rock") in the province of Yamato (now Nara Prefecture). Henjō is said to have lived there at one time and to have had a poetic exchange with Ono no Komachi who visited him, as recorded in the *Gosen Wakashū* (Later Collection of Japanese Poems):

> *Komachi*:
> How cold this rock
> I use as my travel bed
> Please lend to me
> Your blanket of moss

> *Henjō*:
> Having turned away from the world
> My moss blanket has but a single layer
> But it would be cold of me not to lend it
> So let us share it tonight!

40. Takarada Jurai (1740–1796) was a kabuki playwright also known by the name Geki Shinsen. *Seki no To* is the only famous work of his known to us today, but in his time he enjoyed a reputation in the theater world as a deeply knowledgeable man.

41. The Kingdom of Wey was a vassal state located in what is now Henan Province for a period extending from the Zhou dynasty into the Warring States period. In a succession dispute during the Spring and Autumn period, a prince there sacrificed his life for the sake of his older half-brother.
42. Hanzoku Taishi was a legendary king in India who, succumbing to evil heresies, killed a thousand other kings and made a grave mound from their heads in a plot to become the supreme ruler. With the head of the 1,000th king, however, he suddenly repented and achieved enlightenment.
43. Ōtomo no Ōji (648–672) was the son of Emperor Tenji. After his father's death, he challenged Prince Ōama for the throne, sparking the Jinshin War. Losing a battle in Ōmi, he committed suicide.
44. Tomo no Yoshio (811–868) was an early Heian-period nobleman. In 866, the main gate of the Imperial Palace in Kyoto was destroyed by fire, and Tomo no Yoshio accused Minister of the Left Minamoto no Makoto of arson. Secret intelligence, however, identified Tomo no Yoshio and his son as the true culprits, and Tomo no Yoshio was banished to Izu. Linked to a power struggle involving the Fujiwara clan, the affair came to be known as the Ōtenmon Incident.
45. Ōtomo no Yakamochi (718?–785) was a government official in the Nara period and the poet with the most poems included in the *Man'yoshū* anthology. His work is also included in the *Hyakunin Isshu* (One Hundred Poems by One Hundred Poets):

> Frost gleams on the Bridge of Magpies
> That unites lovers but once a year
> Its whiteness tells me
> The night grows old.

46. *Pas de deux* is a ballet term that refers to a dance performed by a male and female dancer. In the nineteenth century, the choreographer Marius Petipa created the *grand pas de deux*,

which typically consists of four parts. The first part is performed by the man and woman together; the second is a solo by the man; the third a solo by the woman; and the fourth reunites the two in an up-tempo duet called the coda.

47. Published in 1782, *Sekai no Makunashi* was written by Honzentei Tsubohira.
48. The Great Tenmei Famine lasted from 1782 to 1788, with crops devastated by cold temperatures and bad weather, compounded by the eruptions of the volcanoes Mount Iwaki and Mount Asama. Starting in northeastern Honshū, the famine spread throughout Japan, causing many deaths and sparking frequent riots at rice storehouses.
49. Tanuma Okitsugu (1719–1788) was a senior counselor who served the tenth Tokugawa shogun, Ieharu. Starting as a lowly page, he achieved rare success, eventually becoming chief senior counselor and lord of the Sagara domain with an annual income of 57,000 *koku* of rice. His reforms of the shogunate's deteriorating financial policies revitalized urban economies, but rural communities were devastated, and corruption grew rampant, making him the target of criticism. With other negative factors like the Great Tenmei Famine also having an effect, Okitsugu lost his position immediately after Ieharu's death.
50. Matsudaira Sadanobu (1759–1829) succeeded Tanuma Okitsugu as chief senior counselor under the eleventh Tokugawa shogun, Ienari. He was appointed to the post partly in recognition for the abilities he demonstrated by surviving the Great Tenmei Famine as lord of the Shirakawa domain. Adopting policies that were the exact opposite of his predecessor, he enacted the Kansei Reforms in an effort to reconstruct the shogunate, including sumptuary edicts and laws regulating public morals.
51. Bandō Mitsugorō III (1775–1831) was a leading actor during the first three decades of the nineteenth century. His quick-change dances, including *Gannin Bōzu* (Priest Gannin)

and *Asazuma Bune* (*Shirabyōshi* Dancer in a Boat) were extremely popular. Hailed as the premier dancer in Edo, he competed with Nakamura Utaemon III, a leading actor in Osaka and Kyoto.

52. *Sagi Musume* premiered at the Ichimura-za in Edo in 1762. It was originally part of a *go henge* (five changes) dance called *Yanagi ni Hina Shochō Saezuri* (Chicks Twittering in a Willow). Accompanied by *nagauta* song, the main character is the spirit of a white heron. The dance begins slowly, with the dancer dressed in a white kimono in the snow. It develops into a nimble depiction of a town girl, and ends with her being tortured by hellfire. Filled with ample costume changes, the piece offers a full portrait of the heart of a woman in love.

53. *Fuji Musume* premiered at the Nakamura-za in Edo in 1826. It was originally part of a *go henge* (five changes) dance called *Kaesu Gaesu Onagori Ōtsue* (Paintings of Ōtsu and the Endlessly Returning Waves) premised on the idea of painted figures coming to life and dancing. In the Showa period (1926–1989) Kikugorō VI changed the main character of the segment into a wisteria spirit, and this is the version usually performed today. The fantastic stage set features a large pine tree festooned with wisteria in full bloom, and the dancer's costumes and hair ornaments all provide variations on the wisteria theme.

54. *Shiokumi* premiered at the Ichimura-za in Edo in 1811. It was originally part of a *shichi henge* (seven changes) piece called *Shichi Mai Tsuzuki Hana no Sugatae* (Seven Continuing Pictures of Flower Figures) performed by Bandō Mitsugorō III but is now performed as an independent piece. Borrowing from the noh play *Matsukaze* (Pining Wind), it depicts a young woman named Matsukaze who ladles brine on the shore to make salt. She longs for her lover Ariwara no Yukihira and performs a dance wearing a robe that he has left behind.

55. *Echigo Jishi* premiered at the Nakamura-za in Edo in 1811. It was originally part of a *shichi henge* (seven changes) piece called *Osozakura Teniha Nana Moji* (The Seven Manifestations of the Late Blooming Cherry). Depicting a street performer from Echigo named Kakubē Jishi who makes his way through town, the piece provided local color that proved popular among Edo audiences.
56. *Tomo Yakko* premiered at the Nakamura-za in Edo in 1828. It was originally part of a *shichi henge* (seven changes) piece called Nijirigaki Nanatsu Iroha (Seven Syllables in Bad Handwriting). In this lighthearted, comical dance, a footman who is supposed to accompany his master to the Yoshiwara licensed district gets separated from him. The foot stamps he performs are a highlight of the piece.

CHAPTER 9

1. *Kanjinchō* (The Subscription List) premiered in 1840 at the Kawarazaki-za in Edo. One of the "18 Favorite Plays" associated with the Ichikawa Danjūrō line of actors, it's based on the noh play *Ataka* and was first performed by Danjūrō VII, with the script written by Namiki Gohei III and the *nagauta* musical accompaniment composed by Kineya Rokusaburō III. The great general Minamoto no Yoshitsune and a few of his trusted retainers (including the warrior-priest Benkei) are on the run disguised as ascetic mountain priests, trying to escape the forces of Yoshitsune's estranged half-brother Yoritomo. Stopped by Togashi, a local noble charged with guarding the Ataka Barrier Gate, Benkei claims that they are traveling around Japan soliciting contributions for the construction of Tōdaiji Temple. Suspicious, Togashi orders Benkei to read the subscription list he's using to raise the funds. Not having a real list, Benkei pulls out a blank scroll and boldly pretends to read, making it up as he goes.

Yoshitsune has meanwhile disguised himself as the group's baggage carrier, and when this ruse is in danger of being exposed, Benkei beats his own lord with a staff to prove to Togashi that Yoshitsune is nothing more than a servant. Sympathizing with Benkei's distress, Togashi lets the group pass.

2. The character Yamamura Sadako, the "woman who's already dead," appears in Suzuki Kōji's horror novel *Ringu* (The Ring) published in 1991. The novel was adapted as a television drama in 1995 and as a feature film in 1998, becoming a forerunner of the current boom in Japanese horror.
3. Onoe Kikugorō III (1784–1849) was a leading Edo actor. The son of a cabinetmaker in Kodenmachō, Edo, he played many of the top roles of his time, including Oiwa in *Yotsuya Kaidan*, Kanpei in *Chūshingura*, and Gonta in *Yoshitsune Senbonzakura*.
4. From *Haiyū Hyakumensō* (One Hundred Faces of Actors), reprinted in *Kinsei Nihon Engekishi* (History of Early Modern Japanese Theater) by Ihara Toshirō.
5. Seki Sanjūrō II (1786–1839) was an actor originally active in Kyoto. In 1808 he moved to Edo where he achieved great success, particularly in *wagoto* and realistic styles, eventually earning the nickname Meijin Sekisan (Master Sekisan).
6. From *Fude Makase* (Letting the Brush Write), reprinted in *Kinsei Nihon Engekishi* (History of Early Modern Japanese Theater) by Ihara Toshirō.
7. From *Sekizen Ō Hikki* (Notes from Old Man Sekizen), reprinted in Kinsei Nihon Engekishi (History of Early Modern Japanese Theater) by Ihara Toshirō.
8. Ibid.
9. Onoe Matsusuke I (1744–1815) was born in Osaka. He apprenticed with Onoe Kikugorō I and made his stage debut in 1761 under the Matsusuke name. Adept from a young age at contriving quick costume changes and using sidelocks to

alter facial appearance, he's considered the founding father of *kaidan kyōgen* (ghost story plays). In 1809, at the age of 66, he assumed the name Onoe Shōroku.

10. In the modern repertory, *kotsuyose* is used in the climactic scene of Kawatake Mokuami's *Kagamiyama Gonichi no Iwafuji* (Iwafuji of Kagamiyama Returns), which premiered in 1860. The scattered bones of the villain Iwafuji reassemble themselves into a skeleton.

11. *Tenjiku Tokubē Ikokubanashi* (India Tokubē's Foreign Tales) premiered in 1804 at the Kawarazaki-za in Edo. It was a kabuki adaptation of a play by Chikamatsu Hanji titled *Tenjiku Tokubē Satokagami* (India Tokubē's Hometown Mirror). Prior to that, there was Namiki Shōzō's play *Tenjiku Tokubē Kikigaki Ōrai* (The Journeys of India Tokubē), based loosely on the true story of a fisherman named Tokubē who visited India during the early Edo period. In that major work, Tokubē is portrayed as a renegade bent on overthrowing Japan.

12. Published in 1858–1859 in Edo, *Okyōgen Gakuya no Honsetsu* (Backstage Stories of Kabuki) is a two-part, four-volume illustrated handbook of kabuki. Written by Santei Shunba II, it contains illustrations by Utagawa Kunisada, Utagawa Yoshitsuya, and Utagawa Kunitsuna and is an excellent resource that reveals the distinctive characteristics of kabuki at that time.

13. Although there are five authors who bore the name Tsuruya Nanboku, the most famous is Nanboku IV (1755–1829), who wrote *Yotsuya Kaidan* and was called Ō Nanboku (Nanboku the Great). With his ultra-realistic *kizewa* (raw domestic) style that accurately depicted the lives and customs of ordinary people, his penchant for dramatic development that emphasized cruel murder scenes, and his taste for the bizarre and eerie, Nanboku revolutionized the kabuki of his day.

14. Matsumoto Kōshirō V (1764–1838) was a kabuki actor active in Edo. The son of Matsumoto Kōshirō IV, he assumed his

stage name in 1801. Although he played *wagoto* roles in his early years, his true forte lay in *jitsu-aku* (villainous rogue) roles. His large nose gave him a unique appearance that endeared him to his audience as "big-nose Kōshirō." He worked frequently with Nanboku, and played the role of Naosuke Gonbē in *Yotsuya Kaidan*.

15. Iwai Hanshirō V (1776–1847) was a leading *onnagata* actor in Edo. The son of Iwai Hanshirō IV, he assumed his stage name in 1804. Blessed with great physical attractiveness and artistic style, he enjoyed such nicknames as Mesenryō (Eyes Worth a Thousand Ryō) and Ō Tayū (Great Chanter). He was particularly adept at playing evil women.

16. Yatō Emoshichi (1686–1703) replaced his father Yatō Nagasuke in the vendetta when the latter died of illness. When the attack was mounted, Emoshichi was just 17 years old and still living at home, making him the second-youngest of the 47 ronin (the youngest being Ōishi Chikara, who was 15).

17. Written by Nakamura Seigorō II, *Chūjō Hime Kyō Biina* (Princess Chūjo, the Doll of Kyoto) premiered at the Nakamura-za in Edo in 1707. According to legends about the origin of the Taima Mandala handed down at Taima Temple in Nara Prefecture, Princess Chūjō was the daughter of Minister Yokohagi and became a nun at the temple during the Nara period (710–794). Praying to Amida Buddha, she received the assistance of the bodhisattva Kannon and used thread she took from the stalk of a lotus to weave the mandala. This legend also provided material for a puppet play called *Hibariyama Hime Sutematsu* (The Forgotten Pine of Hibariyama), which is still in the kabuki repertory.

18. "Greengrocer Oshichi" (1668–1683) was an adopted daughter who lived in the Hongō district of Edo. She met a man at an evacuation site during a fire, and later committed arson so that she might see him again. She was burned at the stake for her crime at Suzukigamori in Shinagawa. Her story

provided material for Ihara Saikaku's collection *Five Women Who Loved Love* as well as many puppet and kabuki plays. Nanboku also referenced her in his *Katakiuchi Yagura no Taiko* (Vengeance and the Drum at the Fire Tower).

19. *Sukeroku* is one of the "18 Favorite Plays" and is usually performed today under the title *Sukeroku Yukari no Edo Zakura* (Sukeroku: The Flower of Edo). The original play, *Hanayakata Aigo no Sakura* (Cherry Blossoms Beloved of the Great Houses), was performed in 1713 by Ichikawa Danjūrō II. Sukeroku (who is actually Soga Gorō in disguise) is searching for his lost sword, the famous Tomokiri-maru, by going each night to the Yoshiwara licensed quarters and quarreling in hopes of provoking the thief to draw it. Ikyū, a villain who desires Sukeroku's lover Agemaki, bears Sukeroku's insults but doesn't draw the stolen sword, which is in his possession. Soga no Jūrō arrives disguised as a saké peddler and reproaches his younger brother for his bad behavior. When he learns that Sukeroku is brawling in order to retrieve his sword, however, Jūrō agrees to help and even accepts a lesson from Sukeroku on how to pick a fight. Ikyū returns and abuses Sukeroku, who bears it patiently until Ikyū gets carried away, draws his sword reprovingly, and slices an incense burner cleanly in half. Seeing that the sword Ikyū wields is indeed his own Tomokiri-maru, Sukeroku kills Ikyū and retrieves it.

20. Sakurada Jisuke (1734–1806) was an Edo native but spent four years working in Kyoto and Osaka when he was in his mid-twenties. After returning to Edo, he became a major playwright and dominated the theater world there for 40 years with works created in collaboration with the leading actors of the day. In his old age he competed fiercely for dominance with Namiki Gohei, who had arrived in Edo from western Japan. Jisuke was especially skilled at writing chanted lyrics, and his catchy titles and blurbs came

to be admired as the "Sakurada style." Plays of his still performed today include *Date Kurabe Okuni Kabuki*, *Ōakinai Hirugakojima*, and *Gohiiki Kanjinchō*, as well as the dance piece *Modoru Kago*.

21. *Sakura Hime Azuma Bunshō* (The Story of Princess Sakura) premiered in 1817 at the Kawarazaki-za in Edo. It tells the story of the monk Jikyū (later called Seigen) of Hase Temple in Kamakura, who falls in love with a young boy named Shiragiku-maru. The two attempt to commit double suicide, but Jikyū inadvertently survives. Seventeen years later, Jikyū (now called Seigen) has become the head priest of Hase Temple. He encounters Princess Sakura of the noble Yoshida clan who, though a young mother, seeks to become a nun. Seigen becomes obsessed with her because he recognizes her as a reincarnation of Shiragiku-maru. Also at the temple is the villain Gonsuke, who raped Princess Sakura some time before and is the father of her child. Princess Sakura had fallen in love with Gonsuke the one night they spent together, and now consents to see him illicitly. When this is discovered, suspicion falls on Seigen as her mysterious lover, and the two are cast out of the temple. Broken and ill, Seigen is poisoned by an evil couple intent on stealing his money, but he is resurrected by a bolt of lightning and eventually reunited with Princess Sakura, who has been abducted by a slave trader. Seigen urges her to commit double suicide with him, but she fends him off and accidentally kills him. She entrusts her fate to Gonsuke who sells her into prostitution in Kozukahara. Meanwhile, Seigen's ghost appears and stays close by her, telling her that it was Gonsuke who killed her father and younger brother and stole an heirloom scroll of the Yoshida family. When she learns the truth, Princess Sakura kills Gonsuke and the child he fathered and recovers the scroll.

22. *Ōakinai Hirugakojima* premiered in 1784 at the Nakamura-za in Edo as a *kaomise* (season opening) play. Act II is set in the world of the *Izu Nikki* (Izu Diary), which describes Minamoto no Yoritomo as he raises an army to defeat his enemies, the Taira clan. In it, Tatsu-hime, the daughter of Lord Itō Sukechika, gradually goes mad with jealousy as she broods upon Yoritomo and his wife Masako while combing her hair. The scene is accompanied by a *meriyasu* (a subgenre of *nagauta*, the length of which can be freely adjusted as needed) piece called *Kurokami* (Black Hair).
23. *Kurokami* (Black Hair) is a famous *meriyasu* piece with words written by Sakurada Jisuke. In principle, *meriyasu* (the word is derived from the Portuguese word *meias*, meaning "socks," referring to the stretchy material from which they're made) are performed mournfully by one singer and one shamisen player. They are relatively short but flexible *nagauta* pieces that provide background music of variable length.
24. *Okuni Gozen Keshō no Sugatami* (Okuni Gozen Putting on Her Makeup) premiered at the Morita-za in Edo in 1809. The chief retainer of the Sasaki clan plots to usurp control of the domain after the death of his lord. The lord's widow Okuni Gozen steals a valuable family heirloom, and the young retainer Kanō Motonobu wins it back by seducing her. But Motonobu is actually in love with another woman, and when Okuni Gozen learns of it, she dies in a fit of rage while combing her hair. Through the magical virtue of a mirror possessed by Tosa Matahei, it appears that Okuni's spirit achieves Buddhahood. Later, however, after Matahei has changed his name to Kizukawa Yoemon, Okuni's vengeful ghost possesses Yoemon's lover Kasane. Transformed into a homely woman and driven mad with jealousy, Kasane is ultimately killed by Yoemon.

## Chapter 10

1. Kawatake Mokuami (1816–1893) was the son of Echizen'ya Kanbē, who traded stock in bathhouses in Edo's Nihonbashi district. Mokuami's birth name was Yoshimura Yoshisaburō. Disinherited at a young age, he found work at a book rental shop, where he read voraciously. He showed a talent for humorous verse based on haiku and studied dance. At age 20 he became a disciple of Tsuruya Nanboku and was granted the name Kawatake Shinshichi in 1843 at age 28. At age 30 he became the head writer of the Kawarazaki-za in Edo. Although he announced his retirement in 1881 to avoid the strictures of a theater reform movement, he continued to write until his death at 78 in 1893. He authored approximately 360 plays and dance pieces in his lifetime.
2. Tsubouchi Shōyō (1859–1935) was a critic, novelist, and playwright. Familiar with Edo literature as well as English and American literature, he helped to usher in Japan's era of modern literature with his novel *Tōsei Shosei Katagi* (The Character of Modern Students) and his book of criticism, *Shōsetsu Shinzui* (The Essence of the Novel). Shōyō contributed to the modern theater movement through his translations of Shakespeare's plays and his original playwriting. His historical plays *Kiri Hitoba* (A Paulownia Leaf) and *Hototogisu Kojō no Rakugetsu* (The Sinking Moon over the Lonely Castle Where the Cuckoo Cries) were both performed as modern kabuki plays.
3. From *Kawatake Mokuami Den* (The Life of Kawatake Mokuami), edited by Kawatake Toshio.
4. *Bonnie and Clyde* is a 1967 American film directed by Arthur Penn starring Warren Beattie (who was also the producer) and Faye Dunaway. Set in the Great Depression, it depicts the life on the road of Bonnie Parker and Clyde Barrow. Clyde, just out of jail and with no prospects, meets Bonnie who works as a waitress and the two go on a crime spree,

moving from town to town robbing banks and killing people. After evading police dragnets for a time, they finally meet their ends in a hail of bullets.

5. The Sakuradamon Incident occurred on March 24, 1860, when ronin from the Mito domain assassinated Chief Minister Ii Naosuke outside the Sakurada Gate of Edo Castle. Ii had made powerful enemies among certain daimyo lords because of his policy of opening Japan to Western trade, his implementation of the Ansei Purge, and his position in the succession dispute involving the shogun Tokugawa Iesada.

6. Ichikawa Kodanji IV (1812–1866) was a famous actor during the final years of the Tokugawa shogunate. He apprenticed as a child with Ichikawa Danjūrō VII and received further training in western Japan while still young. In 1844 he was granted the name Kodanji IV and returned to Edo three years later. Working with Kawatake Mokuami, he created and performed many new plays and incorporated the technique of frequently using *gidayū-bushi* from western Japan as narration in *kizewa-mono* ("raw" domestic plays that realistically depict the lives of the lower classes).

7. *Miyakodori Nagare no Shiranami* (The Bandit Courtesan and the Family Seal) premiered in 1854 at the Kawarazaki-za in Edo. It usually goes by the shortened title *Shinobu no Sōta*. Yamada Rokurō, who calls himself Shinobu no Sōta, was a retainer of the fallen Yoshida clan of Kyoto but is now an *otokodate* (chivalrous commoner) who sells sweet rice cakes on the banks of the Sumida River and works as a gardener. The Yoshida clan was ruined when it lost a precious family seal called *miyakodori*. The lady of the clan and her son Umewaka-maru are forced to flee east and seek Rokurō's help, but when they reach the Sumida River they become separated. Umewaka-maru, in possession of 200 ryō and a scroll containing the Yoshida family lineage, grows ill as he wanders on the riverbank. Sōta (the former Rokurō) happens upon him and gives him comfort, though he doesn't

recognize him. Sōta desperately needs 200 ryō to ransom the courtesan Hanako, whom he knows is actually the (male) heir of the Yoshida clan, Matsuwaka-maru in disguise. Discovering that Umewaka-maru has 200 ryō on him, Sōta asks for a loan, and when Umewaka-maru refuses they get into a scuffle and Sōta accidentally strangles him. The next day, Sōta discovers that the boy he killed was actually the son of his former master, Lord Yoshida (and also the younger brother of Matsuwaka-maru, the very person he was trying to save). Filled with remorse, Sōta decides to kill himself.

8. The Yellow Turban Rebellion was instigated by religious adherents of a secret Taoist society against the Han dynasty in China at the end of the second century. It got its name from the color of the scarves the rebels wore on their heads.

9. *Shiranami Gonin Otoko* (Five Men of the White Waves) premiered in 1862 at the Ichimura-za in Edo. It features five men who form a gang of bandits led by Nihon Daemon and including Benten Kozō Kikunosuke, Tadanobu Rihei, Akaboshi Jūsaburō, and Nangō Rikimaru. Disguised as a young lady of high rank, Benten Kozō attempts to extort 100 ryō from a clothier, but his plot is foiled by Daemon who, disguised as a black-hooded ninja, intentionally exposes Benten as a man in order to gain the trust of the master of the clothing store, Kōbē. Once Kōbē is reassured, Daemon intends to break into his store in the middle of the night and steal a much larger amount. But Benten is actually Kōbē's son, and Daemon is the father of Munenosuke, whom Kōbē raised as his own son. Just as these surprising facts are discovered, the police close in. Surrounded, Benten climbs the main gate of Gokurakuji Temple and commits ritual suicide while standing. Daemon is meanwhile arrested by the virtuous head of police, Aoto Fujitsuna.

10. Storyteller Shōrin Hakuen II (1834–1905) was the son of a magistrate in the Shimodate domain in the Hitachi region.

After apprenticing with Shōrin Hakuen I, he was granted the stage name Shōrin Hakuen II in 1854 and came to be known as "Robber Hakuen" because of his skill in telling *shiranami* tales. He and *rakugo* raconteur San'yūtei Enchō dominated the storytelling field of their time.

11. Mokuami's adaptation of *Tenpō Rokkasen* (Six Great Men of the Tenpō Period) is titled *Kumo ni Magō Ueno no Hatsuhana* (The Celestial Robe and the First Blossoms of Ueno), which premiered in 1881 at the Shintomi-za in Tokyo. Kōchiyama Sōshun, a scheming official in charge of overseeing the tea ceremony for his master, hears from a pawn broker that the broker's daughter Namiji is being held hostage by the lord of the Matsue clan because she refuses to become his concubine. Sensing an opportunity to earn a reward if he saves Namiji, Sōshun disguises himself as a high-ranking priest from Kan'eiji Temple in Ueno, enters the Matsue mansion, and intimidates the lord into releasing Namiji. Although his true identity is exposed just as he's about to leave the mansion, he manages to defiantly talk his way out using threats. Meanwhile, the beautiful Yoshiwara courtesan Michitose's lover Kataoka Naojirō (nicknamed Naozamurai) is on the run because of an illegal gambling debt incurred by one of his friends. Naozamurai bids Michitose goodbye as the police close in, but then manages to escape. He later surrenders to the authorities, but Sōshun promises to use his powers of persuasion to get him paroled.

12. Mokuami's adaptation of *Nezumi Kozō* (The Rat Kid) is titled *Nezumi Komon Haru no Shingata* (The Rat and the Fine Patterned New Spring Fashion). It premiered in 1857 at the Ichimura-za in Edo. Inaba Kōzō (nicknamed Nezumi Kozō, the Rat Kid) is a Robin Hood figure who steals 100 ryō from the mansion of the Inage family in order to help a young swordsmith named Shin'ichi and his lover, the courtesan Omoto. Unfortunately, the money is marked, so that Shin'ichi

is arrested when he attempts to use it to pay off a debt. Also, the elderly mansion guard Yosobē, who gave Kozō assistance during the burglary, is subjected to torture because of Kozō's theft. Kozō then disguises himself as a fortuneteller and learns from a clam seller named Sankichi (who turns out to be Omoto's younger brother) and a footman of the Inage family all of the unhappy consequences stemming from his burglary. Filled with remorse, he decides to surrender to the authorities.

13. The full title of this play as it now stands is *Satomoyō Azami no Ironui*, but it was called *Kosode Soga Azami no Ironui* when it premiered at the Ichimura-za in Edo in 1859. Seishin, a priest at Gokurakuji Temple in Kamakura, has illicitly fallen in love with the courtesan Izayoi. Knowing that their love is doomed, the two decide to commit suicide by drowning in the Inase River, but their attempt is botched. Seishin winds up swimming ashore, where he has an altercation with a young man, demands money from him, and inadvertently kills him, after which he once more decides to kill himself out of remorse. But then a pleasure boat floats by filled with loud revelers, and his heart changes. Realizing that his head will roll whether he kills one person or a thousand, he's suddenly transformed into a black-hearted bandit who assumes the name Seikichi the Thistle. Meanwhile, Izayoi also survives the double suicide attempt and is rescued by a poet named Byakuren, who tries to make her his unwilling mistress. Later, when the lovers are reunited, they try to blackmail Byakuren, only to discover that he is not only a notorious bandit himself but also Seishin's older brother from whom Seishin was separated as an infant. The lovers also discover that the young man Seishin killed by the riverside was Izayoi's younger brother. Horrified by the cruelty of fate, Seishin and Izayoi finally succeed in killing themselves.

14. *Shinpa* (new school) theater, originally called *sōshi shibai* (swaggering drama), was created by young, anti-government

political agitators in the late nineteenth century as a means of winning converts to the Freedom and People's Rights Movement. Its first star and principal originator was Kawakami Otojirō, who scored a hit with his *oppekepē-bushi* pop songs. The genre acquired the name *shinpa* in 1895 (the year it was first performed at the Kabuki-za in Tokyo) to distinguish it from *kyūha* (old school) of kabuki. After many historical twists and turns, the *shinpa* tradition is still carried on today by the theater troupe Gekidan Shinpa (Company Shinpa).

15. Chikamatsu's views on this and other matters were recorded by Hozumi Ikan in his *Naniwa Miyage* (Naniwa Souvenir), which was published in 1738.
16. Ichimura Uzaemon XV (1874–1945) was a famous actor who specialized in the roles of handsome and refined young lovers. The adopted son of Ichimura Uzaemon XIV, he was granted the Uzaemon name in 1903. With his superb physical appearance and masterful line delivery, he played such roles as Sukeroku (in *Sukeroku*) and Yosaburō (in *Yowa Nasake Ukina no Yokogushi*). His performances of domestic dramas in collaboration with Onoe Kikugorō VI won particular acclaim.
17. Onoe Kikugorō VI (1885–1949) was the son of Kikugorō V. As a child he received training from his father and Ichikawa Danjūrō IX and became very proficient at performing both historical and domestic dramas. His dancing, however, was truly unrivaled. He had many opportunities to perform in such demanding pieces as *Musume Dōjōji* (A Maiden at Dōjōji Temple) and *Kagami-jishi* (Mirror Lion). Upon the death of his father in 1903, he was immediately granted the name Kikugorō VI. From the end of the Meiji era (1868–1912) into the early Showa era (1925–1989), he worked with Nakamura Kichiemon I to usher in a golden age of kabuki performance called the Kiku-Kichi Era at the Ichimura-za in

Tokyo. Enthusiastically devoted to developing a new repertory, he often performed works authored by such playwrights as Hasegawa Shin and Uno Nobuo. He was posthumously awarded the Order of Cultural Merit, the first time a kabuki actor was so honored.
18. *Kyakusha Hyōbanki* (Audience Guidebook), with text by Shikitei Sanba and illustrations by Utagawa Kunisada, was published in 1811.

# About the Author

MATSUI KESAKO was born in Kyoto in 1953. After completing her master's degree in theatre and film arts at Waseda University, she joined the production company Shochiku, where she was responsible for the planning and production of kabuki plays. Later as a freelancer, she pursued scriptwriting, directing, and critical writing under the mentorship of stage and film director Takechi Tetsuji. In 1997 Matsui published her first novel, *Tōshū Sharaku-sashi* (Sharaku Goes to Edo). That same year she won the Kodansha Award for Historical Fiction for her novel *Nakazō Kyōran* (Nakazō's Frenzy). In 2007 her *Yoshiwara Tebikigusa* (Revenge in Yoshiwara) won the Naoki Prize. Other major works include *Bakumatsu Adoresan* (Farewell to Edo); *Ichinotomi: Namiki Hyōshirō Tanetorichō* (The Adventures of Namiki Hyōshirō); *Nisemon* (The Imposter); *Sorosoro Tabi Ni* (About Time for Travel); *Hoshi to Kagayaki Hana to Saki* (Shine like a Star, Bloom like a Flower); *Ginza Kaika Omokage Sōshi* (Portrait of Ginza Enlightenment); *Michi Taezuba, Mata* (See You at Road's End); *Kochō no Kairō* (The Coward's Corridor); *Enchō no Onna* (Enchō's Women); *Shifu no Yuigon* (The Master's Last Testament); and *Manga Kabuki Nyūmon* (Manga Introduction to Kabuki).

（英文版）歌舞伎の中の日本
Kabuki, a Mirror of Japan: Ten Plays that Offer a Glimpse into Evolving Sensibilities

2016年3月27日　第1刷発行

著　者　松井今朝子
訳　者　デヴィッド・クランドール
発行所　一般財団法人出版文化産業振興財団
　　　　〒101-0051 東京都千代田区神田神保町3-12-3
　　　　電話　03-5211-7282（代）
　　　　ホームページ　http://www.jpic.or.jp/japanlibrary/

印刷・製本所　大日本印刷株式会社

定価はカバーに表示してあります。
本書の無断複写（コピー）、転載は著作権法の例外を除き、禁じられています。

© 2010 by Matsui Kesako
Printed in Japan
ISBN 978-4-916055-58-3